THE LUCKY ONES

ALSO BY ANNA GODBERSEN

BRIGHT YOUNG THINGS
BEAUTIFUL DAYS

THE LUXE
RUMORS
ENVY
SPLENDOR

THE LUCKY ONES

A BRIGHT YOUNG THINGS NOVEL

ANNA GODBERSEN

HARPER

An Imprint of HarperCollinsPublishers

alloyentertainment

Produced by Alloy Entertainment
151 West 26th Street, New York, NY 10001
www.alloyentertainment.com

Library of Congress Cataloging-in-Publication Data is available.

ISBN 978-0-06-196270-7

Typography by Liz Dresner

12 13 14 15 16 CG/RRDH 10 9 8 7 6 5 4 3 2 1
❖
First Edition

For Farrin

1

ON THE SECOND SUNDAY OF AUGUST, ASTRID HAD
been Mrs. Charlie Grey for exactly two weeks, and she was
beginning to settle into the idea. They lay by the pool, in comfortable silence, as they had every day since the heat got bad.
After dark he went out on his rounds. This was the order of
married life, she was learning. A wife stays in her wifely place
and occupies her mind with wifely thoughts, like who to invite
for luncheon and when the furniture has gone out of style and
needs to be replaced. Meanwhile, a husband goes off in the
mornings to the mysterious world of work. Or, if he happens to
be a bootlegger, he goes at night.

It had not been her intention to marry Charlie. When she

met him he had seemed more exciting than anyone she had ever known—that was all. She had been content to call him her boyfriend without losing her famous taste for flirting, and he had strayed once that she knew of. But they had always had a furious grip on one another, and after his father died so suddenly and horribly they became engaged. Even then it was anybody's guess whether the engagement would last; they always went up and down the roller coaster together, Charlie and Astrid. But that was before the Hales kidnapped her. Everything had been different between them since that night, when he'd broken into the dank warehouse where she had been sure she would die. He had killed the man who had tormented her all those awful hours, and then he had carried her home in his strong arms. That was when she knew for sure she loved him.

And oh, how she loved him. She loved the way he swaggered from some speakeasy to his Daimler having just sealed a deal, and she loved the way he took her face in his hands—the better to put his mouth to hers. She loved the way he surprised her with jewelry, and she loved the way his name looked in the paper, when it was mentioned in connection with "the former Miss Astrid Donal." She loved his body lying next to hers on the double chaise by the pool at Dogwood. *Their* pool. He was big and shiny in the sun, and he wore white swim trunks that matched her white swim costume, which was exactly how she had always pictured marriage.

They had finished the champagne and orange juice that Milly, the maid, had brought down with their lunch, and their skin had dried from their last swim. He was on his back with limbs thrown wide like a star, and she lay on her belly, pushed up on her elbows to look at him. His eyes were closed—whether to protect from the sun or because he was sleeping, she couldn't tell—and his shoulders were relaxed.

"What are you looking at?"

She blinked, surprised. His eyes were still closed, but then she saw the curl at the corner of his lips. "At you, you big lug!"

"Plotting my overthrow, kitten? Poison, penknife, firing squad?"

"Oh, Charlie," Astrid replied, her voice low with mock pity. "When I stage my coup, there shall be no advance warning."

"You'll do it quick and painless, in a kind of sentimental gesture to the love we once shared?"

"Of course! I'm ruthless, darling, not evil."

"I 'preciate that." Charlie furrowed his brow theatrically and waved his index finger like a professor. "However, as your tutor and chief guide in the world of racketeering and vice, I must advise you to be wary of sentimental gestures. Perchance they seem to you small indulgences, but minor errors of the kind have undone men more ruthless than you."

A gasp escaped Astrid's plush lips. "Men more ruthless than me?" she repeated with faux indignation.

He didn't say anything after that, and the joke melted into the humid afternoon.

A silence settled in, and Astrid closed her eyes to the brightness. But just as she was about to doze off, she felt Charlie's hands gripping her shoulders, and with sudden quickness he flipped her over and pinned her from above. Surprise hit her like a stealthy cold breeze.

"See?" he said triumphantly, smiling down. "If you go soft like that, you sorta beg your enemy to make a sneak attack."

He was close now, and she could feel the way his skin had absorbed the warmth of the hazy sun.

"The king lives to rule another day," Astrid replied dryly, wishing that she could move her arms. She squirmed, testing the strength of his grasp, but his hands were as steady and unrelenting as his grin. The sun was so strong overhead that it almost bleached the sky, and she closed her eyes to protect her vision.

"Charlie."

They both turned toward the speaker, and when Charlie saw Elias Jones, who had been his father's right-hand man, he rolled to the other side of Astrid, propping himself up on an elbow but leaving his other arm draped possessively over his wife's torso.

"Hey, Jones! Didn't I catch myself a pretty woman?" he demanded happily, his free hand clutching her waist.

"Yes."

Charlie put a kiss on Astrid's forehead and then glanced up at Jones, as though to say he was ready for the news.

"Tonight, on the road to Rye Haven."

The way he spoke, Astrid knew that each of those words really signified five other ones, too.

"After sunset?"

"We should be in position by sunset."

"All right."

The skin over Charlie's brow rippled, and his voice turned gravelly, but his hand remained on her belly. "Good," he said, as though he had considered the unsaid implications of Jones's message and accepted them.

No words were said in conclusion, and Astrid knew Jones was gone only by the soft crush of grass underfoot as he walked back toward the house. She threw both of her arms around Charlie's neck and rolled on top of him. Two sheets of yellow hair fell down, forming a protective tent that shielded both their faces from the sun. He wrapped his arms around her middle, pressing one hand against the base of her skull and the other against her backside.

"The king rides tonight," she whispered.

When he pulled her tighter for a kiss, his mouth was dry,

and she could faintly taste the champagne and orange juice on his tongue. "Yes, tonight." Charlie pushed her hair behind her ears and studied her face. "But without the queen."

"The queen has another engagement, anyway." Astrid turned her face away and shook her hair out indifferently.

"Oh?" Charlie's hold tightened around her. Now she could feel his heart beating like a drum and was secretly glad he was jealous, even if there was nothing to be jealous of.

"Yes! Dinner at my grandmother Donal's over in Shagbark Hollow. You were supposed to come along, or don't you remember?"

It was obvious from his expression that he did not remember, but he gave a big, showy, regretful sigh anyway. "I'm sorry, kitten. I've been so caught up I forgot somehow."

"Oh, that's all right. Just don't start forgetting important things—like that my favorite flowers are peonies, or what day my birthday is." In a stage whisper, she said: "It's August twenty-third, that's coming up! Anyway," she went on gaily, "Grandmother Donal abhors new people."

"*New* people!"

"Not new to *me*, darling. New to her!" Astrid gave Charlie a quick peck on the mouth and wriggled free of his hot embrace. Tiptoeing toward the pool, she added: "She's just set in her ways—most ladies of her generation are, you know."

"She'd better not think you're too good for me."

Astrid glanced at him over her shoulder and winked girl-ishly. "But of course I'm too good for you." The pillows on the chaise were rumpled from where they had been lolling. Charlie was watching her as though she might abruptly fly away. "You're doing something different tonight, aren't you?" she asked.

"Yes."

"More dangerous than usual?"

"That's nothing for you to worry about—I'm gonna take every precaution. But don't tell anyone where you're going tonight, and when you're done with Grandma, come right home."

Astrid contemplated the still, turquoise surface of the pool. She had been born with a gift for ignoring what was not directly in front of her and avoiding that which might bring her harm. But ever since that night in the warehouse—when she had smelled pickles and onions on the breath of a man she had afterward seen shot dead—she had been nagged by a morbid curiosity about what Charlie did out there without her. The idea frightened her, but it didn't stop the wondering, the sense that she could no longer turn a blind eye to what happened after darkness fell.

Over her shoulder, Charlie went on: "You'll take a body-guard, and he'll wait outside the whole time. I'll tell Victor he's taking care of you tonight—he's the best shot of all my boys, and the best watcher, too."

"All right." Astrid tugged her suit back into place and dove in.

From the balcony of the Calla Lily Suite on the third floor of Dogwood, Cordelia Grey sensed the men positioned among the trees and hedges of her late father's estate. Someone was always invisibly watching these days. Since the night the Hales had nabbed Astrid, neither girl was allowed to leave the property without a bodyguard, and Charlie had been strict about where they could and could not go.

"Oh, Letty, don't leave," she said as she turned away from the vistas of Dogwood and stepped down into the sumptuous bedroom she'd slept in since mid-May.

Letty, her oldest friend, was standing by the bed contemplating an open suitcase and how to make a heap of recently acquired items fit inside. She blinked in her innocent, concerned way, and for a moment Cordelia was back in Ohio on the New York–bound train, breathless with everything she had given up and hungry for everything yet to come. But in the next moment, the quality in Letty's eyes changed; a sweet smile overtook her button of a mouth; she shook her head, almost sadly.

"You know I have to! It's what I came all this way for."

Neither girl much resembled the version of herself that had stepped off the train and into Pennsylvania Station in the first weeks of summer, with a single suitcase in hand and the dreamy look of every newcomer in their eyes. Letty, whose gentleness and shyness had prevented her from auditioning even once over her first few months in New York, had now been taken under wing by Valentine O'Dell, whose movies they used to watch, back in their old lives, at the little theater in Defiance, one town over from Union. After two weeks of Letty taking the commuter train into the city for lessons with Valentine's own voice and acting coaches, he and his wife, Sophia Ray—who was also his costar—had again suggested Letty move into their Park Avenue apartment, the better to oversee her transformation into the thing she'd always wanted to be: a creature of the stage.

"I know." Cordelia sighed and draped herself over the low, stuffed white chair by the balcony's open French doors. A white carpet spread between the two girls like an acre of new-fallen snow. "You're so lucky to be leaving this place!"

"Don't be silly, you'll break free soon enough, and you'll come to visit me, and we'll have tea with movie stars!" Then Letty laughed, that joyful little laugh that was like a bird trilling at twilight, and Cordelia had to laugh, too. Good Egg, Letty's greyhound, who was sitting at her mistress's feet, swayed her head back and forth as though she wanted to be in on the joke, too.

When Letty walked toward the vanity table and began to

sort through the mess of makeup that had accumulated there, Good Egg followed and flopped at her feet. With a little sigh, Cordelia picked up the newspaper from the varnished walnut coffee table and flipped to the society page of the *New York Imperial*.

> *Last night at The Vault we observed the late boot-legger Darius Grey's daughter overseeing her family's business, charging back and forth across that boîte's mosaic floor in a dress of floating black silk, her tawny hair sleek against her scalp and her lips glossy. Though the room was packed to the gills with sports and socialites and gamblers and poets, I never did spot the pilot Max Darby, who is of course known for his distaste of nightclubs almost as much as he is known for his aerial acrobatics. However, he has recently become known for his taste in Cordelia Grey . . . What is happening between the teetotaler and the girl behind The Vault's success? Will we see them together again soon?*

Cordelia's fingers tightened around the edges of the paper as she took in a strange cocktail of pride and irritation. She allowed the columnist Claude Carrion to loiter at her place and drink for free because it was good business; her name had appeared regularly in his column since her arrival in New York, and this attention contributed in no small way to the success of The Vault. If there was an author of the myth of Cordelia Grey, it was him. Yet she had never really liked the man in the expensive, ill-fitting suit with the middle-parted hair and night-owl skin. And she knew that this kind of attention would only make it more difficult to see Max.

"You're so lucky you get to walk around like anybody else, without having to worry about snooping writers or bodyguards!" she said as she folded up the newspaper and put it aside.

Letty stepped away from the mirror. She had been trying on a lipstick, and her mouth was a poppy color that made her eyes vividly blue. For a moment she regarded Cordelia sympathetically. But a mischievous smile soon spread over her lips, and she began to slink across the carpet, at first shimmying her shoulders and then leaping like a fawn, before waving her hands and transitioning into a wild little dance. By the time she reached the chair by the French doors, they had both broken out laughing.

"You can't pretend with *me*, Cord," Letty said, when she'd finished her performance and Cordelia had made room for her on the chair. "I know you secretly like all that fame-and-fortune business, even if you do pretend you're not seeking any spotlight! It's missing Max that's bothering you, and you'll see him soon enough. If I know you, you'll find a way."

As their giggles subsided, Cordelia let out a sigh. Letty was right, of course. The weekend had been long, and Cordelia had worked hard at The Vault, but now the week was new, and she was full of boundless energy. She could feel it in her bones that she was going to see Max any day now. If fate didn't arrange things, she'd just see to it herself.

2

BY THE TIME LETTY REACHED THE CITY, THE SIDES OF her brand-new dress were damp with sweat. She wore a straw cloche to shade her eyes and carried her own suitcase, which felt twice as heavy as it had when she left White Cove. The sidewalks of Park Avenue were mostly abandoned, and she noticed that the poodles and French bulldogs and Malteses were being walked exclusively by maids in uniform. She thought of Good Egg and felt a little sad—when she left Dogwood her greyhound had followed her all the way to the entrance, and then stood there howling dolefully from behind the big gate until the car had rounded the bend. But there wasn't much room for sadness in this particular day, for she was standing at the breathtaking beginning of her next chapter, and she couldn't bring Good Egg with her.

Over the last two weeks, her knowledge of what it was to be a performer had multiplied each day. After a chance encounter with Valentine O'Dell—the movie star whose every expression she knew from the pictures—she had been taking the train into the city so that he could teach her what he knew. They had been full days, and not always easy, and she had danced in front of the big mirrors at his dance teacher's studio for hours until her movements became perfectly effortless and her feet swelled beneath her. This routine was so thrilling and so exhausting that again Valentine had suggested Letty come live in the city with him. Sophia Ray, his wife and favorite leading lady, was returning from the coast, so it wouldn't be unseemly. Plus, Sophia would have a lot to teach her, too.

"Sophia Ray!"

Letty glanced up, bewildered by the sound of a girl's voice behind her saying the name she had just been turning over in her thoughts. She must have gotten distracted and not noticed the numbered streets passing by. Now she saw the elegant dark green awning with THE APOLLONIAN inscribed in gold cursive lettering and knew that she had arrived.

A tall woman with full red lips—whose face was largely obscured by black sunglasses, but whose distinctive halo of peroxided blond hair was not disguised in the slightest—was stepping out of a town car. Even posed like that on a city sidewalk, Sophia Ray glowed with an otherworldly quality that demanded to be looked at.

The redheaded girl who had called Sophia's name had meanwhile rushed past and was reaching for her idol as though she hoped the famous actress would give her a benediction.

"It's such an honor to meet you!" the girl gushed. "I just had to tell you how divine you were in *The Hobo and the Heiress*! I think it's probably my absolute fave O'Dell–Ray picture to date!"

"Oh, well, aren't you the *sweetest!*" Sophia replied while her posture recoiled. Although her eyes crinkled affectionately, there was an undercurrent of disdain in the way she regarded this stranger. It was subtle, but Letty heard it and felt suddenly rather small and insignificant.

"Now," Sophia went on, her words turning saccharine, "why don't you just run along, dear."

In Letty's imagination, Sophia had been her friend, but now that she saw her in person, she shrank in embarrassment—after all, it was Valentine who had been so generous and familiar, and she wondered now if this impressive-looking woman would care about a little girl from the country with her silly big-city dreams.

Letty froze, waiting for the right moment to escape. But before she could, Sophia tipped her head to one side and fixed Letty in her gaze. A radiant smile spread over her red lips, and in a very different voice, she said: "You must be Letty."

The fan swiveled around and regarded Letty with a mixture of envy and awe.

"Yes," Letty tremblingly acknowledged.

"Well, don't just stand there, honey, come on in!" Sophia extended her hand, and with a guilty bob of her head Letty allowed Sophia Ray to shepherd her into the pink marble lobby of her apartment house. "Valentine will be along shortly—we just had lunch at the Plaza, and then some people recognized him on the way out and insisted that he play the piano a little for them, and he's always so giving that way, as I guess you know by now, and he couldn't say no. You see, my dear, how *exhausting* it all is . . ."

It took a few seconds to sink in with Letty that she was the "dear" in question, but once it had, she nodded exuberantly. "Oh, yes!"

"It's a lucky thing Valentine found you before you got too far along in this business. We'll keep an eye on you and show you the ropes."

"Thank you!" Letty gulped. "I feel so grateful that you're letting me come live with me—I mean you—I really do."

"Oh, honey, I'm lucky too. Val's told me all about you, and I can already tell we're gonna be fast friends. You know, it's terribly difficult for a girl like me to make friends. Most other girls are jealous of me, and the ones who aren't just want free hand-me-downs, or to be introduced to someone important, or to be photographed standing next to me. But *you're* not like that, are you?"

"No!" Letty shook her head with as much gusto as she had put into nodding a few seconds before.

"Yes, I can sense it already. *You* I can trust."

Letty beamed up at Sophia. She was so overwhelmed by this welcome that she was more or less speechless, but luckily the elevator made a dinging sound before the silence became awkward, and the large brass doors drew back.

"Well, of course we can trust her!" Both women turned and saw Valentine standing behind them. He was grinning, and his chestnut hair rose in a healthy ridge above his tan forehead. The warm, confident timbre of his voice caused a blush to creep from Letty's cheeks down across her neck.

"Yes, honey, you're one of us now, whether you like it or not!" Sophia led the way into the elevator, and Valentine and then Letty followed. Sophia pressed the button that had no number and instead read PH. As the doors closed, Letty glanced up, her eyes darting from one of her idols to the other, as though if she looked away for too long they might disappear.

She squeezed her eyes, but when she opened them Valentine and Sophia were still there, and the floor beneath her had begun to rise.

The heat had abated not at all when Astrid Donal stepped out of her chauffeured car and heard her grandmother's appraisal of her appearance.

"You look like your mother," Mrs. Earl Donal, née Caroline Oakhurst, announced flatly from the wide wraparound porch of the grand Victorian house where Astrid's father had been born.

This was not precisely a compliment; Astrid had heard plenty of what these two ladies had to say about each other over the years, and she knew what her grandmother really meant. It was as if mother- and daughter-in-law had set out to define one another in opposition, for where Caroline was decorous, Virginia was louche, and where Caroline was regal, Virginia was blowsy. Their disagreements often began at money, but over the years each woman had come to treat the other as a repository of everything one should avoid in life. Astrid, for her part, had learned to hear as little as possible from either party and remain always carelessly above it all, which was more or less the spirit in which she advanced across the lawn now.

"Oh, Nana, please," Astrid replied as she came up the steps and embraced the elegant lady waiting for her. Although her grandmother wore her ash-blond hair in the high pouf of her girlhood, and though her black crocheted dress was cut in the conservative style more commonly seen before the war, she was not strict about the old social ways with her only grandchild—she returned the embrace, as though Astrid were still a little girl and thus exempt from the elaborate formalities she usually preferred. "Don't be unkind—I am far too blond for any of that, and don't you think I have the Donal nose? You always *used* to say so."

"Let us hope and pray." Grandmother Donal took Astrid by the hand and brought her into the house. "The true Donal nose does not fully emerge until one is at least twenty-five, so you have some time yet. I presume that boy loitering by the car is not your husband?"

"No! That's my bodyguard. Charlie's awfully sorry he couldn't come tonight—he did *want* to."

"If you say so," the older lady replied indifferently.

They had come through the long, wide hallway that ran down the middle of the house and into the parlor that faced the Sound.

"Ahhhh . . . " Grandmother Donal sighed, as though she had just returned from a long day in the rough-and-tumble of the world (which she most certainly had not). With a clap of her hands she sank down into a scroll-armed pink satin fainting couch, and within seconds her liveried butler appeared with a silver tray bearing two sweating highballs. "It's good to have you back in civilization, dear."

Astrid accepted her highball and surveyed her grand-mother's definition of *civilization*: walls cluttered with portraits of seven generations of Donals and Oakhursts, rosewood furni-ture that might have once been sat upon by nobility. The house itself was large and airy, but hardly as palatial as Dogwood or Marsh Hall; although her grandmother could afford a more monumental sort of home, she took a snobbish pride in not replacing that which did not need fixing.

Astrid paused to swallow a gulp of cocktail, the lime and tonicness of which provoked a series of involuntary associa-tions. It was the smell of her grandmother's breath when she read her good-night stories, but then it was the smell of her mother's breath, too, when Virginia had scooped her daughter up and taken her on a tour of Europe that lasted years. "Where are you getting your gin these days?"

"Darling, my butler takes care of that; I don't ask." Grandmother Donal turned her face so that her strong pro-file was illuminated against a pink lampshade, which was her signal that she had nothing more to say on the topic. "A grotesque business, from start to finish—I was never one of the sanctimonious women who made themselves hoarse arguing the dry cause, but I love this country still, and I'll not tarnish that love by flouting her laws."

"Well, Nana," Astrid forged blithely on, "perhaps I could help you with all that, or rather *we* could, now that Charlie and I are hitched, for as I'm sure you know he does a good trade in the booze racket."

"Yeee-eee-ees," Grandmother Donal replied ominously, drawing the word out so that its meaning changed as it took on syllables and eventually became everything but affirmative.

The elder lady cleared her throat and walked across the room to a sideboard that bowed under a complete set of Shakespeare with aubergine cloth covers and gold lettering. She paused, her back toward Astrid, and tilted her head to look at the grand portrait of her late husband, whose face was as long and thin and patrician as her own. "It is fortuitous that you came alone tonight—I do want to meet your fellow, of course, some other time. But I have a wedding gift that is for you alone, and it seems that now is the time to give it to you."

"Nana!" Laughter burbled up through Astrid, and she waved her hand at her grandmother before going on buoyantly: "Charlie and I are man and wife, and I am terribly sorry—for your sake, if not for Mother's—that we didn't do it more properly and invite everyone and have it announced beforehand in the papers. But we are married now, really and truly married, which means we share everything."

"Of course." The older woman's voice had turned soft, which was unlike her. Usually she spoke in a high, fluty tone that was an accent all her own. She paused, running her hands over the books on the sideboard, until she reached *Othello* and plucked an envelope from in between its covers. Then she strode back toward her granddaughter, where she began to speak with such urgency that Astrid found she could not maintain her smile of the moment before. "Just the same, humor me. I don't pretend to know how you young people do things nowadays, but criminals are not new to the world, and I have seen the final acts of a few lawbreakers in my time. Money can't save anyone, but it can certainly help those who, in a bad situation, desire to help themselves. It isn't a huge dowry anyway, my dear, just the right amount of money for a woman coming out in the world. My hope is that you and Charlie will live happily for many years and have no need of it, and you can give it to your daughter."

The older woman handed over the envelope, and Astrid—still taken aback by the uncommon tone of their conversation—could think of nothing to do but open it. Inside was a little green booklet with the words WHITE COVE SAVINGS & TRUST embossed on the cover. She ran her fingers over the pages and saw that while her grandmother was right—the figure she had settled on was not outrageous—it was nonetheless far more than Caroline had ever allowed the widowed Virginia, and also much more than even Astrid would ever know what to do with.

"Don't worry, it's in a nice, safe little savings account, and it can remain there comfortably for some time. Only—you must not tell Charlie. The terms of the gift are that you and you alone may withdraw from the account. You understand me? This is to remain a secret."

"Thank you," Astrid mumbled. She wanted to protest that she couldn't keep a secret from Charlie if she tried, but she was stunned by the serious intensity with which her grandmother was regarding her. She blinked and put the booklet back in the envelope. For the first time, she resented Charlie for not coming tonight—if he was there, her grand-mother would have seen that they were a married couple, and that he could be trusted. Plus, Charlie would have known what to do with the money, instead of leaving her to deal with it alone.

"Wonderful!" Grandmother Donal clapped her hands, her tone once again aristocratic and detached. "Come, darling," she went on, taking Astrid by the elbow and drawing her up from her chair. "I'm sure dinner is ready by now—oysters and a light fish soup—and I believe we'll have some champagne to celebrate your being married and so grown-up-looking."

As they came into the hall, Astrid caught a glimpse of

Victor, the bodyguard, keeping watch on the lawn, and for the first time since becoming Mrs. Charlie Grey, the notion of being married and so grown-up-looking seemed a little less than a glittering, endless party.

3

"ANTHONY," CORDELIA CALLED FROM THE ENTRY TO the second-floor poolroom, leaning against the door frame and crossing one driving moccasin over the other. Her hair was in a loose braid, and she was wearing a man's blue work shirt—tied at the waist and with the arms rolled to the elbows—over a black slip dress. To a man she probably looked like a girl ready to spend an evening reading fashion magazines at home, but Astrid—still in the chic black dress she had worn to her grand-mother's earlier—gave her friend the up/down, and a little crescent moon appeared at the corner of her lips. With a spark of female imagination, she had seen what her friend was up to. "Anthony?"

"Yes?" he answered without turning to look. He was bent over about to take his shot and did not sound pleased about the disturbance. Charlie was out already, going about the business that had kept him and Jones tense all day, and he had his best men with him. His second-best men were on the perimeter of the property and stationed on the rooftop with rifles, so the poolroom at that hour was occupied by the youngest members of the Grey outfit, their faces pink between what scrubby facial hair they could grow. "One of the headlights on the Marmon needs fixing. Will you take me?"

Anthony took his shot and turned around, so that he missed the cue ball going wide of its mark and bouncing harmlessly against the green felt side barrier. "Now?"

"Yes, now." Cordelia stared back at him, letting the steady, unblinking quality of her sweet brown eyes dispel the peculiarity of her request. "If I take it now it will be ready tomorrow," she added firmly, as though that explained everything.

"But we're in the middle of a game—"

He cut himself off when Cordelia stepped away from the door and raised her chin imperiously. "Yes, but if we go now we'll be back before dark. Charlie says we're not to leave the property after dark, and I want to make sure it's ready for tomorrow."

When Anthony realized that Cordelia was not to be argued with, he threw the cue down on the table and walked huffily toward the door ahead of his boss's sister, who twirled her feet around before giving Astrid a wink and following him down the big main stairwell. They didn't speak as they crossed the grass toward the garage. He was still angry about the interrupted game and didn't notice that both headlights on the Marmon were working fine when she started up the motor and honked at him to follow her in one of the old Model T sedans that the Greys kept on hand for minor missions of this kind.

As they drove through the wooded lanes toward Old Oyster Town, she watched Anthony in the rearview mirror, noting the fierce expression he wore and the distraction in his eyes. The expression was unchanged as he pulled into the filling station, and so she didn't bother to talk to him, only signaled that she was heading into the garage to find the mechanic. He waved at her indifferently and unfolded a newspaper to read while he waited.

Inside the office, an old man in grease-stained overalls sat behind a desk with his feet up. When he saw Cordelia come through the door, he hastily put away the bottle that had been next to his feet and finished what was in his paper cup. His body was thinning in the arms and legs, but the lost mass appeared to have repositioned itself around his gut.

"You needn't worry about me," she said with a smile.

"Silly of me, I suppose, but it's hard to know who to trust

these days," he grumbled, as he reached for his bottle. "Now I get a look at you, you seem all right. Even so, we're closed for the day, miss."

"Oh, I don't mind. I was just wondering if I could leave my car on your property till tomorrow; would that be all right? The Marmon coupé out there." The man's eyes must have been blue when he was younger, but they were almost silver now when he narrowed them. "There's ten dollars in it for you if you say yes."

"That's a lot of money to pay a night watchman," he observed.

"Not if you include the fee for letting me slip out the back door." She smiled brilliantly, and added: "Plus the cost of a shot of that whiskey. And of course, you'll have to give a note to my friend Anthony when he comes after me."

The man took another paper cup out of the drawer where he'd been keeping his whiskey and poured out a shot. Cordelia stepped toward him and put a ten-dollar bill on the table along with a folded piece of paper that had Anthony's name written on it. Inside was a note explaining that she wasn't in any trouble, and that if he didn't want to be, he should keep his mouth shut, and that she'd be home before Charlie noticed. Meeting the old man's eyes, she raised her cup to his. As she drained it, she was reminded that the Indians were said to call alcohol *firewater*.

"Thank you," she said, and then scrawled a number on the newspaper lying on the desk. "That's how you reach my brother Charlie, if you ever want to get some imported whiskey. He doesn't usually do small accounts, but if you tell him you're a friend of mine, he'll make an exception. My name's Cordelia."

Realization came slowly into those silver eyes. "Thanks, miss," he said.

She smiled again and went to the window, where she motioned to the driver of a black roadster that had been idling by the pump. Its lights went on, and it rolled slowly into motion. She watched Anthony glance up from his paper and glance away when the roadster turned so that its snout was pointed in the direction of the city.

"Will you keep this for me too?" Cordelia said, taking off the blue work shirt and hanging it on the hook by the door.

"Sure thing, miss."

Dusk was settling in as she stepped through the back door and made her way across the dusty lot. It was that hour when the light is strange and plays tricks on unaccustomed eyes and making out much of anything is difficult, particularly if what one ought to be watching for is dressed in black.

They didn't speak until they were a half-mile down the road. Once they left the Old Oyster Town road for the main county

ed over suddenly and reached for her. The
back and forth for several seconds until
lled away, smiling. "I'm sorry, I must taste
hiskey. I didn't think the old man trusted me,
so I took a shot with him."

"I don't care," he said, starting up the car again. She had
forgotten how handsome he was, with his short dark hair just a
dark shadow on his skull, and his pale blue eyes as serious and
unwavering as ever. He held her gaze and swallowed. Then a
rare and genuine smile began to spread beneath the stern out-
cropping of his nose. "I'm just happy to be with you."

The feeling Max stirred in her now was the same one
she'd experienced when she first saw him. She had just
arrived in New York, and he had been flying his airplane
above Pennsylvania Station, leaving puffy white lettering
behind him in the sky. "That's Max Darby," an onlooker had
told her impatiently when she'd inquired, and the name
would always hold for her the wonder of that first breath
of the city. She was not even really surprised—only a little
awestruck—when, a few weeks later, after everything had
gone terribly wrong, he had fallen out of the sky right in
front of her, forcing them both to see her true mettle. That
was the way she always felt when he turned his quiet, intent
gaze on her—that he was capable of great things, and so she
must be, too.

She reached for his hand and went on holding it as they talked idly of the days since they had last seen each other. Mostly what Cordelia could remember of them was how often she had replayed the scene out in front of The Vault in her thoughts, savoring the memory of how urgently he had kissed her on the sidewalk that night.

Not until they reached Harlem did his shoulders begin to relax a little. Still, as they crossed the street to the brown townhouse where his mother lived, he kept looking over his shoulder as though someone might be following them. But the tension dissolved when they came up to the second-floor landing and the door with the number two hand-painted on it flew open.

"Cordelia! So good to see you again, sugar," Mrs. Darby exclaimed once she had hugged her son. Taking Cordelia's arm, she said, "I've been after Max to bring you by again. Anyway, come on in. Food's getting cold."

Everything was neat in Mrs. Darby's parlor—the old Victorian-style furniture was polished and simply arranged and the light was warm and the table was set for three. A fan whirred in the kitchen, and a phonograph was playing a piano concerto in the next room. There were children shouting on the street, and she could faintly hear the people moving around in the apartment upstairs. Here was a room where secrets did not need to be revealed, because—unlike in the rest of the world—none were kept, and for a moment, as they bent their heads while Max said grace, she forgot the things that she had come to New York in search of and was perfectly content.

Elsewhere in Manhattan the evening was only just beginning. In Harlem, wide-eyed voyeurs from the white parts of town, who had come in search of long-legged brown girls and exotic stage shows, were staring through car windows at the spectacle of the streets. They would likely have been surprised by the tranquility of the scene on the second-floor flat of an old brick townhouse, where two of the tabloids' newest stars were privately enjoying one another's company. For Cordelia, there was no place else to be. Whenever she glanced at Max's pure, handsome face she felt a ripple of pride to think he was hers and he was capable of something few people could do. And for his part, he kept looking at her and then looking away, as though he couldn't quite believe he had a girl like her in his mother's parlor.

After dinner, Mrs. Darby had retired in order that the young people might have some time alone, and Max sat on one side of his mother's yellow chintz sofa with Cordelia's head rested on his lap. Her body ran the length of the sofa, with her feet on the armrest, and she had let her eyes sink closed as Max played with her hair.

"You know, when I lived in Union, I used to go to the library to read the New York papers whenever I had a spare hour . . ." Cordelia began in a quiet, musing way. "I'd pore over the crime columns and the gossip columns in the hope of catching some mention of my dad. I loved reading about New York, too. I used to collect old guidebooks so I could learn the streets and the subways and the neighborhoods, so that when I came here, I'd never be lost."

"Did it look like what you imagined?"

"Not exactly. It was so much more than I expected! But the funny thing is, I always assumed that once I got here my real life would begin, that I wouldn't have to be imagining it all the time. But I found out I could be trapped here, too. And I kept reading the papers anyway. And you know whose name I looked for?"

Max smiled faintly. "Mine?" he answered. His eyes had a quality as though they were contemplating something he was afraid of but that he was determined to do anyway.

She bit her lip. "Did you ever seek out mine?"

Leaning forward, he replaced a tendril of hair behind her ear. "Yes. First by accident, and then so I could figure out where the hell a girl like you comes from. Once I knew who you were, I thought I'd better not try to know you any better, but I kept searching for your name anyway, not knowing why."

"Do you know why now?"

"Yes. It's because you're the bravest girl I've ever met."

Cordelia lowered her eyes. Her childhood had taught her how to swat away insults, but she did not yet know how to gracefully take a compliment. Neither said anything for a while after that, and Cordelia would have been happy to let the comfortable silence stretch out a while longer, except that a thought from earlier in the day kept nagging her.

"Charlie's up to something tonight."

"How do you know?"

"I'm not sure, really. I can just tell. He was preoccupied—they all were—and when he left he told me I was to stay close to my bodyguard and that under no circumstances was I to leave Dogwood." A faint smile played on her lips, and she opened her eyes and met his gaze.

To her surprise he did not smile back. "What's he up to, do you think?"

"I guess it probably has something to do with the Hales, although I can't be sure. Why are you frowning like that? Aren't you happy that I'm here?"

"Of course. But if Charlie thought it wasn't safe for you to go out tonight, maybe it's not safe for you to be out."

"But I—"

"Just promise me that in the future you'll stay put if it seems dangerous, and let me come to you?"

"All right. I promise."

"Good." Max pushed the hair away from her forehead, as though he wanted an unobstructed view of her face before he kissed her.

The kiss was sweet, and when it was over, Cordelia felt pleasantly fatigued and lay her head on his shoulder. "I wish I could stay here all night . . . but that would scandalize your mother, wouldn't it? And anyway, my poor bodyguard is probably sweating right now, terrified I won't be back before the boss."

"I know," Max said sadly. Yet they did not get up immediately, and when they did, they moved slowly and a little regretfully out of that quiet room and its low, warm light. At the door, he removed his leather flying jacket from the hook and handed it to her. "Take this."

"But Max, you need that! Anyway, it must be near ninety outside; I won't be cold."

He nodded in agreement. "Take it anyway," he said, and Cordelia realized that what he really wanted was for her not to go out with naked arms.

"All right." As they went down the stairs to the ground floor, she slipped it over her shoulders.

Outside, it was almost as light as day with the streetlights and the passing cars. They could hear music from somewhere, and shouting and laughter filtering from the windows of the higher stories. He reached for her hand and stepped ahead of her off the curb, shielding her from any oncoming cars, and raised an arm. A yellow cab pulled over, and he leaned in the front window to negotiate the price of the long drive.

"He'll take you," Max announced, turning to face Cordelia.

"Thank you."

"I'm glad you came."

"Me too."

"I should drive you," he said suddenly.

"No . . . You need to be at the airfield early, and if you take me now it'll be almost morning by the time you get back."

For a moment there was the old stiffness between them, a curious air of formality. Then, gazing at her, he gave a faint little shake of his head, as though he still couldn't quite believe she was real. His lips parted, and her breath caught, because she was briefly sure he was going to tell her that he loved her. Instead he opened the back door, and watched solicitously as she arranged herself on the backseat.

"I'll call you soon," he said and grinned, and they both knew he had thought it.

"Good." She grinned back at him as he closed the door and went on grinning as they pulled away from the curb. Although she did not so much as glance over her shoulder, she knew that he kept on watching. She sank back happily against the leather seat and didn't notice the silver sedan on the other side of the street making a swift U-turn so that it could follow her cab as it traveled south toward the Fifty-ninth Street Bridge.

4

VEHICLES ON A CITY STREET AT NIGHT WEAR POKER faces, their features stony and their eyes as steady as the moon. There was that rhythm of headlights as cars zoomed past, and Astrid liked how whenever a beam went over them she got a good picture of her husband, the line of his jaw and the way he filled up his shirt. When she woke up that morning she had been tempted to tell him her grandmother Donal's secret, but then she remembered her promise to the lady. Instead Astrid had cooed that she couldn't be apart from him and asked if he'd take her on his nocturnal rounds, and by now anticipation was at a high fizz inside her.

The world Charlie was taking her into was not one that

her mother would ever see, nor any of the girls who were going back to Connecticut to finish at Miss Porter's in the fall, perfecting themselves only so that they could be married to bores like Beau Ridley—the boy who had taken her first kiss—who would soon enough turn into the kind of musty old husband her mother collected. Virginia Donal de Gruyter Marsh had always been competitive with her daughter, for the silly and incontrovertible reason that she would forever be precisely twenty-two years younger than her, but Astrid had never heard such desperate jealousy in her mother's voice as she had on the telephone that afternoon. The old lady had been trying to invite herself out with the bright young things, on the flimsy pretext that she missed her daughter. But Astrid knew the real reason—Virginia couldn't stand that Astrid had chosen to be not at all like her mother and had forgone the chance to collect expensive surnames in order to collect nights like these.

As they flew down Sixth Avenue, Charlie leaned forward, his elbows on his knees, his brown eyes intent on the task ahead. Astrid let a hand rest on his back protectively. He worked so hard, her Charlie. After his father had died he had become a little obsessed with it, and he had pushed hard to make the business grow, especially where it meant stealing clients from the Hales. The Hales had struck back, of course—by kidnapping Astrid—but Charlie had saved her. And now she would save him, however she could, and see to it that he didn't work *too* hard, and that there was always lightness at his side, in the pretty form of herself.

"Here," Charlie announced, and the driver pulled the Daimler off the wide avenue and onto a tree-lined side street.

Astrid pressed her shoulders up toward her ears, and a low murmur of expectation escaped her lips as they passed the redbrick buildings of the Village, where markers of the old family neighborhood life were still mixed in with the new fun. She had been down here plenty of times with Charlie and with the fast set from White Cove—young people like her who wanted their evenings frothy and were more likely to see the sunrise at the end of a day than at its beginning. But she had never been in the Village like this—moving stealthily, instead of with the intention of making a scene.

"Here," Charlie said again, and the driver stopped the car in front of an old storefront, the windows of which had been painted black from the inside. Over the front door a neon sign blinked PHARMACY. Without looking back at Astrid, Charlie pushed open the door. Astrid scooted toward him on the seat and stuck a leg out, her high-heeled shoe reaching for the pavement. She let out an angry yelp when she felt the steel of the door closing against her calf.

"Charlie!"

"What are you doing?" His face was wide open with surprise, and it was only after he saw his wife's crumpled mouth that he realized her leg was smarting. "I'm sorry, baby. You stay here."

"Charlie." Astrid scowled. "You said I could tag along."

"I'll be right inside, baby, and then I'm gonna take you to the sweetest little Italian place around the corner, all right? Ted will stay with you," he went on, meaning the driver. "He's armed."

The gold dress Astrid wore glimmered in her wake as she descended to the sidewalk and closed the car door behind her. She brushed a lock of blond hair out of her face and met Charlie's gaze. He turned his chin up in silent argument, but he blinked first, and Astrid, knowing she had won, spread her full lips into a smile. After another second he gave in completely. With a subtle tilt of the head, Charlie indicated that his bodyguard should precede him. He took Astrid's hand and moved ahead of her to the door, and she shimmied in her slinky dress to keep up.

The bodyguard poked the bell with a sturdy finger.

For what seemed a long time there was no noise within. Then the door was drawn back and a long, wan face with a pair of spectacles balanced on its nose appeared in the crack of the door frame.

The man's eyes scanned the three young people in the street. He stared at Charlie and then at Astrid and then at Charlie again, letting his eyes linger the longest on the young heir of the Grey bootlegging fortune. "What seems to be your ailment?" he said suspiciously.

The bodyguard looked at Charlie, and Charlie said: "I can't sleep at night."

"How long has it been since you've slept through the night?" the man asked—incuriously, Astrid noticed with a sly upturn at the corner of her mouth, for she had been a witness to this sort of password ritual before.

"Eight days," Charlie replied.

The man nodded and pulled open the door so that they could follow him through an empty pharmacy, where the medicine bottles hung like ghosts on the mirrored shelves, and into a back room. Several small tables were illuminated by hanging lampshades, their Victorian tassels faded and their cloth coverings threadbare. "Runnin' Wild" played from an old phonograph. Five couples occupied the room, none of them the type who might be found playing croquet on a White Cove lawn on a Sunday.

"I see plenty of wedding rings, but I think we're the only man and wife in the room!" Astrid whispered delightedly into Charlie's ear as the fellow with the glasses showed them to their table. This seemed funny to her, that they had landed in the kind of out-of-the-way place where people went when they were up to no good.

"What can I get you?" the man with the glasses asked

as Astrid lowered herself into an old wooden chair.

"I'd like to speak to the owner," Charlie said without sitting down.

"Oh, Charlie, let's warm up a minute! We'll have two of your finest whatever it is you serve here," Astrid said with a careless wave of her hand and a theatrical wink. When the man saw her wink, his features relaxed for the first time since they'd entered, and Astrid decided that she liked his face, which was shadowy in some parts and protruded in others.

Reluctantly, Charlie sat down beside her, and the bodyguard retreated to the corner of the room as their host disappeared behind a curtain. "You see, Charlie, pretty soon I'm going to be indispensable to you! I suspect you needed a little ladylike touch for this sort of business. You can be *awfully* intimidating, you know."

The veins on Charlie's thick neck were popping slightly, so she softened her eyes at him. She didn't let up until some sweetness came into his gaze, and then she leaned toward him and said: "Charlie, promise me you'll never come to a joint like this with some girl who isn't me."

"Why would I ever—"

Astrid rolled her eyes in the direction of the other patrons, urging him to look around. "You know."

"Astrid." Charlie put both hands at her waist, encircling it. "Astrid, I would never."

"I know, I know, just *tell* me."

He lowered himself so that his mouth was close to her ear. "I would never," he said, his stern voice breaking over the sincerity of the sentiment. She sensed a kiss coming, but their drinks came first, served in chipped white coffee cups.

Beaming, Astrid brought the coffee cup to her face. But the taste of the whiskey was terrible, so she put it down definitively into its saucer. "Oh, Charlie, don't tell Mr. Specs, but this tastes awful!"

A twinkling little laugh escaped her lips, and it broke the sweetness of the previous moment. Charlie turned from her slowly and signaled the host, who came away from the wall toward their table. A new song had come on, another old one—Astrid couldn't remember the name, but she knew they'd been playing it in the cafés in Paris the year after her mother's second divorce, when they'd lived out of suitcases in Europe.

"I'm sorry," Charlie told the man coldly, "but my wife says this stuff is terrible."

"Oh, well, terrible is such a strong word!" Astrid trilled.

"I apologize." The man with the glasses kept his voice just as cold and did not look at Astrid again. "But that's all we serve here. Perhaps Madame would like it better at another kind of establishment."

"My wife likes it here fine." Charlie stood and pushed his chair back. "I'd like to talk to the owner about it."

"I am the owner, sir."

"Then I'd like to talk to you about it. Alone."

The man turned down the corners of his mouth and swung his head, as though he didn't see the point but was willing to accommodate this unusual request, and then he gestured toward the back of the room. Charlie shot a meaningful look at his bodyguard, and Astrid gave a soft squeal as she hurried along behind Charlie, through the curtain and into a small, dingy office. A desk took up most of the room, and the rest was occupied by a filing cabinet, the top drawer of which was unlocked and open to reveal stacked bottles full of amber liquid.

"My name is Charlie Grey," Charlie said, dragging a chair back so that he could sit in it.

"I know who you are, Mr. Grey."

Astrid's eyes went excitedly to Charlie at this evidence of what a big, important person he was and how his reputation spread even to holes-in-the-wall like this one. Though he didn't return her look, she stood behind him anyway, delicately placing her ringed fingers on his shoulder, thinking what an impressive accessory she surely was for him.

"I import liquor. Good liquor. Not like what you've been serving."

"I know what you do, Mr. Grey."

"Try it. We just brought it in through the Bahamas. It's top-notch."

Charlie brought out a flask from the inside pocket of his coat and poured a thimbleful of brown liquid into two of the coffee cups that were lined up neatly on the desk. Both men drank and then set their glasses back down and regarded one another. Although Astrid had spent the whole day in anticipation of this part of the evening—when she would be ushered behind a curtain and get to see how things were really done—she couldn't stop her attention from drifting now. The room was small, after all, and not very interesting, and she couldn't stop herself from wondering, just for an instant, what was happening at the Ritz's roof that evening. Then her gaze settled on the room's lone decoration, a framed picture of two children wearing frilly white getups, which she supposed were meant to be fancy.

"How many cases can I order you?" Charlie was saying.

"Mr. Grey, I'm not sure we understand each other," the man replied.

"Why, mister!" Astrid broke in. "Are those your children?"

Startled, the man followed her pointed finger. "Yes," he said cautiously.

"Oh, they're *very* darling," she gushed.

"Thank you." Astrid smiled at him, and he smiled back. "Those are my two oldest, Rosie and Matthew."

Charlie pushed back his chair as he rose up. "How many cases can I order you?"

"Mr. Grey, your liquor is very good. But I can't buy from you. I buy from Coyle Mink." The man paused while his drooping eyes focused on Charlie. "He runs the Bronx."

Charlie put his fists on the table and leaned forward so that when he spoke his spittle landed on the man's nose. "I've heard of Coyle Mink, and I've even heard of the Bronx, but this isn't the Bronx, and you're buying from me now."

"Mr. Grey, I—"

"How many cases?" Suddenly Charlie was yelling.

"But I—"

"How many cases?" This time Charlie's voice was lower, but no less menacing. He'd spit a little more, and the spittle remained glistening on the man's long, worn forehead.

"Five . . . ," the man ventured, as though he hoped this would do.

"Five." Charlie brought his shoulders back and spoke the word as though savoring it. "Five cases to start. I'll have my boys be by tomorrow with your five cases." The flask disappeared under Charlie's jacket, and he produced a card, which he twirled in the air between two fingers before placing it on the desk. "A pleasure doing business with you. This is my wife, Astrid, by the way. Isn't she the prettiest wife a man can buy?"

"Yes," the man answered, but his voice was hollow and empty of conviction. It was the opposite of the voice he had used to say "Rosie and Matthew."

A sadness crept into Astrid's heart when she heard in the man's tone how little he cared whether she was pretty or not. Before she could say anything, Charlie's arm was gripping her, pulling her out of the office. She glanced back, but the man was still staring down at his desk with that blank and weary expression of defeat.

In Charlie's body she sensed triumph. He was springy with what he had done. When they went back through the speakeasy he was strutting, and the men and women huddled at their tables turned their faces toward him a little meekly, as villagers might look up at a Viking. He did not have to say anything to the bodyguard stationed by the door—the man just followed along as they went quickly through the pharmacy and out onto the sidewalk. Holding the car door for her, Charlie ushered Astrid in. She heard metal slam against metal, and then Charlie was beside her, pressing her against the backseat, his mouth pushing on her mouth to open it up.

He was proud of himself, and she wished she could be proud of him too, but the pathetic condition they'd left that man in—his face all slack as though he'd just absorbed another of life's many blows—had soured her evening.

"Charlie, I just got so tired," she said, pushing him away. "Do you think you could take me home?"

"Not a chance, doll!" His dark eyes were shot through

with electricity as he pulled her toward him. "I'm not letting go of you now."

City dwellers are people who won't sit still. Every year they move faster and find new activities to absorb their manic energy. They parade and they cheer, they showboat and they observe, they play elaborate games of hide-and-go-seek as though the concrete canyons were some kind of buzzed-up jungle gym and, as long as they keep playing, none of them will ever grow old. Any newcomer to the great metropolis might find it strange that the first showing of a motion picture is also an excuse for a rabble of newspaper photographers to push and shove against a velvet rope, calling out names often printed in columns or referred to reverentially on the radio. But the proud owners of those names had dressed in such finery that it was perfectly obvious they expected more from their evening than to sit in the darkness watching themselves projected onscreen.

On the way into the Loews theater on Forty-Fifth Street and Broadway, Letty had not seemed at all out of place on the arms of her two patrons. She had paused and smiled for the cameras, wearing a dress of rippling persimmon that highlighted the luminescence of her shoulders. A narrow silver ribbon went around her bobbed and shiny helmet of hair, fixing a magnolia in full bloom over her left ear. That afternoon, Sophia had given Letty *her* lessons in how to be a star, which were different from

Valentine's lessons. Sophia had taught Letty how to pose for a picture, how to smile for the public, how to radiate an aura of importance and glamour. And perhaps this was more valuable information, all things considered, because she was following all of Sophia's rules, and the cameramen were calling out to her as though she, too, were in the pictures.

Even so, when the lights went down in the theater, she was transported to the world of Minetta Carrington, a witty and passionate socialite, married to a vapid playboy but still attracted to the tennis champion she had been in love with as a girl. As the heroine traveled to the South Seas and Europe in search of meaning, Letty's heart got tender over her story and all its beautiful impossibility.

"Did you like it?" she whispered, still a little awestruck, when the lights went up.

"Like what?" Sophia was draped over the back of her seat, her attention focused, as it had been for the last ten minutes or so, on the two bow-tied gentlemen behind them, both of whom were vaguely familiar to Letty, although whether from the whirligig of her recent nights or from some movie she'd seen once, she couldn't be certain. "Oh," she went on in a changed tone, dropping her wrist—which was heavy with a cuff of diamonds—over Letty's hand. "The movie. Delightful, didn't you think so?"

"In the beginning, maybe. But after that it was so much

more! It was so *sad*, and I almost can't believe that . . ." Letty trailed off, thinking of how it had ended for the heroine, alone on a boat going back to a New York that had nothing left to offer her.

"I thought it was exquisite," Valentine, leaning around his wife's back, told Letty in a low voice. Then he grinned, and she realized that he had been watching just as reverently as she had.

All around them, well-heeled men and women were rising, smoothing out silk dresses and straightening jacket cuffs. Their eyes were on the door, as though the next thing might start without them and that knowledge was making their skin crawl. Even though she knew she shouldn't be, Letty was a little surprised that they were able to break so quickly from the world of the movie. It bothered her, almost. But it bothered her less when she remembered that Valentine had been watching rapturously, too.

"Shall we, my dear?" he was saying now, to Sophia.

"Yes, darling," she replied. "Save me before I bore these two to death!"

"No! How could you possibly ever?" the two gentlemen exclaimed, almost in tandem, as though they were twins. After that there was a great deal of blowing kisses and exchanging of promises, and Sophia begged them to send all her love and best wishes to their pugs.

"Are those men brothers?" Letty whispered, once they began making their way down the grand curved staircase to the lobby.

"Brothers!" Sophia hooted and leaned in conspiratorially. "I suppose they might be more or less like brothers now, but for a long time they were more akin to Mr. and Mrs."

Letty's eyes got wide, and her mouth made a circle around her confusion. How could that be, she wanted to ask, when they were two men and everyone could see it? But Sophia gave her a wink, and Letty understood. To be let in on this gossip triggered a small spasm of satisfaction within her, and as they swept down toward the lobby she was reminded of Sophia's earlier prediction that they would be fast friends. A great chandelier hung over the crowd on the first floor, dappling their faces, many of which were turned up in expectation at the descending movie stars. She was feeling so important that it only surprised her a little when the first person to approach their group of three thrust his hand in her direction.

"Why, you must be Letty Larkspur! I've been dying to meet you."

Letty gave the tall, blond gentleman—whose blandly handsome face was somehow familiar to her—a goofy smile but managed to simply nod in a vague way instead of saying anything in reply. Saying little created mystery—that was the advice Sophia had echoed earlier, while they'd gotten dressed.

"I'm Laurence Peters," he went on. "I played the part of the tennis champion's rival, remember, in the middle of the picture? The one who throws his racket down in a huff?"

"Yes, of course. I didn't recognize you without the visor."

"You look stunning!" he gushed.

Sophia cleared her throat, and Laurence's eyes darted from Letty to her patrons, who were drawn up quite impressively and regarding him with skeptical eyes.

"Well, uh—" Laurence faltered, as though he were embarrassed by the sudden realization of his true place in the firmament. "Will you be going on to Jack Montrose's party, I hope?"

This time Letty didn't respond immediately because she had no idea who Jack Montrose was, or why she would be going to his party. But Sophia answered for her. "Of course we're going to Jack's party," she said haughtily. Then she put her arm around Letty and drew her toward the exit.

"What kind of a party is it?" Letty asked, as they stepped out and the cameras began to flash again.

"The kind of party people like us go to." Sophia laughed and shook her hair out.

"In order that we might be bored stiff," Valentine put in, less enthusiastically.

"Darling, don't *say* that!" Sophia's smile grew bright and her grip on Letty tightened. "Someone might overhear you and think you mean it."

Valentine gave an apologetic half-smile to Letty. "I want to go over my lines for *The Good Lieutenant*, and anyway, my costume screen test is tomorrow and I want to be well-rested."

"You see, my dear, he's vainer than I am!" Sophia was signaling to their driver and did not see the fretfulness her comment caused in Valentine's brow.

"But don't leave us!" Letty blurted without thinking.

"You ladies will have much more fun without me." Valentine's smile returned now, and he bowed gallantly in Letty's direction.

"Darling, don't be ridiculous, we will miss you every second." Sophia turned and kissed her husband as her cream-colored limousine approached. Then she removed her glove so she could use her thumb to wipe the lipstick off his lips. "That is too dark a shade for you," she laughed. "Better now. But listen, lover, will you take a taxi home? Suddenly I am in *such* a hurry to get to the party . . ."

Letty wasn't sure if this suggestion pained Valentine, or if she felt pained for him, or if what she was really feeling was disappointment. She wanted to talk to someone about the movie, and Valentine was the only person, as far as she could tell, who had been watching it.

"Of course, my dearest," he replied. He kissed Sophia, and then Letty, on the cheek before striding off along the sidewalk, in the direction of Park Avenue, as though he were just any ordinary person. For a moment Letty watched him disappear into the crush of bodies, but then she heard Sophia calling her, and she followed the turquoise train of her dress into the limousine, and, like that, they were on to the next attraction.

Astrid didn't know how long she'd been asleep when Charlie came in, waking her. The turret room that had once belonged to Darius Grey, but was now theirs, was strewn with clothes not yet put away from their travels. Light from the guard tower slanted in through the high windows. She turned away from the door so that he would not know she was wide-eyed, and she stared at the window wishing she could sleep as she normally did—the happy, solid sleep of girls who are just the right amount selfish and do not have to begin their days at any particular hour. The light was already in the sky, and on the other side of the room she could hear Charlie careening back and forth.

The evening came back to her, a series of ugly scenes. How Charlie had dragged her all over Manhattan, bragging about her looks and family and his bootlegging prowess, how he was going to be bigger than Coyle Mink. When she'd finally prevailed upon him to take her back to Dogwood, they had been intercepted at the door by Jones, and when Astrid went up to bed ahead of him, she heard Charlie shouting from the second floor. The fight must have gone on all this time.

Now Astrid listened to Charlie wrestling with his jacket and with his shoes, and she knew that he was even drunker than before. Finally he got himself undressed and fell, hard, against the mattress beside her. Immediately he began to snore. Snoring was not something she had minded particularly while they were on their honeymoon—she had not wanted to sleep while they were away, and anyway, snoring seemed like something that men did, and for that reason it had delighted instead of tortured her. But now she knew that it was torture.

She turned over so that she wouldn't have to look at him, and then she turned back over again. The beginning of the dawn was on his high slab cheekbones and the curve of his closed eyelids. For hours, it seemed, she stared at that face, wondering what went on behind it, until she had the idea to disentangle herself from the white bedclothes and go to the sofa, where she lay herself down and closed her eyes.

5

"WHAT DID I TELL YOU? SOMETIMES IT'S MORE FUN just us girls."

To punctuate her point, Sophia flagged down a passing waiter and took two champagne flutes off his brass tray, although Letty was pretty well convinced already. By then she'd realized how disappointing it would have been to go home and talk about the movies when she had a real party like this one to go to that was as grand as anything she'd ever seen on screen.

"Val's a romantic, you know. He's absolutely in love with the pictures, worries himself sick about his lines and all that. But it's just as important to leave the house now and then, especially on nights like these, when the important people are out and in a good mood, and there are so many people to see you looking your best!"

"Oh, yes, I can see that."

Glancing around the great expanse of Jack Montrose's living room, Letty thought how the gentlemen in tuxedoes and women in the latest styles did practically glow with importance. Although she was also pretty sure that just about anyone would feel important in such a setting. The dimensions of the room were almost improbable—it seemed to go on forever in two directions. Behind them was a wall of gold-flecked mirrors, and in front of them a series of glass doors were thrown open onto a terrace that floated above the soft topography of Central Park treetops. Clustered seating areas were scattered throughout the room, low white sofas and chaises separated from each other by potted rosebushes. At their feet lay a bearskin rug.

"You never know who you'll meet at a party—if you remember nothing else I tell you, honey, remember that. Get yourself invited to as many parties as possible, and when you're there, practice picking out the most important man in the room. When I was coming up, I used to time myself—I got so good I could pick out the heavy before the boy had even taken my coat." Sophia fixed a cigarette into her cigarette holder and paused her monologue long enough to let a man materialize and light it for her. "Thank you," she said dismissively. "Now," she went on, when the man was gone, "you try it."

Letty sat up straight and brushed her hands across the bright lap of her dress. Her blue eyes went right and left, taking in the faces of the guests. They were interesting, proud faces, wily and shining and gay, and for a moment Letty couldn't see how any one of them might be singled out as special. Almost every one of them looked as though they had been to Europe twice and kept their own chauffeur and a charge account at Bendel's. The columnist Claude Carrion, whom she recognized from The Vault, was walking across the floor with his shoulders thrown back, and Letty, who had heard Sophia mention his name several times while they were getting ready, wondered if this were a kind of test and *he* might be the most important man in the room.

Then she caught sight of a face that made her smile involuntarily, and she forgot what she had been searching for in the previous moment.

"Oh . . . Will you excuse me? I see someone I know."

"I don't think you found the heavy, doll." Sophia gave Letty's shoulder a light slap as her red lips parted in a beneficent smile. "But if you must. A man who is not important today may be important tomorrow, and one can't always tell who happens to be the second cousin of a king."

"Thank you," Letty said gratefully, as though she needed special permission to walk over to the man leaning on the marble balustrade outside on the porch. When he noticed her, he stepped in her direction with his hand lifted in greeting.

The way it had been the last time she had spoken to Grady Lodge did not fully occur to her until she was beside him. The memory turned her cheeks pink. It was the night he had been planning to introduce her to his parents, but she had behaved badly and forgotten, and by the time she had turned up he hadn't wanted to anymore. That was the night she learned that he chose to live on the pennies he made as a writer, even though the Lodges were millionaires. She'd seen him only once since, and they hadn't spoken. He had been escorting a girl named Peachy Whitburn, who was from the same world as Astrid Donal and already knew how to walk across a room like she owned it.

"How," Letty said, mimicking his hand gesture.

"How," he replied with a laugh. "I am glad to see you still blush," he went on, and the tone of his voice told her that he wasn't angry anymore. "It's a telltale sign that you're still human, no matter the company you keep."

"Oh." Wishing she could stop blushing now, Letty placed a palm on her cheek.

"I'm sorry. Did that sound harsh? It was a pretentious thing to say. I only meant that I read about your ascent almost every day."

"It can't be *every* day." Averting her gaze, Letty caught

a glimpse of Sophia, watching her from the sofa. "I certainly haven't done anything to deserve that kind of attention."

"Perhaps the current coverage is an advance on your future activities. I'd like to think I'm the only one who knows you're special, but that doesn't seem very likely." Saying this, Grady smiled, almost sadly, and put his hands deeper into the pockets of his trousers.

The flattery sent a pleasant ripple over the naked skin of Letty's arms that lasted until she saw the sadness persisting in his deep-set gray eyes. "Are you courting Peachy Whitburn now?" she asked awkwardly. "I saw you together that time at The Vault, and you seemed so happy together."

"Oh, yes—Peachy," he replied without sounding any happier. "I suppose I ought to marry her. Everyone says I should."

Letty was almost pleased now to see that he didn't really want to marry Peachy Whitburn, but then she remembered Sophia's most recent instruction, that she should try to pick out the most important man in the room, and she felt a touch ashamed to think that she had occupied herself with the one fellow present she knew for certain couldn't get her a part. Guiltily, she turned to see what Sophia thought of her now—but her guilt was washed away by surprise when she realized that Sophia was no longer on the sofa near the polar bear rug.

She shrank a little at the thought that Sophia had gotten miffed with her and left the party. How alone she would be if that were the case—and in a room like this one, it was as terrifying a thought as she'd had in weeks. Stepping away from Grady and toward the center of music and chatter, she craned her neck in search of her mentor and saw women in every shade *but* turquoise.

By the time she spotted Sophia's waterfall of a dress, Letty had drifted from the balustrade to the doorway to the grand ballroom. But suddenly Letty wasn't sure if the woman was Sophia at all. An arm clothed in red velvet was wrapped around the woman's waist, and the hand that emerged from that same red velvet was rested familiarly on the upper flank of her thigh.

"Grady, will you excuse me just a moment?" Letty murmured as she moved back into the room. He answered, but Letty wasn't sure she heard all of the words, because at just that moment the woman turned and Letty saw for sure that it was Sophia. Her face was shining up at the man in the red velvet smoking jacket, showing him a daffy smile. He wasn't handsome exactly, but he had large, carved features, and his body was big, as though he played a lot of sports and ate a lot of meat. He was important, that was obvious, and he was old enough that his hair was going gray. Old enough that he might have been Letty's father, or Sophia's.

As she moved to follow them through the crowd, Letty realized that the man in the red jacket was their host, Jack Montrose, and that Sophia must have gone to him because she wasn't feeling well. That was why he was holding her close; she could no longer stand on her own, and he was taking her somewhere she could rest. They were passing through a doorway on the far side of the ballroom, and Letty had almost caught up when a black tuxedo jacket blocked her way.

"Letty Larkspur!"

She glanced up at the fair, beaming face of Laurence Peters. "I can't talk right now," she said quickly.

"Talk—who wants to talk?" He guffawed good-naturedly and picked up one of her hands as though he meant to waltz her across the floor. "There's some real second-rate dancing going on over there, and I thought we could show 'em how it's done."

"No, I—" Letty glanced back and saw that Grady was framed in the doorway to the terrace, looking at her. She knew how she must appear right now, in that bright, flimsy dress, with Laurence almost ready to pick her up off the floor. But she couldn't think about that. The woman who had taken her under wing and promised to teach her everything she knew had fallen ill, and Letty had to help her.

"Miss Larkspur, I know I'm not as big as Valentine or Sophia." Laurence's brow had somehow or other gotten stormy, and his mouth puckered. "But I don't think that's any reason for you to treat me badly."

"I'm sorry, I didn't mean to." Letty pulled away—already she had lost sight of Sophia and Jack Montrose. "But you'll have to excuse me now."

"Well, I expect you to make it up to me!" Laurence called after her, but by then she was turning the corner where she'd last seen Sophia draped over Jack Montrose's arm. Through the doorway was a dimly lit hall, which Letty hurried down. After it turned, she could scarcely hear the party anymore, and she came to two doors that faced each other. Sophia must have gone behind one of these. Letty went to one and knocked timidly. There was no reply, and she had just turned toward the other when she heard a low moan from within, as though Sophia were in pain.

"Sophia!" Letty gasped and knocked on the door.

No one answered, but there was a sound as though someone was being pushed against the door from the other side, and another moan. Letty's heart quivered. She raised her hand and knocked harder. "Sophia!"

The noises stopped, and then the door opened a crack.

"What?" Jack Montrose's cheeks were ruddier than before, and his tie was undone, and she knew right away that he was angry. She swallowed and forced herself to hold his gaze.

"Where's Sophia?" she said wildly. "Is she all right?"

He stared at her, almost quizzically, and then a smile crept across the lower part of his face. The smile was much worse than the scowl it replaced, and for a moment Letty felt as rotten and small and sad as on the night she'd almost been duped into performing at a stag party, when a room full of men had wolf-called her and demanded that she remove her clothes.

"She's indisposed. That's all." He said it slowly, drawing each word out lasciviously, so that they both knew it was a lie. "I'm taking care of her. She'll be better in a minute."

The door slammed shut before Letty could say anything more. She stumbled backward, shocked to the core by this irrefutable evidence that a woman might have the love of Valentine O'Dell and still seek amorous attention elsewhere. If more sounds came from inside the room, she didn't want to hear them. She wished that Sophia would emerge and explain that it wasn't what it looked like at all, but she didn't, and after a while Letty hung her head and began to move slowly back toward the party. All she could think of was Valentine, how anonymous he had been as he walked away from them along the sidewalk, and how impossible it was going to be to keep what she had seen Sophia doing from him.

6

IT WAS THE HEAT THAT WOKE CORDELIA. SHE ROLLED over in the twist of her sheets and saw that the maid had been there. A polished wood standing tray had been erected, and there was a pot of coffee and a carafe of orange juice waiting for her. The newspaper had not come with the rest of the breakfast things, and for a moment she felt short-tempered with Milly, who never could seem to concentrate on a single thing at a time long enough to do it right and ought to know by now how Cordelia liked to start her morning.

But then she remembered how hard Milly had taken it about Danny, who died from bullet wounds the night Astrid was kidnapped, and also how busy Astrid kept her now that she lived at Dogwood, and decided that there was no use in being irritated. The Vault had been full last night, and Max Darby loved her—at least, she was pretty sure he'd thought it. Anyway, that habit of newspaper reading, of trying to learn about the world from smudgy broadsheets, seemed like a relic of her old life. Especially when she stood up and walked across the thick white carpets, past the low, fashionable white furniture of the Calla Lily Suite—which even now was stocked daily with fresh deliveries of its namesake flower—and peeked down on the rolling landscape of soft green velvet that was Dogwood's west lawn. She was looking at her father's vision of what life ought to be, and she knew that she had found it, too.

With a sigh of satisfaction, Cordelia determined to go find Charlie and tell him how well they had done the night before. It was a fine thing to have a brother, and though they never needed to say it out loud, they could glance at each and silently know how proud Darius would have been of them. She stepped into a pair of wide-legged trousers and an ivory camisole that fluttered at the neckline, and pinned her hair away from her face so that the skin of her neck would remain as cool as possible. Then she poured herself a cup of coffee and went downstairs.

As she came onto the second-floor landing, she saw Keller, one of Charlie's boys, coming out of the billiards room, and she smiled brightly. "Morning," she said.

He averted his eyes. "Afternoon now."

Before she could reply, he was past her down the stairs.

"Is something wrong with Keller?" she asked as she walked into Charlie's office and sank into the big chair opposite his desk.

He was facing the window and didn't turn around to look at her right away. Outside, the sky was hazing over, and she wondered if more rain wasn't on the way.

"Who?"

"Keller! The new man. The one who can't seem to grow a beard." A few seconds passed without a response from Charlie, and her fine mood began to flicker. She wanted Charlie to feel as light with good fortune as she did, but he wouldn't even look at her.

"Nothing is wrong. He just didn't get much sleep last night, and I expect he's feeling it today." The chair groaned when Charlie took his feet off the sill and began to slowly swivel.

"Charlie!" she exclaimed, once he was facing her. "You look like hell. You might think about getting more sleep yourself."

He smiled thinly and lit a cigarette before putting his oxfords up on the desk. "Dad never slept," Charlie said after a while.

"He didn't?"

"Said he didn't like it. Said when he slept he just mostly tossed and turned and worried he was missing something."

"Doesn't mean he wouldn't have wanted you to."

The focus of Charlie's eyes drifted and became indistinct. They were milky, tired eyes, and the skin beneath them had a punched-out quality. "He would have wanted *you* to sleep. He always said you were just as pretty as your mother, and just as precious, and that you should be pampered the way he wasn't able to pamper Fanny when she was alive." He held the cigarette between his index finger and thumb, contemplating it. "I have one memory of her, did I ever tell you?"

Cordelia took in a breath. "No, you didn't."

"Well, it's not a memory so much. More like a picture in my mind of a shack somewhere, probably some hideout of Dad's, and they were listening to the radio and dancing. Duluth Hale was there, it was when they were still friends, and I can remember his fat face with its big gaping pie-hole, and dancing around Mrs. Hale, and everyone laughed a lot."

"That sounds nice," Cordelia said with a smile. She hadn't known that Duluth Hale and her father had been friends like that, but it didn't sound so bad, now that she was hearing it.

"They were probably drunk, and Dad probably smacked me later and told me I should have come from a nice, pretty girl like Fanny instead of the no-good one I actually crawled out of."

Charlie still wouldn't meet Cordelia's eyes, and she was somewhat glad of this, because her face had grown long. She didn't like to think that there was any difference between her and Charlie, or that their father could have said a mean thing like that. But she didn't have to conjure a reply, because Elias Jones came in then and walked straight for the desk.

"Cordelia, I need to talk to Charlie." The way he spoke, Cordelia knew he meant alone.

"Of course." She stood up awkwardly, glad to go but also wishing she could have thought of something to say to her brother.

"I'll want to talk to you, too. Later."

She nodded and, after a few seconds of unsuccessfully trying to catch Charlie's eye, went out of the room.

The dark mahogany of the second-floor landing had an icing of pale blue light from the skylight high above, and Cordelia paused, staring at it, wondering why she felt so ill at ease. She had seen Charlie in foul moods before, and there were always things that Jones wanted to discuss with him alone. For a while she hovered there, frozen, unsure whether to go back to her room or downstairs. Then the door to the billiard room opened and one of the boys came out. He paused when he saw Cordelia, and then his eyelids half sank and his mouth curled in a funny way.

"What?" she demanded indignantly.

But he only shrugged and went down, taking the stairs two at a time. The door to the billiard room was ajar and she paused for a moment in the door frame, as though she might catch someone doing something that would explain the pall that hung over Dogwood. But there was only one person left in the room—Victor, Astrid's bodyguard, sitting on the worn sofa by the window, his legs crossed and a newspaper open in front of him.

"Miss Cordelia." He stood up when he saw her and put the paper away.

"Where's Astrid?"

"I don't know, I haven't seen her all morning, is she all right?" He said it too quickly, then afterward cracked his knuckles as though he was embarrassed.

"I suppose there's nothing strange about her being in bed past noon," Cordelia replied slowly. "That's how she was brought up."

"Right." Victor cleared his throat. "Of course."

"Victor, what's wrong?"

"They didn't tell you?"

"Tell me what?"

But before he could reply, she heard her name being said on the radio, and she forgot about Victor and charged toward the droning sound.

". . . ever since Miss Grey entered the young pilot's life,

his golden touch seemed compromised. Whereas before he was incapable of doing wrong, now he erred, his interest in flying went slack, and though he was reputed never to touch alcohol, he was spotted in clubs where drinking was known to be the main draw. Of course, there were many in the sporting world who thought he would return to form once the bootlegger's daughter was out of his life, but as was reported in the Night Owl column this morning, it appears they've been seeing each other regularly, that in fact Cordelia was visiting Max Darby in his mother's Harlem apartment and was apparently in on the secret that he was a Negro by birth . . ."

Cordelia's eyes rolled slowly toward Victor. Her face was numb, and she couldn't begin to think of what to say. "It's in the paper, too, isn't it?"

"I don't know—"

"Never mind." She crossed toward him and snatched the paper out of his hand and flipped to the gossip section. There, taking up almost a quarter of the page, was a photo of her and Max stepping out of Mrs. Darby's apartment, and then a smaller one of Max the next morning saying good-bye to his mother on the street. In the black-and-white photo the difference in their skin tone was exaggerated, but you could perfectly see the family resemblance.

After that she was deaf to the radio and the ceiling fan and anything Victor might have tried to say to her.

"If Jones comes looking for me, tell him I've gone on a long walk."

She didn't gauge Victor's reaction. By the time the last word was out of her mouth she was at the door, and shortly thereafter she had arrived in the first-floor library, where she asked to be connected to the Hudson Laurels' place.

"Mrs. Hudson Laurel's line." It was a strange, prim voice, and though Cordelia had never met Max's patrons, she sensed that this was a secretary and not the lady of the house herself.

"Is Max at home?"

"I'm sorry." There was a long pause. "I don't know who you're talking about."

Cordelia's eyes sank closed, and she set her teeth. The horrid coldness of this statement made her want to lash out, but she knew that wouldn't help her any. All that mattered in that moment was finding Max. "Yes," she said evenly, "you do."

On the other end of the line there was a sharp exhalation. "Well, he's not here. Mrs. Laurel can't have him in the house anymore. He was like a member of the family, you know, and that just wouldn't do anymore. She was a suffragette! She's still sore *they* got the vote before we did."

Cordelia put her forehead into her palm, and then drew her long fingers across her face until they were massaging her temples. "Please," she whispered. "Please just tell me where he is."

After a long pause the woman went on in a changed tone. "There only ever was one place he seemed to like going. Mr. and Mrs. Laurel had a terrible row this morning, and I suppose he hasn't had the heart to tell the boy that he won't be able to fund him anymore."

"Thank you." Cordelia put the receiver down and allowed herself one long moment with her eyelids pressed closed. After that, instinct took over. She drove fast toward the gates, ignoring the shouting of the guard who wanted to know where she was going and if Charlie had approved it. Ignoring him was easy, because she could barely hear anything over her self-recriminating thoughts.

When Letty cracked an eye she saw that the light filtering in through the window was not yet strong. It cast the white expanse of wall next to her with the pale greenish color of six A.M., which meant that she was already late in getting up and that her father would be coming soon to rouse her. She burrowed deeper and closed her eyes and wished she could stay like that a while longer instead of going to the dairy. She pulled the sheet up close to her chin and let the silkiness settle over her, so that its cool surface caressed her skin. It was the silk sheet that jolted her. She opened both eyes again and blinked, remembering that she wasn't in Union at all but in Manhattan, in the home of movie stars, one of whom she'd witnessed disappearing into a room with a man who was not her husband.

In Union, and even at Dogwood, she'd always dressed carefully before leaving her room and beginning her day, but she was too hungry for all that, so instead she stepped over the thick carpet and sat in front of her vanity in the pale peach ankle-length slip that Sophia had given her, along with several other items that the actress no longer had use for. She threw the cream-colored kimono that hung in her closet over her shoulders and tiptoed out into the apartment, just like that. The hall was quiet and lit by sconces, and she padded over its soft carpets toward the sunken living room, which was decorated with simple furniture that nonetheless seemed very expensive, and pampas grass erupting from gold urns, and gigantic portraits of Valentine and Sophia. The room was a little strange to her—somehow too grand to really be a home—and she was happy to step into a kitchen fragrant with the smell of cooking bacon.

"Ah, Miss Larkspur, the lady of the hour!" Valentine said in booming, perfectly enunciated syllables. He was sitting at the round pedestal table by the large double windows with the morning papers strewn before him. Letty couldn't stop herself from smiling at that—she was helpless around compliments; she lit up when she got one, like a child who has been offered sweets. The kitchen made her happy, too—it was clean and simple compared to the rest of the house. The uniformed maid was busy chopping potatoes on the tiled sideboard, and the aroma of coffee emanated from the stove.

"Are you hungry?" he asked solicitously.

"Yes, I'm starving!" Letty said, sliding into a chair and putting her elbows on the sturdy surface of the table.

Valentine grinned. "Beryl, make Miss Larkspur an omelet, would you?"

"Yes, Mr. O'Dell," the maid replied as she advanced toward the table with a porcelain coffee cup and saucer in one hand and a coffee pitcher in the other.

"My dear, what a phenomenon you are! You see, already your name is on everyone's lips . . ." Jovially he turned open the paper near Letty's hand to the society page and bent forward, putting his head close to hers as he drew his index finger across a photograph that took up almost a quarter of the page. In it, a girl with short dark hair sweeping over her pale cheeks was being moved across a dance floor by a tall, smiling boy in a tuxedo jacket, her body not so much tiny as exquisitely delicate in his arms.

"Is that me?" she heard herself say.

"Yes, if the *New York Troubadour* knows anything at all. 'Miss Letty Larkspur, who has fast become inseparable from our leading light Sophia Ray, was seen dancing on the Ritz roof with the up-and-coming player for Montrose Filmic Company,

Laurence Peters, at dawn . . . '" Valentine pushed the paper toward Letty, and she quickly scanned the column, as though she were afraid he might have made it all up. "Sound like you?"

"I guess, it's only that . . . ," Letty whispered, as she began to read the item again from the top. "Well, the funny thing is, I don't remember being on the Ritz roof."

"No?" Valentine chuckled. "I suppose that doesn't surprise me, really. You fell asleep in one of their salons sometime after eating breakfast late last night, and Hector had to carry you to the car. Must have been quite a party. Seems Sophia fell ill and had to take a room at the Ritz for the night."

"Oh." Letty couldn't bring herself to look at Valentine. The image of Jack Montrose's sneer rose up in her thoughts, and she felt a little sick.

"Yes. Must have been quite a night you girls had."

If she heard any more details of the evening, Letty feared she might reveal what she suspected had transpired between Sophia and Montrose. There were a few seconds when she even thought she ought to. Seeing Valentine as he was now— ruffled in the morning and so kind and handsome—she knew that he deserved better. But she couldn't bring herself to tell on the woman who had already taught her so much about how to be a New York girl, and she changed the subject in the only way she could think of: "Do you suppose they get the *Troubadour* in Ohio?"

Valentine met her eyes. "Why, do you have some fellow waiting for you back there?"

"No." Letty shook her head emphatically, as though that would prevent her blush from lingering.

"Sophia thinks the world of you," Valentine was saying as he turned his body toward the window. She watched the workings of his neck as he swallowed, and momentarily forgot the extraordinary fact of her name being in the paper as she gazed at the perfect line of his profile against the bright skyline. "Perhaps," he went on quietly, "she sees something of her young self in you. Only—" He exhaled, and his eyelids sank closed, and when he spoke again it was with a tone that she'd never heard him use. "Only, don't end up *too* much like her."

"But isn't that why I'm here?" Letty said before she could think how it would sound, or even what it meant.

Valentine stared at her, his eyes as deep as pools. The sunshine lancing through the window made him appear golden as he never could in the movies. "Show business is a hard business, and it has made Sophia tough; that is all I mean. You must not lose your sensitivity, and—and I would hate to see you hurt."

The weight of his hands hovered over hers, and the room melted away. Letty felt the same way she had when she first met Valentine; his brown gaze was warm and steady in her direction, as though for the first time she was completely understood. The connection between them hung in the air, beautiful and ephemeral.

"There you go, miss," Beryl said as she roughly slid a plate in front of Letty. The omelet was perfectly formed, on a white oval plate, garnished with a sprig of parsley and a twist of grapefruit that frowned up at her accusatorily.

"What a happy sight this is!"

Letty's head swiveled and she saw Sophia, framed in the doorway to the living room, her hair rather limp but her lipstick freshly applied, wearing a tuxedo jacket over her turquoise evening gown. It took Letty several seconds to realize that Sophia was not being sarcastic, that she was truly pleased by the sight of her husband and her protégée cozily eating breakfast together. Then she realized that Sophia must have been out on the street like that, and a sense of scandal rippled through her.

Valentine issued a hearty "Good morning, my dear!" as his wife advanced toward him and planted a kiss on his lips.

"Well, what are they saying about us this morning?"

"A lot—isn't that the only thing that matters?" Valentine replied lightly, and they both laughed as Sophia opened the newspaper and began to search for her name. They continued to chatter, but Letty couldn't hear them. She could still feel the place on her hands where Valentine had touched her; the spot was vibrating with the warmth of his skin against hers.

"Coffee?" Beryl was addressing Sophia, but she was staring at Letty. Suddenly Letty was conscious of her appearance, that she was wearing her bedclothes. The way the silk slip caressed her skin made her feel only a little better than naked. Shame and confusion washed over her, and for a moment she almost wished that she *had* woken up in Ohio. Just a few seconds ago she had been gazing longingly at a married man—her new friend's *husband*—and she was certain that her guilt was radiating from every point of her body. But then there was that other hideous fact, like a screw in her belly, that Sophia had cheated on that husband and that Letty had seen it.

"I ought to get dressed," Letty said stupidly.

"But what about your breakfast?" Valentine asked.

Letty stood up, pushing back her chair. "I'm not so hungry anymore," she lied, and backed toward the door.

"Well, hurry up." Sophia winked at her chummily. "I have big plans for today."

"All right." But Letty was hurrying away from the kitchen just to avoid meeting Sophia's eyes.

In her room, Letty wasted no time in undoing the kimono and pulling the slip over her head. As quickly as possible she secured her plain cotton underclothes, and over that, a pleated skirt that covered her knees and a boxy sailor-style shirt. She sat at her vanity again, taking in short breaths. Now she recognized herself; here was the small-town girl she had briefly misplaced.

It was all very well for movie stars to wait until dusk to dress properly, but she had grown up among simpler folks.

The day she had spent with Sophia had felt so fancy and fun, and Letty knew that a movie star of her caliber could teach her things she'd never learn elsewhere. But the price was so heavy. The secret she was being asked to keep, disgusting to her. She remembered now that she had learned to adore Valentine O'Dell on her weekly sojourns to the movie house— she had loved him a long time really, from afar, and she hated the idea of him being mistreated. Of course, that love had been the silly fantasy of a little girl; she had understood that after a few days in his company. But now, thinking again of his touch, and the magnitude of Sophia's betrayal, she wondered if her kind of affection wasn't what he needed after all.

When Cordelia got to the airfield and saw how Max was flying, all of the color drained from her face. Even the roar of his airplane sounded angry. When he turned sideways or upside down or did flips in the air, the effect was just as furious. She had seen him do these tricks before, and though they always made her frightened for him, they had seemed playful then, and artful, a perfectly executed imitation of danger. The way he was flying now, it looked like a direct challenge to Death himself.

Relief washed over her when he finally brought the plane down and she could run toward him across the ruined grass. Their eyes met, and Cordelia briefly saw the storm in his. Then he turned away from her and stalked toward the hangar.

"Max, wait!"

She had to run to catch up to him. When she did, she grabbed his hand. It was slight, but she could feel his rage ebb a tiny bit with the touch.

"Max," she said. "I'm so sorry."

They stood like that a while, an arm's distance apart, holding hands. He stared off into the distance, and she stared at the back of his head.

"You don't have anything to be sorry for," he said eventually. But the words were so full of bitterness that she knew he wanted everyone he had ever met to be sorry.

"Come. Just come on. Come with me. All right?"

Her hands went up his forearm, gently pulling. Eventually he turned and she saw how twisted up his face had gotten with all the nasty things being said about him. At first he came reluctantly, but by the time they reached the car they were both moving quickly. They didn't discuss where they were going, or talk at all, until they had driven a good ways and were close enough to the Sound that they could smell it.

Out on the water, birds went up and down with the small, soft waves, which emanated from some unseen source and were continually lapping against the pebble shore. She thought if Max looked up and saw that, something inside him might settle and perhaps he wouldn't feel so hopeless.

"You know, I think everything is going to be all right," she began in as sure and soothing a tone as she could muster. "It'll blow over. Everything always does. It'll blow over, and everything will be the same. Or maybe even better. Why, I was reading in the newspaper just the other day how they formed the first Negro Aviation Club, in Los Angeles, and—"

"I don't live in Los Angeles. I live in New York."

"Of course, yes, I only meant—"

"And I don't want to be part of any club. I don't want to be an exotic sideshow. What I do—I'm the best at it."

"All right, but—"

"Cordelia."

She took her eyes off the road to glance at him. They had reached an uneven patch of road and she had to hold the steering wheel firmly with both hands to keep from veering. Max was staring at his hands, as though trying to think of what to say. Then he made a fist and punched the dashboard.

"You'll hurt yourself," she whispered.

"What does it matter?"

"It matters to me."

"You have no idea." He put his hands over his face. "You have no idea how bad this is. It's not just that I'm black. I'm a black boy with a white girl. You know what they do to boys like me? Not just in the South, either. Here in Queens County they put sheets over their heads and . . ."

He didn't finish, and Cordelia winced at what he had started to say. She wanted to reply with something sweet and uplifting, but nothing came to her, and she stared out at the road in front of them, the grand houses on the bluffs, the dense clouds lurking overhead.

"Just take me home," he told her.

"Home?"

There was an extended silence and then Max said, "Back to the Laurels', I guess, is what I meant."

They didn't speak again, except Max's mumbled directions, until they were at the hedgerow that separated his patrons' property from the road. She recognized the stately white building, although she had only seen it from above, when they had been flying. From this perspective, down at the bottom of a hill, the house seemed more imposing, as though it were regarding her with skeptical eyes situated at the top of a long, proud nose.

"Max, I love you," she heard herself say. Those weren't the words she had intended, but when she heard them come out of her mouth she was almost overwhelmed by how much she meant them.

He sat there long enough that she knew he'd heard her, but he didn't meet her eyes. "Thank you for the ride" was all he said, and then he got out of the car and started up the hill at a steady pace.

She waited to see if he would glance back or wave at her. She wondered too if he might change his mind, if the prospect of going into that house where he had once been celebrated, only to be treated cruelly when his secret was revealed, would prove too much for him. But he didn't. He kept moving in that determined way toward the grand white house where he had once been groomed to be a hero. Her heart struggled and gasped. She wanted to call out to him and tell him she would wait, but she knew that would do no good. He was too far gone from her now.

7

DOGWOOD WAS LOUSY WITH MEN, A SPECIES IN WHICH
Astrid had shown great interest before she was married. As a
debutante she had been unembarrassed by her reputation as a
flirt, and she had collected the affections of the old and young,
the gallant and erudite and shy, like so many postage stamps.
But men were abhorrent to her now. Their voices emanated
from the remote corners of the house, and they crossed the
lawn in pairs with rifles rested arrogantly against their shoulders. Even at a great distance she knew the way sweat clung
to their skin, fouling the air around them, and the cruelty they
were capable of.

In silent protest of men and all the messes they caused,

Astrid had spent as much of the day as possible in a bubble bath and only emerged from the confines of the suite she shared with her husband when she ran out of reading material. She had let her hair dry naturally in the warm summer air and had used none of the usual feminine tricks to make it less fluffy afterward. She had selected a dress that Charlie had given her, a white pinafore-style thing, not because it was his gift but because she had never bothered to have it taken in—Charlie always bought dresses two sizes too big for her, and this one was so large it concealed her slender frame. Despite these efforts, her reflection, as she glimpsed it on the second-floor landing, didn't appear undesirable, only winningly careless in a way that fit the hot season and the voluminous styles girls were wearing that year.

Oh, well—she took the latest magazines from the library and shut herself up with Good Egg in the glass-enclosed porch where nobody liked to go anymore, because it was where Darius had been shot. She put Rudy Vallée on the phonograph, which all the toughs playing pool on the second floor would surely deride as music for silly women. Then she rang for Len, the cook, and asked him for chicken salad and potato chips and lemonade, in order to ruin her appetite, just in case Charlie had any designs on dining with her. She couldn't stand the idea of sitting across from him while he thoughtlessly digested food that he had earned by pushing around nice old men who wanted nothing more than a better life for their children. With exquisite carelessness, she lay herself down on the faded rose velvet daybed in between the potted palms and crossed her ankles and lost herself in a *Fame* story about Eloise Aligash, the lady who did the voice of Cara Gatling for the radio.

These small triumphs carried her a while, until she heard the heavy footsteps sounding above her. Good Egg raised her head from the ground and yipped at the ceiling. Someone was putting their full weight onto those old floorboards, and she was sure it was Charlie. She scowled and muttered out loud and even considered going upstairs to tell him he ought to be considerate of the people below, except that would mean seeing his big face, and she didn't want that. Instead she rang for more potato chips, and turned her attentions to *Vanity Fair* magazine.

The *Vanity Fair* was full of high-tone musings about plays she hadn't seen and probably never would, but she was grateful to it when the hall door creaked open and Charlie's heavy footfalls headed toward her. Her shoulders stiffened, but she issued an order to her ankles that they would remain as still and careless as before.

"Wake up, kitten, it's time to go to work!"

Charlie's body went down on the other end of the couch, jostling Astrid. Her ankles held firm, and she raised the magazine so that it would continue to shield her from his brutish features. The sound of his linen pants against the velvet daybed was among the most grating she had ever heard—but it was put to shame by the whisper of his fingers among the potato chips, and then again by the horror of his molars as he munched them.

"Kitten?" Charlie rested a hand on Astrid's ankle, but she ordered it to remain frozen, impervious to his touch. "I'm going out, and I need my girl by my side."

"I don't much feel like it tonight," she said, after a long pause, mostly hoping this would get his hand off her ankle.

"Aw, don't be sour." Charlie stood up, jostling the daybed again, and strode across the room. The way he spoke—rather breezier than the situation called for—Astrid knew he thought he was going to get his way. She peeked beyond the pages of her magazine and saw Charlie still putting potato chips in his mouth with one hand as he fiddled with an ornate cigarette box on a rosewood end table. From behind, she had to admit, he still had something about him. Maybe the way his shoulders stretched out his beige linen jacket. But she tried to remind herself how rank his kisses were just after he smoked. "I know it probably wasn't the funnest joint I took you to last night," he went on, as he got the cigarette lit. "But tonight'll be different. More the way you like it. More class."

He was turning back around, so Astrid quickly drew the

magazine up to cover her eyes. "I'm really not in the mood, darling," she answered aridly.

"Oh, come off it!" Charlie snapped, grabbing the magazine and ripping it from Astrid's hands. For a moment they stared at each other—his face pulled down in irritation, hers wide open with surprise, her hands slightly raised, holding their position from before the magazine was snatched away. She blinked, and he averted his gaze, as though embarrassed by what he had done. "I'm sorry, Astrid. I just don't get what's come over you. I just wanna show you off."

Astrid folded her arms over her chest and gave him her profile. "Show me off?"

Charlie sighed and made an attempt to smooth the crumpled magazine, before tossing it aside and sitting down next to Astrid on the daybed. "Come on, don't be like this. You'll like the place we're going tonight—the Saxton Hotel on the East Side, old clients of Dad's. They say they just got a new delivery of wine and champagne, classy stuff, down from Canada, so they don't need us anymore. Well, we got plenty of class, and I aim to convince them they need us, damned as they ever did. Then I'm taking you for dinner, kitten."

Astrid took her time in answering. She flattened the bodice of her dress over her stomach and examined her nails, which were due for some pampering. It occurred to her that Rudy Vallée was no longer crooning to her from the phonograph, and she lamented this lack of background music in her thoughts. She cast her eyes about the room before letting them roll back to meet Charlie's with exquisite languor. "I'm not hungry."

"But—"

"I'm not *going* to be hungry."

Charlie regarded her, his head thrust back on his neck and his eyes burning. "All right, stay here. Stay here all night. But don't think you're leaving this property." He turned away from her quickly, as though already his attention had moved on to other matters. "I'll tell Victor he's watching you tonight, and this time, there'll be no little forays into the city . . ."

He was still issuing commands when the door swung shut behind him, and Astrid began to think of all the things she might have said to put him in his place.

"Evening, Cordelia." Paulette, the hostess of The Vault, had greeted her boss at the door of the club with a pleasant smile, but there was a telltale sign of surprise in her eyes. Perhaps she knew it was obvious, because she added, "We weren't expecting you."

"I know." Cordelia tucked a few wayward strands into her low bun and surveyed the tables, which were half-full on a hot night when the humidity was so oppressive that nobody seemed to want to move if they didn't have to. "But I had an intuition it might be busy."

The truth was she only *hoped* it would be busy, or at least busy enough to take her mind off Max—how his feelings for her had ruined his career, and how he'd walked away from her declaration of love without a single backward glance.

"Might be," Paulette said doubtfully.

"You'll find me in the office if you need me." Cordelia kept her voice formal and aloof, trying to sound like Paulette's superior instead of a girl searching for distractions. Even when she'd thought of something happy or amusing that day, it had led her back to Max, because then she had longed to tell him about it, and after that came the realization that she might never be able to tell him about anything again.

As she strode toward the back of the club she made little nods of acknowledgment to the men behind the bar and patrons that she recognized. A few cigarette girls were leaning against the rear wall, near the big brass doors that led to the old bank president's office, and though they began to move when they saw Cordelia coming, their eyes searched her a few seconds longer than they ordinarily would have.

"Go on." Cordelia shooed them as she went through the brass doors and into the hallway, not glancing back to see if they obeyed. She knew what they had been thinking, of course. They were thinking that she had been going with a black man and were wondering if she had known all along or found out with everybody else.

In the month following her father's death she had been so full of self-recrimination and nervous agitation, and she had gotten in a bad way, lurking around the house and lying in the bath long after the water had gone cold, smoking one cigarette after another. She hadn't stopped until she met Max's mother, and Mrs. Darby had made it obvious what she thought of girls who smoked. It had been easy to give up, once Cordelia saw what it meant to Mrs. Darby, and she hadn't really wanted one till now.

But she was still Max's girl. At least, she wanted to be. Just because he seemed far away didn't mean she could go back to her old ways. So she straightened her dress, a loose-fitting flowered chiffon that fell away from her shoulders in tiers, and went to find the distractions she'd come all the way to the city for.

Someone, it seemed, had been listening to her prayers. A pack of young men in bow ties celebrating the coming wedding of one of their members had taken up noisy residence at the bar, and a flock of chorus girls still in their feathered getups had filled the remaining tables surrounding the dance floor. An alliance between the two groups was in the early stages of negotiation, still as acrimonious as it was flirtatious, and the electricity of the exchange was spreading through the room, and even the music was speedier now. It was no longer an evening for quiet, languid drinking. The bar was low on supplies, and Cordelia was needed downstairs immediately to determine what should be opened next.

After that there was a rush on drinks and a shortage of ice, and she had to send Anthony out for more. Cordelia joined the men behind what were once the teller windows of the bank to keep up with the demand, shaking and stirring drinks and then passing them to the uniformed bartenders on the other side. When she stepped back onto the club floor, she saw that every seat was full now and two of the chorus girls had climbed onto the bar and were doing an old-fashioned cancan with the enthusiastic support of the band.

She sent one of Charlie's men to help Anthony with the ice and the other two to stand under the chorus girls in case they slipped.

"Don't ruin anyone's fun," she instructed, "but I won't have either of those girls breaking their necks in my place."

"But then there's nobody at the door," one of the men protested.

"Never mind that. Anthony will be back in a minute, and anyway, from what I can see, all the troublemakers are already in here. Let them dance a little longer, and then get them down safe and buy them a bottle of champagne."

There was a lot of shouting, customers in bright colors moving excitedly back and forth, and her frenetic labors continued until she went to the front of the place to check on the ice and saw someone who stalled her forward motion. The stillness with which he regarded her was so disquieting that she did not realize for several seconds to whom those eyes belonged.

"Thom Hale," she said flatly, as though hearing the name out loud might tell her what his presence there portended. He was standing at the bar twirling a drink like any other customer; the fit of his white linen suit was urbane and roomy, and she remembered with irritation how comfortable he made himself everywhere. The last time she had seen him, it had been in someone else's speakeasy, where he had been just as free of care, so that it came of something of a surprise when she heard how he had presided over Astrid's kidnapping some days later.

"Cordelia Grey," he replied, and the corners of his mouth shot upward like a schoolboy's. His face was as handsome as always, although more suntanned—almost as dark as Darius used to get—and his coppery hair was combed neatly to one side. Although his father was a gangster, his mother was from the society family that owned the White Cove Country Club, and his features had an aristocratic and knowing aspect. He always seemed a few steps ahead of everyone else.

"What are you doing in my place?"

"I thought I might have a cocktail, see what the competition was doing." He let his eyes scan the room as he sipped his drink, as if to demonstrate to her the innocence of his mission. "That's not against the law, is it?"

Cordelia let the tension in her chest dissolve and stepped toward the place he occupied by the bar, in between two groups becoming joyously oblivious to everything around them. She cocked her head and regarded him, and when she spoke again, her voice was light. "No more than anything else we do."

He laughed, too quickly, and twirled his drink in the other direction.

Cordelia gave him a cool stare. "It wasn't that funny."

"No, I suppose it wasn't." Thom shrugged and looked away. The bones of his face were strong and fine, and he had the slender height and careless manner that Cordelia had come to recognize in the privileged—in people who had never been deprived of anything. He was gorgeous; even after everything, she was not blind to that. "Actually, I came to talk to you about business."

Cordelia's eyebrows floated upward in surprise. "Why would you want to talk to me?"

"Because I know you," he said quietly. He coughed into a closed fist and cast his eyes about the room before continuing. "You know your brother hijacked a shipment of ours the other night?"

"Is that why he's so full of bluster these days?"

"Yes, well, Dad wants to burn Dogwood to the ground, as you can imagine. But I don't want any more of this back-and-forth."

"You want a truce." Cordelia let this information settle in with her. "But why?"

"It's not practical," Thom said simply, and sipped his drink.

"You'll have a hell of a time convincing Charlie that's a good reason."

"That's why I only want to talk to you."

Cordelia nodded but did not reply.

"I'm sorry about your friend Max, by the way. I never thought he was right for you, but it's ugly when a man distinguishes himself only to lose his backing and reputation over a thing like that. Aren't many white men can fly a plane like he can."

The mention of Max made Cordelia flush, but it wasn't exactly embarrassment she was feeling. She was almost angry that Thom was thinking about Max at all. Then she noticed Thom's eyes on her again, how they scanned the length of her dress when he thought she had glanced away. The memory of what they had done together returned to her, of Thom's skin on her skin, that they had been naked and he had whispered her name over and over. A feeling of shame seeped into her belly, and she hoped that Max never knew what she had done with other boys before she knew him. When she felt fingertips against the skin of her arm, she almost jumped. But to her relief it was only Paulette at her shoulder.

"Phone call for you," she said, before being absorbed back into the crowd.

Cordelia nodded. When she turned back on Thom, she found that though she ought to hate him, she no longer did. "You look like you've been spending too much time in the sun," she observed. One of the bartenders had ventured in their direction, and she called out to him: "Carl, do you know Mr. Hale?"

Carl's attention was being sought from every direction, but he did briefly glance at Thom and nod at Cordelia.

"See he pays for his drinks!" she yelled. In a voice neither hostile nor kind, she addressed Thom, saying, "It's good to see you," before quickly making her way to the back offices.

The lavender hour had come and gone, and Astrid was still arguing with Charlie in her head. She had been staring at the same page of *Vanity Fair* for as long as she could remember—it might have been two years—and meanwhile the onset of darkness had done nothing to cool the room.

"'There'll be no little forays into the city,'" she said out loud, pinching up her face and mimicking Charlie's bossy tone. She went over to the phonograph and started Rudy Vallée again, conjuring in her memory the last time there had been a little foray into the city. It was the night—one of the nights, how many had there been?—when Charlie abandoned her so that he could play dirty with the Hales and she had been ordered to stay in. She had twisted Charlie's man Victor's arm until he drove into the city in pursuit of Cordelia and Letty and Billie Marsh, her stepsister. What a grand night that had been! The four of them traipsing from one speak to another, never paying for a drink and being lauded everywhere they went.

"That was the last time I remember being happy," she sighed into the gilt-framed mirror by the enameled bar cart. But the phrase was heavy with melodrama, and she knew it wasn't true. She had been happy in her sewn-together wedding dress, and she had been happy on the pleasure cruiser that she and Charlie had taken to sail through the Caribbean. She had been happy last night with Charlie, before she saw what a grubby business bootlegging really was. Once upon a time she had been good at forgetting all the miserable things in life, and it seemed silly that she couldn't now rid her mind of that doleful man with the inno-cent children and the sad little speakeasy behind a pharmacy in the Village.

"Oh, hell, the heat is getting to you," she went on, again to the reflection of her pretty, heart-shaped face. "Knock it off, darling, you'll give yourself permanent lines."

So she sashayed across the room, twirling on the old Persian carpets while Good Egg ran circles around her, picking an orchid from one of the potted plants and putting it behind her ear, telling herself she didn't care what Charlie was up to and that it didn't matter to her that her best friends were all out in the world, being romanced by new beaux and living very noteworthy lives. After that she felt a little sad and decided that a garden party was the only cure, and called everyone she could think of and told them to come tomorrow at three.

It was only when the final chords of "If I Had a Girl Like You" sounded that she realized that she'd come down with a bad case of cabin fever, and that she might preserve her sanity if she told Charlie's boys that Cordelia needed her at The Vault. She straightened her silly dress and smoothed a fluff of yellow hair and headed for the hall.

But her way was blocked sooner than she anticipated.

"I'm going out," she said with expert blitheness.

Victor blocked her path, his arms crossed over his chest. She sensed that he had been standing there a long time already. "No, you're not." His voice wasn't unkind, but he had something like a smirk on his face, and his stance was wide, as though he were bracing to physically prevent her from leaving.

"Oh, *come*." Astrid smiled in her special plush way, and her posture loosened. There had been a night—the night she tried to cook Charlie a real meal, to disastrous results—when Victor had been assigned to watch her and they'd played cards and had champagne for dinner. It seemed to her that right before she'd laid her head on the big, ponderous dining room table and dozed off, he had said something just a touch flirta-tious. Perhaps, she thought, he would still be susceptible to her charms now. "Remember what fun we had last time?"

"I remember how much *trouble* you got me in last time."

"Oh, it couldn't have been so bad, or why would Charlie have left me with you again?"

"He knows I haven't forgotten." The smirk was gone, and there was no hint of a joke in Victor's dark eyes. They just stared at her, placid but unyielding, over that serious Roman nose. "He knows I learned my lesson about being bossed by a girl."

"Well!" Astrid exclaimed, as she ducked around him.

Victor didn't answer except by following her—he stepped lightly, but the wax floor in the ballroom was hard and there wasn't much furniture there to absorb the echo. As she went through the billowy white curtains and down the big stone steps of the verandah, she hoped he would stay behind and watch her from the porch of the house so that she could be alone with her thoughts. But by the time the grass was under her bare feet and she was striding beyond the light that Dogwood's high windows cast across the lawn, she feared he was no longer following her. For a while her pride won out over her curiosity, but when she reached the place on the lawn where the earth began to slope upward, she couldn't stand it anymore, and she turned sharply.

There was Victor, not even five yards behind her. He had frozen, but there was something nimble about the way he hovered—he had the cautious watchfulness of an Indian tracker on the hunt.

"Oh!" she gasped, and then a cascade of laughter flowed through her.

He was trying to look stern, but her laughter disarmed them both, and a smile that began in fits and starts finally got the better of his face.

"I thought I'd given you the slip." She winked at him, and the absurdity of her statement made them both chuckle.

"Miss Astrid, I'm sorry to say, your technique leaves something to be desired."

"Damn! And I thought I'd been so clever."

"You are very clever in some ways, but when it comes to not being noticed, you are a little . . . stupid."

"Stupid!" Astrid put her fists against her waist and pouted theatrically. "Charlie would have your hide if he knew you called me names."

"I'm pretty sure all Charlie cares about is that I don't let you leave this property, whether by your own doing or 'cause the Hales want you."

Astrid bowed her head and batted her lashes contritely. "Oh, dear, I see I *did* get you in some trouble."

Victor's slender shoulders rose and fell, and he turned his face away. For a moment Astrid watched him—though his hands were scarred and blistered, and he had the face of a tough, his tall, lean body was almost too thin, and you could see it, the way his work shirt was tucked into his denim pants.

"Well," she went on, when she realized he wasn't going to answer that. "I may have gotten you in trouble, but *you* very nearly got me killed! Sending a girl of my type to a place like that West Side tavern of yours." Her tone was light and joking, but she couldn't quite bring herself to say the name of the place that Victor had told her about, where the two men had put a bag over her head before stuffing her in a car.

"I know, I'm sorry for that." He kept his gaze averted, and he spoke in a solemn tone that did not match her own. "I never meant for you to go there. Not without me, anyway."

"Well." Astrid clapped her hands, as though that would scare away the lingering moroseness. "I guess we're square!"

Victor's dark eyes met hers, and he nodded.

Astrid thrust her hand forward for him to shake. "Friends, then?"

"Friends."

They shook on it, heartily, like men who had recently argued over baseball but have since come to their senses. When Astrid let go of his hand they turned and began ambling, not exactly in the direction that Astrid had been going before, but not back toward the house. A few stars winked hazily, and a muted quarter moon lolled somewhere above the black tree-tops. The grass was soft beneath her feet, and it dimly occurred to her that it might feel very sweet to lie down on it. Victor walked along next to her at an easy distance, and they didn't speak. The cicadas and mosquitoes were saying plenty.

It was not until they had reached the stone patio surrounding the pool that she had any thought worth saying out loud. "You know," she began philosophically, "all day I was thinking what detestable beasts men are."

"Oh, yes?"

"Yes." Astrid nodded. She caught one of her hands with the other behind her back and turned her face up girlishly to regard the heavens. "In fact, I was trying very hard to hate you back there in the house, but that was a more difficult task than I had anticipated! *You're* not beastly at all."

He paused on the stone tiles—she could see his reflection in the pool—so she stopped to face him. A hot, dry wind picked up, pushing Astrid's skirt around and the bodice of her dress against her skin. She smiled from the corner of her mouth. A light passed through his black pupils, and his long lashes lowered with his blink.

"What are you saying?" he asked.

Astrid dropped her lower, bee-stung lip. "Only this—" But she knew if she said any more she would burst out laughing. So she took a shy step in his direction and then, with a cat's swiftness, put both her hands forward and pushed. She stared at him, suspended over the glassy surface, his face wide and flat with shock. Her mouth was buckled with a coming laugh, but before it had a chance to escape, he had grasped her arm, and then they were both falling, very slowly. It might have been a whole hour that they hung there, like constellations against the dome of the sky, smiling at each other, happy and dry, before the water hit them, enveloped them, and they were sinking into its cool quiet.

Then, suddenly, Victor had his arm around her waist and was dragging her back toward air. There was no utilitarian purpose for this, as Astrid was a strong swimmer, but she let herself be pulled, and when they surfaced she gasped and pushed her hair back from her forehead as he kicked and paddled the water to keep them afloat. Their clothes were heavy, and she could feel his heartbeat.

"Is that the kind of thing friends do?" He had meant it as a joke, but his tone wasn't humorous, which changed the meaning of the sentence.

Her chest heaved under the sopping white bodice of her dress, which was now plastered to her skin, and her high, ringing laugh echoed off the surface of the water. She pushed away from him, took two long strokes to the side of the pool, and lifted herself up onto the cement ledge.

"See what happens when you go soft?" she admonished. For a moment she let her feet dangle in the water, watching Victor's head and shoulders bob above the deep end. "I'm gonna give you the slip yet!"

Then she leapt to her feet and went running out across the lawn, cartwheeling once she had reached the illuminated circle that surrounded the house, and darting through the ballroom before anyone could see the state of her clothes. She did not wonder if Victor was behind her this time; she knew he wasn't. It would be stupid of him to follow her, and she knew he wasn't stupid. Anyway, once she had the drenched dress off her body and was safely buried in her second bubble bath of the day, she would have no need for monitoring. Milly, her maid, would tell him where she was, and then he could knock off for the rest of the evening. Meanwhile she would be relaxing, satisfied that she had enacted some small revenge on the men of this world. And if that thought wasn't enough to put her to sleep, there was always that picture of Victor, how trusting and handsome he'd looked right before she pushed him over the edge.

8

AS SOON AS LETTY LEFT MANHATTAN, HER SHOULDERS softened. She had not been completely honest with her patrons about her reasons for going to White Cove—although of course it was *possible* that Cordelia and Astrid needed her and *mostly* true that neither of them was free to leave Dogwood to come into the city. If she had told Sophia and Val the real reason for going—that Mrs. Charlie Grey was having a spur-of-the-moment garden party, and Letty was desperate for a chance to be around old friends—she ran the risk that they would invite themselves along. The heat wave had yet to abate, and just about anybody would have jumped at the chance to go to the country and escape the stifling sidewalks. At first Sophia had frowned theatrically at the news, but then she'd insisted that Hector drive Letty.

"What a good friend you are to me." Sophia had sighed happily. "I want to make sure you are always as comfortable as possible."

That did stir up some guilt inside Letty, and now, riding comfortably in the back of the O'Dells' town car, it hurt her a little to think how generous Sophia was, even when Letty couldn't stop her mind from returning to what Sophia may have done with Jack Montrose, and then Letty would have to wonder if she was hurting Valentine by not telling him about it, and the confusion rose up and started to overwhelm her again, and she was glad that she was speeding through the suburbs away from The Apollonian.

As she began to walk up the slope toward the west lawn she saw Good Egg, and her relief was complete. The greyhound was trotting along beside a boy whose face she could not quite make out, and when she spotted Letty she paused for a moment with her snout in the air. She woofed once in greeting and then came down the hill at a gallop.

"Hello, girl!" Letty exclaimed as Good Egg leapt up, almost embracing her with her long legs.

Once girl and dog had greeted one another, Good Egg began to walk back toward the boy, as though leading Letty to him. As they approached, Letty recognized Grady's boyish features, and she smiled widely. He was wearing a loose-fitting white suit that made him appear more like the scion of one of the old White Cove families than the city scribbler she'd originally gotten to know. Meanwhile, Good Egg ran ahead and did a few laps around Grady's legs.

"I think she remembers you," Letty called out.

"Could that be possible?"

"It was only a few months ago." Good Egg was panting, and her head swung back and forth as her chocolate eyes went from Letty to Grady. "Plus, you saved her life."

"It was you who did that. I was scared witless and wouldn't have known what to do if you hadn't been there." Grady glanced at Good Egg, as though to apologize for bringing up a painful memory. "You look lovely," he went on, in the slightly choked voice that people use when they are saying things they cannot help.

"Oh—thank you." Smiling at the compliment, Letty looked down on the navy-and-white striped tank dress that hung off her narrow shoulders. Her first choice had been rather more girlish, but Sophia had told her that you never know who you'll meet or what will happen when you leave the house and that a more sophisticated frock was preferable. Now she was glad she'd taken the advice. "I'm sorry I didn't get to talk to you more the other night. Sophia fell ill—Sophia Ray, that is, the actress, with whom I am studying these days—"

"I know of Miss Ray, of course," Grady interrupted.

"Yes, well, once I knew she was ill, I had to go to her."

"Naturally." The sadness was back in Grady's eyes, and Letty realized that the newspapers had run photographs of her dancing with Laurence Peters at dawn, and that it was probable that Grady knew she had not spent the entire evening acting as nursemaid. "Well, I suppose you want to see your friends," he said, rather conclusively.

They began to amble toward the tent, where young men and women dressed in white idled under the protective shade of the tent's white arc. Milly was circulating with trays of drinks, and Astrid was standing at the middle of a circle of boys who looked like they might be off to college in the fall, all of whom were listening attentively to the story she was telling.

"There you are!" It was Peachy Whitburn, her strawberry-blond hair parted sharply on the left side, wearing a sleeveless, high-necked dress of ice blue. She did not exactly smile when she saw Letty, and for a moment Letty was reminded of the second time they'd met, and how Peachy had seemed to have forgotten the first time, and wondered if she wasn't going to pretend not to know her now. But then she reached out for Grady's hand and met Letty's eyes directly. "Ah, the famous Letty Larkspur."

"Oh, I don't know about famous." Letty shifted awkwardly in her high-heeled shoes.

"Well, what would *you* call someone whose name appears in the paper every day?" Peachy returned, as though Letty had said something very simple.

Before Letty could think how to reply, the person standing just behind Peachy turned around. "Letty, there you are!" Billie Marsh, Astrid's stepsister, exclaimed. She gave a roll of her eyes in Peachy's direction and then, putting her arm around Letty, went on: "You won't mind if I steal her, will you? I haven't seen her in *ages*. Good! I didn't think so."

Before either Peachy or Grady could reply, Billie drew Letty away from them and into the tent. Billie's hair was as dark as Letty's and shorter, too, though she wore hers slicked back from her face and tucked behind the ears, which gave her a rather Spanish aspect. She was wearing wide-legged navy trousers and a white blouse that might have been feminine if it hadn't been two sizes too big for her.

"Sorry I couldn't save you earlier, darling; those two are punishingly dull," Billie said as she went about fixing drinks for them.

"Oh, but—Grady is all right, isn't he?"

"He *used* to be—I was really rather impressed when he dropped out of Columbia and started lurking around the Village. But now that he's back with Peachy I'm afraid I've given up all hope. Or he has. Or something. He's well on his way to entrapped."

"That's too bad," Letty said before she could think to guard her disappointment.

Billie handed Letty a drink and regarded her over the rim of her own. "Why the long face, doll? Aren't you coming from some fabulous party or other?"

Letty colored and averted her eyes. "I'm fine, really, just a little tired. There *have* been a lot of parties. But this is a nice one, isn't it? So many people came, and Astrid invited them only yesterday . . ."

"Yes, well, you know how infectious Astrid can be. When she gets a notion to do something gay, she's like a magnet: No one can stay away."

"Who are all those boys?" Letty jutted her head in the direction of the small crowd that surrounded Astrid.

"White Cove boys, some of them home from school for the summer. That tall blond with the pink face is Beau Ridley, the senator's son. *Never* turns down an invitation to a party— complete and utter boor. He's famous for his practical jokes, or at least he'd like to think he is. Have you heard the one about him bribing a hansom driver to lend him his horse, and then a bellhop at the Ritz to let him take it up the service elevator? A lot of broken glass that night, and naturally his father had to pay through the nose to keep it all hush-hush. But Astrid enjoys those sorts of antics, I suppose." Billie rolled her eyes and sniffed her julep. "The other four are all the same story but with different names."

The corners of Letty's mouth curled up, and she felt a little braver just knowing that Billie was her friend. "Where's Charlie?"

"Up at the house, I gather. Everyone is on high alert today, it seems." She tilted her head in the direction of the bodyguard on the edge of the tent, the one named Victor with the slender frame and the prominent nose. "Plus when he was down here before, Astrid kept avoiding him, and I think he got a little sick of it."

"And Cordelia?"

"She went on one of her moody walks. That business with the Darby fellow has got her down, I think, though she's not really talking about it."

"Well," Letty said with a sigh, "it's good to see you, anyway."

"Drink up, dolly." Billie raised her class to clink it against Letty's. "Then you'll tell me what ails you."

For a few minutes they stood by the table quietly observing the twenty or so well-heeled young people mingling in the shade. Then Astrid caught sight of the newest arrival and called out to her. "Letty, darling, when did you get here? How I've missed you—come *here!*"

A yellow sheaf of Astrid's hair had fallen over one eye, and her hand was extended demandingly toward her friend. Letty paused and glanced at Billie, but Billie only nodded, encouraging Letty to go mingle. Taking a few steps forward, Astrid grabbed her hand and pulled her in.

"Boys, this is Letty Larkspur, who was maid of honor at my wedding! Letty, these are the boys. Don't bother learning their names. They all dress the same anyway, so it's impossible to know which name goes with which face."

All the boys laughed loudly at this, as though a putdown from a girl like Astrid was a kind of honor, and then they all started asking Letty questions about herself in their funny, fancy accents. After that the party continued to go around like a carousel. The heat mellowed, and the sun got big as it sank toward the horizon. Just as Beau Ridley, or one of his look-alikes, was asking if he could get her another julep, Letty spotted Cordelia sitting a ways off from the party, on slightly higher ground, her arms wrapped around her knees.

"Yes, thank you." Letty waited until the fellow had gone off to the table, and then she walked out from under the tent toward her friend.

"You looked like you were having a good time." Cordelia's hair was down and didn't appear to have been brushed that day; it streamed over her shoulders and over her sleeveless midnight-blue chiffon dress.

Letty sat down next to Cordelia. "Nice to have my mind off things," she replied after a time.

"What things? You were so excited when you left for the city."

"Yes." Down at the party the music had grown louder and faster, and Beau Ridley had arrived at the edge of the tent. He was standing there with a julep in his hand and confusion on his face. "I am still. Only . . . they're so different from the people where we're from." A sigh worked its way through Letty's whole top half. Meanwhile, Astrid had come alongside Beau and was saying something to him through coy, twisted-up lips. With a little laugh, she removed the julep from his hand and shook her head at whatever he was saying. Then she grabbed for Billie and lit out across the lawn with her stepsister in tow. "They're just awfully sophisticated, is all."

"What are you two talking about?" Astrid demanded gaily as she approached.

"How sophisticated the Valentine O'Dells are!" Cordelia called out. "Seems all that sophistication has gotten Letty down."

"Well, they can't be more sophisticated than *we* are." Astrid shot Billie a glance as though for confirmation.

"Can't be," Billie affirmed as she sprawled on the grass before Letty and Cordelia.

"And you like *us* fine!" Astrid handed Letty the julep and, oblivious to the possibility of grass stains, arranged her white poplin skirt over her long legs.

"But none of you are quite so confusing," Letty protested shyly as she sipped her drink. "I feel like I *should* be Sophia's friend. My whole life I've wanted to be just like her! But now that I see how she really is, I wonder . . ."

"Is she acting better than you?" Cordelia demanded. "Because if she's acting better than you . . ."

"That's not it." Letty shook her head. "I saw her . . . and this big important fellow Jack Montrose . . . and they . . ."

Astrid gasped dramatically. *"No!"*

"And meanwhile, Valentine is so good and kind, and he seems to have no idea . . ." As soon as she said the name Valentine, her eyelids got heavy and color burst on her cheekbones.

"Oh, dear." Billie's wry smile cracked open one side of her face. "So Sophia is cheating, and Valentine is giving you swoony eyes?"

"I wouldn't say that, exactly . . ."

"He's an actor; he *wants* you to love him," Billie went on, ignoring Letty's demure vagueness.

"You're worried because a married man is flirting with you?" Astrid laughed and leaned back on her lean arms. "You're there to meet movie people, darling, not for moral instruction! Let the O'Dells take you to their parties, and so *what* about the flirting? Sounds like Sophia is making eyes, or worse, with plenty of fellows. Show business folks are used to following different rules, you know."

"All you have to do is remember that you're there because you can sing better than any of them," Cordelia put in.

"Yes, and if they don't get you in pictures, they'll introduce you to someone who will."

"So keep your chin up and laugh it off and down the hatch and et cetera, all right?"

"All right." Letty shook her drink so that the ice rattled against the glass. "Now it's Cordelia's turn."

"Oh, no." Astrid reached for Letty's glass and took a long sip of the julep. "None of that! What's got Cord so gloomy is what's happened to Max, and there's nothing to say about it till she sees him again."

"But—" Letty began to protest.

"She's right." Cordelia inhaled significantly and shook her hair off her shoulders. "There's nothing to do till I see him. And maybe that's just what I'll do. Only let's sit like this for another hour or so first, can we?"

"Yes," said the other three at once. So they went on sitting on the rise and watched the guests under the tent as the blue sky ripened in the afternoon. They laughed about what had been said already that afternoon, and what might happen yet, and were happy to leave challenging things until later, when the sun went down and the air wasn't quite so thick.

Charlie had been adamant that neither Cordelia nor Astrid was to leave Dogwood, even with bodyguards, so when the party started breaking up, Cordelia asked Grady for a ride to the Old

Oyster Town filling station and ducked in the backseat while they went through the gates. With the events of the last few days, she had forgotten about leaving the Marmon there. But once she'd waved to the old man in the office and was steering the coupé in the direction of Manhattan, she realized that she could not have planned her escape better. The leather seats were hot from the day, and the sky was tinged lavender. She rested her elbow on the window and felt the breeze in her hair as she went over the Queensborough Bridge. When Max came out of the church on 145th Street, he had no trouble spotting her. She was leaning against the hood of the car, and she was the only white girl on the block.

With a gentle gesture, he leaned toward his mother and whispered in her ear. Mrs. Darby squinted in Cordelia's direction, nodding but not otherwise acknowledging her. Then Max crossed the street in swift, purposeful strides until they were standing face to face. The day was almost done and the light was romantic, and Cordelia's frank, red lips curled up at the edges because, for a minute or two, she and Max were just like any girl and boy who are shy about seeing each other after a separation.

"If you want to talk, we'd better drive somewhere else. They aren't going to like you talking to me here any more than they'd like me talking to you in White Cove."

Cordelia's smile faded, but she nodded, understanding, and she walked around to the driver's seat and started up the motor without comment. They drove cross-town, through streets filled with children running through fire hydrants that had been mercifully opened. The spray of the water looked like gold in the late afternoon light. Eventually they found themselves on the West Side, and parked on a sloping street just past an old cemetery.

"I bet your mother is happy to have you home," Cordelia said after a time. They came to a park bench and sat down, a foot apart, as the sun melted over the river. The bank of trees on the other side were orange with sunset, and the water surrounding the sun's reflection was silver and still and dotted with boats of all sizes—lazy barges and small fisherman's barks with their lines cast out.

"She is, but she'd rather I was doing what I was meant to do. Anyway, it doesn't feel much like home now. Harlem, I mean, not Ma's apartment."

"They aren't proud to have you?"

"Nobody likes a prodigal. Not really. They'll take me, but it doesn't mean they like that I got famous while I was passing as white." Max laughed a joyless kind of laugh and leaned forward, propping his elbows against his knees. The sun washed out his pale blue eyes, but he was staring back, just as intensely, as though he were challenging it. After a while Cordelia rested her hand on his arm, and he glanced up at her. He shook his head and leaned back against the bench, draping his arm around her shoulders. "You think if you went back to Ohio now they'd be happy to see you?"

"I know they wouldn't." Cordelia's throat was dry and bitter, thinking of her hometown. There were so many reasons they wouldn't want her back that were impossible to explain, so she just whispered, as sweetly as she knew how: "But nobody ever looked up to me."

"They think you were kind of uppity back there?" His grip tightened on her, and she leaned against him, toward the affectionate way he pronounced *uppity*, as though it were a good thing.

"Yes."

"Me too."

She nodded and knew that it wasn't important to tell him how she'd come to leave, the memory of John Field standing at the altar with that hopeful grin, and then his face when she spotted him from the train and how it had been long with sorrow. Or the things her Aunt Ida used to call her, or the probable prohibition against saying her name out loud in their house now. They were alike, she and Max, and it was the characteristics they had in common that had driven her to the city, more than any of those other things.

"Max?"

"Yes?"

"They want me to negotiate with them."

"Who does?"

"The Hales." His arm against the back of her neck stiffened, so Cordelia opened her eyes and saw how fiercely Max was staring at her. The blue eyes were striking against his olive skin, and she could see the constriction in his neck. "Negotiate what?"

"A truce, between my family and theirs. Thom Hale came to see me the other night at The Vault. I haven't told anyone yet—I think they're waiting for me to say something to Charlie."

"But why you?"

Cordelia shrugged. "I guess they think I'll be easy to push around." A half smile emerged on one side of her face. "I suppose you could tell them they shouldn't count on that."

But Max did not pick up the joke. "Don't" was all he said.

Averting her gaze, Cordelia replied, "But why not? If they think they can push me around, they'll find themselves disappointed, and anyway, there's too much fighting as is. One of our boys died the night Astrid was kidnapped, and they lost a few, too, and I don't want any more of that."

"Don't," he repeated. Shaking his head, he went on, "They killed your father. What would stop them from hurting you? Please, Cordelia."

"What use would it be, killing me?" Cordelia sat up so that she was next to Max with her legs tucked under her. "They may be killers, but I hardly think a dead girl would do them any good. It just wouldn't make any sense."

"Don't talk that way."

"Well." Cordelia sighed, wishing she'd said nothing and hoping her breath would blow the topic away. Half of her had wanted him to talk this way, but half chafed at it. "Lucky for you, Charlie'd never have it, so I think I'll have to put off my dream of brokering peace between warring tribes for another day."

"Good." Max ran his fingers over her hair, and she closed her eyes, letting his touch send little tremors through her skull and down into her lips. Then something else occurred to him, and he stood up abruptly. "If there's trouble, you should get home before dark," he said as he offered his hand.

She stood without his assistance, and they walked slowly back to where she had left the car. They didn't speak again, not even when she slowed the car to a stop in front of his mother's house. His eyes darted from one window to the other, trying to determine whether they were being watched, and then he leaned in, holding her steady at the waist with his hand. The kiss wasn't a shy kiss this time. He kissed her as though he needed to, as though he couldn't stand not to, and she kissed him back, wishing it would go on and on. When he got out of the car he bent and gazed at her for a few moments, before disappearing behind that brownstone facade.

An exquisite sigh traveled across Cordelia's whole body once he was gone and she knew for sure how it was between them: that she was in his mind, as he was in hers, but that she couldn't know when she'd see him next.

9

WHEN SHE DESCENDED THE STAIRS THE NEXT MORN-
ing, Cordelia heard yelling from behind doors and knew
that something had not gone Charlie's way. Jones was speaking, too, in his more quiet and measured voice, which told
Cordelia that it was something to do with the business and
that she would learn of it eventually. But her body was still
pliant with sleep, and she didn't feel like talking to her
brother when he was angry. Twisting her long, loose braid
over her shoulder, Cordelia proceeded to the first floor and
found Len, the cook, reading that morning's funnies with his
foot up on a chair.

"What can I get you, Miss Grey?"

"I'll have coffee and orange juice and a croissant," she replied, and then went out to the verandah.

It was a little strange, saying the word *croissant* to a man like Len, who had only one leg and whose talents tended more to spaghetti with meatballs. But Darius had always liked fine things, and his daughter was getting used to asking for them. On the verandah, she adjusted her light linen shift and sat down in the elaborately curving white iron chair.

The sky was thick with formless, gray clouds tinged slightly yellow by a sun that was—Cordelia assumed, though she could not see it—approaching its height. Dogwood was peaceful at that hour, and the weather wasn't so bad today, at least under the stone arches that protected the south side of the house.

"Thank you, Len," she said as the cook placed her breakfast tray down on the white iron table. "Thanks," she repeated, more gratefully, when she saw that he had folded up the newspaper he'd been reading before and tucked it next to the silver coffee carafe.

She looked for Max's name in the sports pages of the paper but found it instead in the local section. Her anger flared when she saw why. The article mostly consisted of an interview with Mrs. Laurel about how she didn't have any problem with Negroes personally, it was only that she, like most people, abhorred dishonesty, and that was the reason that her husband had to cut funding to his former prodigy. She went on to endorse a dry politician for the upcoming governor's race and to make various allusions to the tide of immigrants—the Irish and Italians and Germans—who were ruining the country with their native drinking habits and strange-smelling foods.

A loud groan of exasperation escaped Cordelia's lips, and she threw the paper aside, just before Charlie came charging through the French doors and strode past her.

"What's the matter with you?" she said to his broad back.

Charlie stood on the lowest stone step, staring out at the lawns that rolled into orchards and fields and great clusters of trees as far as the eye could see.

"Astrid," Charlie said darkly.

"Is that all?" Charlie shot her a suspicious, over-the-shoulder glance, so she added: "I heard you and Jones . . . talking."

The only acknowledgment Charlie made of this observation was a snort. "She won't look me in the eyes," he went on. "Maybe she caught the cabin fever, having to live with a bodyguard and never goin' out."

"It's been rough for me, too, with someone always on my tail."

"Yeah, well. Get used to it."

"Charlie . . ." Cordelia sat up straight and tucked her braid into her dress. An idea was taking shape in her mind, and she wasn't going to let Charlie's sourness arrest it. "You know, it really is no way to live . . . Perhaps it's time we called a truce with the Hales?"

It took a while for Charlie to turn around. Once he was facing Cordelia she saw that he was wearing an expression like he'd just been called ugly. "Why would we do something like that?"

"They asked for it, for starters."

"They asked *you*?"

"Thom did. He came in to The Vault the other night and told me he'd like to negotiate a truce."

Charlie's eyes glinted with anger. "Thom Hale was in our place!" he shouted. It was not a question. He repeated himself and then stormed back up toward Cordelia, grabbing the table with both hands so that it shook, sloshing coffee and orange juice onto the white iron curlicues of its surface. "Thom Hale was in my place and you *didn't tell me*?"

"I was going to tell you." Cordelia leveled her gaze at her brother. "I was thinking over what he said to me."

"That we should pretend like they didn't murder our dad? Or try to kill Astrid? All so we can make it a little easier on them business-wise?" One side of Charlie's mouth was curled up, and he stared at Cordelia disgustedly before turning away. When he sat down on the top step and put his elbows on his big knees, she saw how his dress shirt was rolled to the elbows. Suddenly she knew that he had been up a long time already, worrying.

"Why did you hijack their shipment?" she asked.

He swung his head to look at her. "How did you know about that?"

She met his gaze evenly until he turned back to the landscape.

"We took a lot of clients from the Hales after Dad was killed," he began slowly. "You know that?"

Cordelia put down her coffee cup and began to redo the plait of her hair. "Yes, I know that."

"We lost some of them while I was away. Plus some old-timers, clients who'd been with Dad since the beginning."

"Oh, Charlie, you weren't away *that* long, I don't believe—"

"We didn't lose 'em because I was away. We lost 'em because the Hales got some new supply, real primo stuff. Through Nova Scotia, I guess."

"If the Hales can get this stuff, surely we can, too," Cordelia replied calmly. She had finished redoing her braid, but now it felt too tight, so she pushed her fingers in, trying to loosen it.

"That's what Jones said." Charlie gave a mirthless laugh. "But I couldn't have that. Takes too long."

Cordelia paused and watched her brother light a ciga-rette. She didn't like the way he was talking, the ominous way he'd said *Takes too long*. "What did you do?"

"You seem to know already. We hijacked their delivery. Big one. Few days ago, on the road to Rye Haven."

Cordelia took in a breath. With a shudder she thought how cavalier she had been, going into the city to see Max by herself. If Charlie had hijacked the Hales, she knew they were likely to strike back one way or another, and she had made it back last night only by being lucky—Max had been right. "What are you going to do with it?" was all she could think to say.

"I'm going to sell it! At a markup, to those same bastards who thought they could do better without us."

Cordelia nodded. Though she still didn't like the way Charlie was talking, she couldn't really argue with him. She supposed that was what Darius would have done. "You aren't nervous they'll come back at us?"

Charlie lit a cigarette, striking the match hard against the stone. "Stop sounding so much like Jones," he muttered. "Of course they'll come back at us."

"Unless we negotiate with them."

Charlie stood and faced his sister. His cigarette was between his teeth and his meaty arms were folded tensely over his middle, and he regarded her for several seconds without saying anything. To her surprise he asked, "Did they give any conditions?"

Cordelia blinked. She was remembering Thom at The Vault that night, how he had watched her. That smug look on his face, and the audacity of him coming into her club. How it had been difficult to think of him as more than a boy who meant some harm to her heart, when in fact he was a boy who threatened everything she held dear. But what did any of that matter? Thom had stood there in his expensive suit wearing his tennis-court tan, and she had not been afraid of him. "Only that they want to talk to me."

"You?" Charlie laughed out loud. "Why you?"

Cordelia shrugged. "I'd like to know the answer to that one, too."

A cloud of smoke unfurled slowly from Charlie's mouth. He was squinting, and for a moment he held the cigarette forward between his index and middle finger before dropping it and stubbing it out.

"Let me do it," Cordelia said, switching the cross of her long legs.

"Hell no." With a firm shake of his head Charlie came back up the steps and sat down next to her. He picked up her coffee cup and took a big gulp.

Cordelia sat back in her chair, heavy with a mysterious disappointment. "What's coming if we don't talk to them, Charlie?" she asked softly.

"I don't know." They were both looking south, in the direction of the city, and they saw the two figures coming over the rise at the same time. "I don't know, but we'd all better prepare. Oh, and this came for you." From his pants pocket he took a folded yellow square and placed it on the table-top. "I don't know what you two are up to, and I'll do you the courtesy of not asking. You can take care of yourself, I guess."

Charlie was up again, staring at something in the distance. In seconds she had unfolded the paper and read the telegram. The sender had been left blank, but Cordelia knew perfectly well whom it was from.

Thank you for coming to me yesterday. I wasn't much fun, and probably didn't deserve your visit. But seeing your face made me believe the sun might come up again, and sure enough it did.

"Are there any games you *are* good at?" Astrid demanded. She had won the first game of croquet handily, and now, just when she had been going easy on Victor, he had put his orange ball in position for her to knock him out. "Whenever I remember your abysmal rummy game I have a private shudder and fix myself a drink, you know."

Light played in Victor's dark eyes, and he smiled in a quiet, untroubled way. He was standing with his mallet rested on his opposite shoulder, and he took his time answering her. "I know enough not to show you my hand that way," he replied eventually. "You'll just have to try to beat me at all of them and find out."

"Oh, really?" Astrid gave him a little smirk before twirling around and walking over to her ball, the green one, and assuming a wide stance. The thin white cotton of her sleeveless V-necked dress just barely touched her skin, and the oxfords she wore without socks were beaten in and fit comfortably to her feet. She shook her hair away from her face and gripped the shaft with both hands. She took two practice swings, stopping short of the ball, before letting her mallet hit its mark. A loud *thwap* was followed by a quieter *cluck* when the green ball rolled against the orange one. "Ha!" Astrid pumped her fist in the air. "That's the game, darling—you'll never recover from this."

"You could always take the extra turn."

When she revolved to face him she saw that he didn't really care one way or another—he was smiling at her in a happy way, and she knew that he wasn't suggesting it because he wanted to win. He only wanted the game to go on longer. She wanted the game to go on longer, too, and she liked him for being so peculiarly indifferent to winning; but she could see the way the sky was darkening overhead, and anyway she herself hated to lose. "Not a chance, mister," she said with a wink.

Victor ambled toward her as she put her foot on her own ball to steady it. With one long swing she knocked the orange ball high into the air. They both sucked in breath as it sailed, farther than she'd meant it to, up the hill and over the wall of the hedge maze. "Damn!" she said, when she saw it was gone.

"Come on." Victor reached for her hand and pulled her toward the maze. "Don't worry, we'll find it."

"No." He glanced at her face and then at her hand, as though it had suddenly occurred to him that holding it wasn't the best idea. She waited for him to let go, but he didn't, so she went on, "It's going to rain, can't you see? I'll send Milly out for it later."

"All right."

The air was full of that dry, earthy smell that comes just before a downpour, and the atmospheric static was playing in her yellow hair. She smiled and pulled him in the opposite direction, back toward the house. "I think I'll beat you at back-gammon next," she mused as they walked over the grass.

"As you wish."

"I *do* wish. And after that, I don't know, maybe table tennis? Although I will have to ask Charlie to buy a set, I guess, because there isn't one in the house . . . Are you good at table tennis?"

"I wouldn't ruin the suspense for you." He grinned. "Although perhaps we should start with billiards, since Dogwood already has a billiards table."

"Aha! So *that's* where your abilities lie. And you thought

you could hide it from me. I'll tell you what, Victor, I'm going to give you a shot, one shot . . ." She trailed off as they came to the rise that separated the south lawn from the less tended meadow where they had been playing. At first it was because she realized that she had been squeezing his hand, and then it was because she saw Dogwood sitting there below, like the country castle of some English lord. She didn't want to let go— the surface of his palm was large and dry, and she liked the way it felt against hers—but then she saw a tall figure emerging from the shadows of the verandah on the south side of the house and her pulse quickened. She couldn't remember what she had been trying to say, so she released her grip and went striding ahead of him across the grass.

They didn't speak again until she was within shouting distance of the house and could make out the features of her husband, standing on the first flight of steps. "Thanks for giving my ego a little boost, darling. If you insist I'll return the favor sometime soon over billiards." Then, raising her arm above her head and calling out in a voice loud enough that Charlie could hear her: "There you are!"

The scowl she saw at a distance was still on Charlie's face when she began to climb the steps. Behind him, at the breakfast table, was Cordelia, but she was absorbed in a telegram and didn't acknowledge her friend. Astrid spread her vermillion lips in a brilliant smile that held steady even when he didn't reciprocate it, and she threw both arms around his middle. "Don't look cross," she said with a laugh, shaking out her hair.

"Where have you been all morning?"

"Playing croquet." Glancing over her shoulder she saw that Victor had remained below, leaning against one of the stone statues and staring in the direction of the city as though something might come at them from there. "Where have you been?"

"Business, I've been seeing about the business." His voice was still gruff, and he was staring down at her as though he didn't know her very well. "You spend more time with your bodyguard these days than you do with me," he spat out resentfully.

Astrid's heart dropped, and a cold fear settled in around her temples. But her smile was unwavering, and her voice was fine and clear. "Well, that's because my own husband is too busy for me!" His torso was stiff to her, but she pressed firmly against him and went on. "Pay attention to me, take me out once in a while, and I wouldn't be forced to waste time with what's-his-name down there!"

For a minute Astrid thought Charlie was going to be furious. That he somehow knew about what had happened in the pool last night, and she and Victor were both in big trouble. A clap of thunder sounded somewhere off in the distance, and the first drops went *splat* on the verandah. Then she felt his middle relax and his arms fold around her. "I'm sorry, baby, I've just had so much on my mind," he said. He buried his face against her neck and kissed her there. Though it embarrassed her, the touch made her lips part, and she wanted him to go on putting his mouth along her hairline. "Friday night!" he said, lifting her so that her feet came off the ground. "Friday night I'm taking you out."

If she could have she would have turned to see if Victor was watching them, but it was impossible from that position.

In the next moment Charlie shouted, "You hear that, Victor? I'm taking my wife out Friday night—till then your job is to see she's entertained!"

After that, there was no chance that Victor had not seen how Charlie was holding her. He had said Victor's name in that self-important, threatening way, and she hated him for it, and she hated him for holding her so that she was pinned against him, and she hated that Victor had to stand there watching them. She didn't quite know why, but it made her insides crumble to think that her bodyguard saw her husband handling her as though she belonged to him and only him.

"And Cord," Charlie said when he put her down. Cordelia glanced up, surprised, and half waved at Astrid. "I changed my mind. Let's call those bastards and tell them yes."

10

"YOU DON'T HAVE TO."

"I know."

"You were supposed to be my *little* sister," Charlie said, almost like a complaint, but when he bent down to put his meaty arms around her, Cordelia could smell his guilt. "Now here you are cleaning up my messes."

"I'll be all right, Charlie." She squeezed him and then pushed up on her tiptoes to kiss his forehead. He twisted his face away, as though he didn't want the others to see how he savored this gesture of affection, but she sensed it was so rare for him that he almost didn't know how to accept it.

"We'll be here till you get back," Jones said, and lifted

the yellow slicker so that Cordelia could put her arms into its sleeves.

After midnight last night a rain had come through while the three of them sat in Charlie's office, talking over what terms they would accept and what they wouldn't. It was still drizzling now as she set off in the motorboat. One of the Hales's men operated the rudder—he, too, was wearing a slicker. As they sailed out to sea, she looked back at the little crowd of men whose features were soon indistinct but whose black umbrellas cut perfectly through the dense atmosphere. Duluth Hale was with them, unarmed, and he had promised he would wait there that way until Cordelia was returned safe from the boat that Thom Hale had anchored some distance offshore. She hadn't spoken to Thom's father—*that*, she would never do—but he had ogled her with those little pig's eyes that were set too close together in his big platter face.

She'd only seen that face once before, the night she'd driven to Avalon, the Hales's place on the Sound, with the intention of killing Thom for what he'd done to her family. For a quarter of an hour she had pretended that she still loved Thom, and they had swayed together on the dance floor. Somewhere in between that dance and the moment when Thom had tried to get her alone in the dark, Duluth had spotted her, and she had shuddered under his gaze. The way he moved, that heavy preying gait, had revolted her then, and she felt no less suspicious of him today as they took off from Rock Point.

A wave came at the motorboat from behind, and her heart leapt as the craft shot up and went down beneath her.

The Hales's man smirked. "Hope you don't get seasick."

"No."

The men on the Point were too small to see now, so she turned and gazed out in the direction of New York Harbor instead, letting tendrils of tawny hair blow across her chin. She had told Charlie that everything would be all right, but in fact she wasn't sure of that herself. The whole plan had taken shape so quickly, and now all the ways it could go wrong began springing up haphazardly in her thoughts. Maybe the Hales really did want a war, and nabbing Cordelia would be the confirmation. Maybe this was Thom's idea alone, and he was going to make her pay for what she'd wanted to do that night at Avalon. But she tried to remember how Thom had seemed to her the other night—just a rival like any other, and one she happened to know how to talk to.

At Dogwood they had been up late last night, drinking black coffee and debating whether to let Cordelia talk to the Hales, and she'd woken up tired. She was still tired, but her fatigue was due to something more than lost sleep. She had done so many things, made so many mistakes. Back in Ohio, she'd always thought that if she met her father, her life would magically start to make sense, but instead she had blundered in ways that led to his death. And of course there was John Field, whom she had promised to have and to hold forever on the same day that she slipped off in the night. Finally there was Max, who, because of her, had lost everything he'd ever worked for. If she did this one thing right—if she reached an agreement with the Hales and ended the violent tit-for-tat the two families had been engaged in—then perhaps she would be able to put her head down and rest awhile.

The shore receded until it was just a misty blue line, and she held tight to the side of the boat. When the man across from her cut the engine abruptly and stood up with his arm raised, she twisted in her seat and saw the hull of Thom's ship rising above.

Hands reached for her, pulling her up, and then she was standing on the blond plank deck next to Thom Hale. His coppery hair was a little overgrown now and his eyes were more lucid than she remembered them being, and he wore a blue-and-white plaid shirt tucked into beige pants. These were the simplest clothes she'd ever seen him wear.

"Here I am." She lengthened her neck and spoke with as much indifference as possible.

"Yes." He observed her in the same way he always had before—his chin lifted, his eyes taking in everything and offering nothing. The line of his patrician lips curled on one side, as though he were amused or disgusted or otherwise onto something nobody else was. Suddenly Cordelia wished the slicker weren't two sizes too big for her and that its hood didn't flop stupidly over her face.

"This is your boat?"

"My father's. Just one of his toys; he never used it much. Dad gave up on social climbing a long time ago."

"What do you do with it?"

"*You* know. Your family stole my cargo."

Cordelia's eyes widened. Earlier, he'd spoken of the hijacking almost neutrally, but now she saw how it angered him to have his loot taken.

"You brought that shipment down yourself, then?"

Thom shrugged, but she caught a fugitive light in his eyes and knew he was proud. "I'd show you around, but then you'd just tell Charlie my secrets."

"We have our own ways, Thom." The wind and the salt spray were so relentless against her face that she could only squint at him. "Shouldn't we talk?"

"Yes."

Just then the sea lurched under them. A wave broke over the deck, sending a sheet of water across its surface and soaking her tennis shoes. She froze, shocked by the sudden wetness of her feet and the growing realization that she was not on equal terms with Thom and his crew. No matter what she had to offer him in negotiation, out here she was at his mercy. Then she felt Thom's arm against her back, pushing her toward the pilothouse. The others were on the far side of the deck—even though they were Thom's men, she had felt better knowing there were witnesses. Now it was too late for that.

Inside, the ocean was less fierce-sounding, and the large panel of levers and dials framed by shining blond wood seemed to promise control over the elements. Now that they were alone together in an enclosed space, she was suddenly aware of Thom's breathing. The rhythm of her heart became fast and erratic, and she tried to tell herself this was only because she was frightened.

"We haven't been alone together since the night you . . ." He trailed off and hung his head.

"The night I pointed a gun at you?" There was no chance either of them had forgotten the fact, so she figured she might as well just say it.

"It wasn't me. You know that, don't you?"

Cordelia's features folded quizzically. "It wasn't you who what?"

"Told my father. About the tunnel."

"No?" She gave him a hard look and crossed her arms over her chest. The mention of her father and his murder made her want to tell Thom to forget the whole thing. But then she realized that he was only trying to make her angry, that it was a clever trick with which to begin a negotiation. Thom always had been clever. "He's dead," she pronounced with precise and quiet fury. "Change that, and I'll agree to whatever you like."

Thom put his hands in his pants pocket and gazed out through the window. "I'm sorry, I didn't mean—" He worked his jaw angrily and shook his head once.

"So you brought in that champagne yourself?" Cordelia said, to change the subject.

"Yes, from Canada."

"That's how you got so much sun."

"Yes." He made a gesture like he might take the wet slicker from Cordelia, but she waved him off. Instead she pushed the hood back and brought herself to her full height. "Drink?" he offered.

"No, thanks." The ocean lifted the boat up beneath her, but she forced herself to hold his gaze and made believe the rocking didn't trouble her. "I guess you want those crates back."

"No—we'll let you sell them."

Cordelia arched an eyebrow.

"You can sell those crates, but when your clients want more they're going to have to come to me. If they want quality French champagne, that is."

Tilting her head back, Cordelia regarded him with a wry smile. "And here I thought all champagne was French."

A dimple emerged in his cheek, the ripple of a smile

suppressed. Thom's eyes remained on her as he pulled a pack of cigarettes out of his front pocket and offered one, and she felt almost as she had in those first days of knowing him, when there was such camaraderie, when even his smallest gestures seemed brilliant and exciting. *Shake your head*, she told herself. Once she had refused the cigarette she knew that it was going to be easier to harden her voice. "All right, we keep those crates, but we won't be giving you back any of the clients we took."

"How 'bout the ones you took from Coyle Mink?"

The name startled Cordelia. What did Coyle Mink have to do with this, and what hadn't Charlie told her? "I guess you know all our business," she said coolly.

"And I'm sure you know ours," Thom replied with matching detachment. He left his cigarette between his teeth as he inhaled and exhaled, watching her. She had never wanted to smoke so badly in her whole life.

"Listen, Thom, I don't like it, and I don't like your father, and I don't like you. But we don't want to fight you anymore."

"Sure." Thom sneered. "I figured that's why you came."

With a little sigh and a gaze tossed out to sea, Cordelia concluded: "We will fight if we have to."

A cloud of smoke escaped Thom's mouth and filled the cabin. "No, we don't want to fight you, either."

"Why? You did before."

"That was when Darius was around. You're more manageable now."

After that there was more stone in Cordelia's heart. "What do you want, then? You seem to have it all figured. Why don't you just tell me, and we can wrap this delightful chat," she spat, her lips twisting with sudden sarcasm.

"No more hijackings, no more kidnappings, no more blown-up warehouses."

"No more murders."

Thom glanced away and took two furtive drags of his cigarette. "No more murders," he said eventually.

"And in exchange?"

"Nothing. Territories stay as they are. We got two of the big hotels with our new stuff—we keep those. But otherwise, the Greys continue to supply the hotels, the Hales keep their speaks. Whoever you sell to now, you keep; same with us, so long as there's no poaching in the future."

"Is that all?"

"Yes."

"Agreed." Cordelia put her hand forward and gave Thom's a quick, firm shake. He met her eyes, as though to make sure she was for real, and she returned his gaze steadily. "Well," she went on, now blithe, bringing the hood of her slicker over her wind-tossed hair as she moved toward the door, "I guess that's that."

"Wait." His voice had changed, as threatening as that of a radio villain. When she felt his fingers grabbing for her wrist, her heart dropped and she saw how stupid she had been to think it would be that easy, coming out here alone. He spun her around hard; his expression was fierce, all lightness and camaraderie drained away. An instinctual fear passed through her, darkening her eyes. With an ominous shake of his head, he repeated: "You're not going yet."

"That's enough for me," said Dave, the biggest and blondest of Charlie's men, who also happened to be the worst of them at hiding what he was thinking.

"But the game isn't over!" Astrid protested. Her eyes rolled innocently to Victor, who was leaning against the wall behind Dave and watching her with arms crossed and an amused expression. She tried to appear a little confused and entirely surprised by this turn of events, as though all three of them had not seen her cheat. It hadn't been *much* of a cheat, really. After her last shot, the white cue ball had bounced off the far embankment and seemed likely to hit the eight ball—which would have ended the game too soon for her liking—and she had only jostled the table slightly to change its course. Anyway, she wasn't entirely successful at appearing confused; the way Victor was looking at her, she couldn't quite control the smile that was tugging at the corners of her mouth.

"All the same." Dave handed his cue stick to Victor and feigned a yawn. "I'm tired of it."

Most of the boys had gone with Charlie and Cordelia when they had driven off the property on whatever super-secret important mission they had been up all last night talking about. The rain had been intermittent since then, occasionally gusting across the lawn and splattering the windows, so the boys who were left came in to drink beer and talk about the local girls. But they had thinned out since, from ten, to five, to three. Now there were just two, but Astrid averted her eyes and fiddled with the lace hem of her dress as though she might be able to pretend she hadn't noticed that.

"They won't call the boss's girl a cheat, not to her face." Victor lifted the cue up and rested it on his shoulders, with his arms dangling over it. "But that doesn't mean they'll keep on playing with you."

"Oh, to hell with them, they're all goons with poor personal hygiene habits anyway." Astrid flipped her hair and pranced across the room toward a sweating silver plant holder now being used as a champagne bucket. She refilled her glass and regarded him with her drink aloft. "I like to win, you know, and anyway I've always thought scruples were sort of boring, do you know what I mean?"

Victor shrugged, as though he were considering her point of view but wasn't convinced by it. In the moments of silence that followed, Astrid became aware of the labored wheezing of the ceiling fan (it had been straining against the tropical air all week) and also that the phonograph was no longer playing. The quiet unnerved her, so she exclaimed, "Odd weather!" and looked away.

"Yeah, they were calling it a hurricane till yesterday. Knocked out some towns in the Carolinas. But we're just getting the tail end. They say it's going to hit this evening and be gone by tomorrow."

"Oh." She took a gulp of champagne, which made her feel dizzy and happy and light-headed. As a consequence, she didn't think to argue with Victor over what he said next.

"I could teach you to play. Then you could win without cheating."

"All right, darling, teach me everything you know!" She giggled and came slinking back in the direction of the table.

Victor slid the cue off his back. "The thing to remember," he said, his voice growing low and official, "is that it's all just geometry. Did you study geometry at that fancy school of yours?"

"Classical geometry," she replied without removing her lips from the rim of her champagne glass.

"Well." Victor whistled low. "You *are* fancy."

"You bet your life." Astrid raised her chin and dragged her fingertips languorously along the walnut edge of the pool table.

"Think I'd rather just take your word for it." Victor winked and stepped backward. "You take my word on this: It's a game of angles. You want the ball to go in the pocket, right? So for the ball to roll in a perfect trajectory from where it rests to the pocket, you have to hit it at the right angle." He drew his finger over the green felt slowly, showing her how one would have to hit the white cue ball so that it would hit the green one, knocking it into the side pocket. "You see?"

For a moment Astrid hesitated, but when Victor thrust the cue stick in her direction she took it and moved so that she could examine the green ball as he again traced a line to the side pocket.

"Then, go back to the cue ball and get low to the table. Imagine you're the ball. Look at the table from the ball's point of view."

"I'm the ball? You *must* be joking." Astrid hooted, but was met only with the brilliance of Victor's teeth.

"I'll show you."

He moved around to her other side and, with a gentle palm between her shoulder blades, urged her to bend forward. Once she had, she saw what he'd been trying to explain: The balls lay before her like a model of the solar system, as though she were looking at the Earth over the shoulder of the moon. If she hit the Earth square on, it would bounce off the wall; she needed the moon to hit on the right side, so that the Earth would skew left. She raised her cue, ready to take her shot, but he gently corrected her.

"Here, move this way," he said, guiding her body left. She had always thought of Victor as such a slender fellow, almost as though he were no bigger than she was. But now she saw how much larger he was, really. His wingspan was so great that his arms went around her without touching her arms or back as he repositioned the stick in her hands. "And keep the cue low, closer to the angle of the table. Now, do you remember where the cue ball needs to hit?"

"Yes."

"Hit it with confidence—not so hard it bounces the green ball out, but with force."

"All right." Holding her breath, Astrid drew one arm back; with an exhale she let it fly forward. The way the moon moved across the felt, the smack it gave the earth, and the clean silence with which the earth sank into the side pocket were all so gratifying that Astrid couldn't help but leap back and jump up and down. "I did it!"

"You did it!"

She turned, and Victor was so close behind her that their chests almost touched. His smile was bright as hers, and for a moment she thought he might jump up and down, too. But he didn't. He only stared at her with stars in his dark eyes.

"Oh," she said as her smile fell away. "Oh," she repeated, once she'd managed to avert her gaze.

"You're a natural."

"Naturally fatigued," she said quickly, and then laughed a weak laugh to hide the lameness of the joke.

Victor stepped back and spoke with a formal intonation. "Yes, of course. I can give you another lesson some other time. If you want, that is."

"Perhaps." Astrid turned and carefully placed the cue back on the table. "But right now I think I'd better go take a nap! Charlie is taking me out tonight, you know, and I'd better get a little rest first."

"I'll escort you. As your bodyguard. Just to make sure you're all right."

Astrid nodded distractedly and downed the remainder of her champagne. Had the idea been that this would make her feel drowsy, when in fact all of her senses were intensely alive? She knew that if she spoke her voice would be far softer and sweeter than was appropriate, so instead of replying she just let him follow her as she moved into the hall and up the stairs.

As she climbed toward her bedroom she thought of Charlie and the way he had looked on the verandah that day and how jealous he used to get when she flirted with another boy. Usually she *had* been flirting, but that was a long time ago, before she was married, and she knew she ought not to flirt now. Yet she was acutely aware of the lightness of Victor's feet against the floorboards, and the rhythm of his breathing, and his smell, which suggested that he had recently shaved with Ivory soap. All the inches between them suddenly seemed like an agony she wouldn't be able to bear, and she wished that she were the girl she used to be, free to do as she pleased. But she wasn't, she reminded herself, and Charlie would be taking her out tonight.

Then she saw things as they truly were. This was just another moment, unconnected from all the moments in the past and all the moments yet to come. There was no one around, and Victor was a sweet boy, and she was doing nothing wrong, playing cards and croquet and billiards with him. So she pressed up on tiptoes and kissed him on the mouth.

She had meant it chastely (at least she thought she had), but he staggered backward as though the kiss had been a big, wet passionate one.

"Good-bye," he warbled.

By then she was thinking about the softness and yearning in his lips, and she wanted to know what a big, wet passionate kiss with him would be like. Before she knew her own mind, she'd thrown her arms around his neck and they were joined at the mouth. A few seconds passed before his hands found her lower back, bunching up her dress there while the kiss went on and on.

"Oh, *dear*." She pulled back and wiped her mouth with the back of her hand.

"I'm sorry, I—"

"Sorry for what?" The chagrin that had been in her voice a few moments before was gone, and a mischievous glimmer passed over her eyes.

When he hung his head she darted backward, opening the door behind her and slipping inside the darkened room. "See you later!" she called before slamming the door and running to the bed, where she threw herself down and wrapped herself in the covers and told her heart it had better stop causing such an uproar, or else.

11

"WAIT. PLEASE."

Cordelia's heartbeat was so out of order that she'd been briefly deaf to the plaintiveness in Thom's voice. But she saw now that his menacing tone had been all in her mind. Had she ever heard him say the word *please* and mean it? His face was almost unrecognizable, he wanted so badly for her to listen.

"Wait," he said again. "Let me explain."

"Explain what?" Her throat was scratchy, and her stomach felt weak in anticipation of what he might say—for a moment, he looked like he might ask if she could love him again.

"How it happened—how my father's man got into Dogwood."

"Oh."

Thom drew his hand over his face, and then words began to tumble from his mouth: "At first I thought it really was my fault—that they'd followed me, and that's how they found out about the tunnel. I was ashamed, I think, and afraid that I might have something to do with it. That's why I didn't call or—or—I don't know."

Cordelia closed her eyes and forced air into her lungs. "But how can you be sure they didn't follow you?"

"Because I made my father tell me. I went away for a while, and I thought about things, and I realized I couldn't feel right about avoiding what had happened—that night. That's why I was there, after they nabbed Astrid. I had to make sure for myself that it didn't happen that way again. When I came back this time I told him I wouldn't speak to him again unless he explained how he got into Dogwood."

By now Cordelia's stomach was in such a knot that she couldn't produce words, but she nodded at Thom that she was listening.

"You see, my father always knew about the tunnel."

"What? How?" Cordelia demanded.

"He knew because my mother grew up at Dogwood. It was her parents' house, and she used to play in that tunnel when she was a child. Her family is one of White Cove's best families, you know—her father was paranoid that thieves would come after him, or try to kidnap his daughter for ransom. So he had the tunnel built as an escape route."

To Cordelia, the idea of a child at Dogwood sounded bizarre and a little sad. She had never pictured it as anything but a bootlegger's home, the staging ground for raucous parties. But that was shortsighted, she knew—who but the local aristocracy would build a house that grand? "Well," she said eventually. "That's quite a coincidence, isn't it? My father owning your mother's childhood home."

Thom blinked at her. "Darius never told you, did he? About how he and my father fell apart?"

Slowly Cordelia shook her head.

"I suppose you know that in the early days they were best friends. It was Dad's outfit, but Darius was his right-hand man. Small-time operation, robbing banks mostly. Darius was just a driver most of the time. But as soon as they started making real dough, Dad got social pretensions, started going to parties with fancy people. That's how he met my mother. I think he wooed her just to prove he could get a girl from the snooty set. Anyway, they eloped, and he took her back to Minnesota to show her off to all the little people where he came from. It was on the way back through Ohio that they met Fanny. The way Dad tells the story, you know he's still sore about it—they saw her at the same time, sitting on a porch at sunset, and she was the most perfect girl either of them had ever seen. Beautiful, but brave, too. Of course, Darius had the advantage, not being a newlywed and all, and she chose him. When they left town, she went with them."

"That's why they fell out?" Cordelia said incredulously.

"No." Thom took a long, painful breath. "When they got back to New York City, they'd spent all their loot buying bespoke suits and gold watch chains and showing off in the Midwest, and meanwhile Ma's people had disowned her, and she was bitter about having a husband who didn't really love her and living in a no-good part of town. For a while they tried to be family men and work normal jobs, but they weren't cut out for it. Eventually they robbed a bank they probably shouldn't have and had to hide out a long time in some shack out in the Pine Barrens. Funny to think we both must have been there and known each other as babies, isn't it?"

Thom rolled his eyes up to meet Cordelia's, but she was so focused on his story that she wasn't able to make any kind of expression.

"There wasn't much to do there but drink, and that's what they mostly did," he went on. "One night they had too much, and Dad got romantic with Fanny. Ma started screaming, and Darius was waving his gun around. He was threatening to kill Dad, and though he probably didn't mean it really, the gun went off. Well, the bullet ricocheted off something and caught Fanny in the belly."

Cordelia's hands flew to her face. "That's how she died?" she managed to whisper.

Thom was watching her carefully. "It wasn't that bad a wound, just painful, but there was a bounty out for them so they didn't get help right away. Five days later, when they finally found a doctor who promised not to ask questions, the gangrene had set in, and it was too late. Darius blamed Dad and never forgave him. He became obsessed with doing everything bigger and better than him, and they've been rivals ever since. Dogwood was the culmination of all that. Dad wanted to buy it to appease Mother for all the things he'd done, but Darius got there first. He bought Dogwood out of spite."

"But if Duluth knew about the tunnel all those years, why didn't he come after Dad sooner?"

Thom shrugged. "I didn't ask him that. I think it had something to do with you coming back, how much you look like her, and that Darius was hell-bent on keeping us apart. All that opened the old wound, I guess, and Dad couldn't have it."

Cordelia squeezed her eyes shut and told herself not to cry. What Thom had told her was so much, the whole story of her life, and she couldn't stop herself from shaking, now that she heard it so plainly for the first time. "Oh, God," she whispered hoarsely. "That's so awful."

When she felt Thom's arms around her she was too weak to do anything but lean into him. "I'm sorry," he said, pushing the hair that was becoming wet and clumped with tears away from her face.

"He must have thought it was his fault. The way I thought it was my fault about him." She looked up at Thom, as though hoping he might agree with her.

But he didn't seem to be thinking about that at all. His eyes glinted, and then he lowered his face to hers. He kissed her as though he had been thinking about kissing her for a long time, and she kissed him back thirstily, the way she might've drunk in the first glass of water after a winter's hibernation. For a while she was lost in the sweet wetness of the kiss, her body melting against his. But when he pulled back smiling, the past few days came back to her—Max and Charlie, how she had been going to set things right—and her brow folded. It seemed to her that all her years had been calculated by some misguided romantic so that she would end up here, in Thom's arms.

"This isn't right," she mumbled, stepping away from him. When she saw his crestfallen face she knew that she would never be angry at him again. But the truth didn't change the animosity between their families, the ugly history they shared, nor the terrible thing that had happened. "I have to go."

She put her shoulder against the door and went out onto the deck. The salt spray met her face immediately, and she was grateful for the way it cooled her face after the warm kiss.

"I don't think that's a good idea." Thom had followed her

and was squinting to the south. "Don't think it will be safe in the little boat, not in a few minutes. That squall is moving fast."

Cordelia's heart quickened. She wanted to be back with her brother, tell him that everything was set.

Thom seemed to have anticipated her thoughts. "I'll call ashore, talk to Dad. I know he's waiting with Charlie; he can tell them you're all right."

"No." A moment ago her heart had been a fist, but now it opened. "No, that won't be necessary." The men on the other end of the deck were pointing at a dot growing large against the western sky. They didn't speak about it, they just watched and waited. No rain was falling just then, and the wind was warm and dense. The restless weather made her skin tingle. "I'm glad we have a truce."

"I am, too."

They stared at each other for a few moments as the airplane grew larger and began to descend toward the surface of the water.

"Did you know it would be like this?" He glanced sidelong at her question, and his lips parted. Hurriedly she added: "The ocean, I mean."

His lips closed and opened again as though he wanted to say something, but in the end nothing came out. She could now make out Max in the cockpit of the seaplane, and she stepped to the railing with her arm raised in greeting. She thought she saw him raise his hand back at her, but she could tell he was concentrating on how to land on the rough surface.

"There's something that's bothering me, Thom. You could have struck that deal on the phone with Jones in a few minutes. Even Charlie would have agreed to that without getting too troublesome. Why make me come out here, in this weather?"

Thom shrugged and tried to get another cigarette lit. He cupped his hands to protect the match, but even so the wind was too strong. Eventually he threw away the match and put the cigarettes back in his pocket. "I go back north tomorrow," he said, meeting her eyes again. His chin was drawn down, his eyes cast upward at her. "I just—had to see you."

A smile broke over her face before she could stop it. As soon as she had control of herself, she folded it away.

"Come with me," he said with sudden urgency. "It's going to be bad, you know that, right? Now that Charlie has challenged Coyle Mink. You can't fight him, Cord; he's organized, violent, into all kinds of rackets. He's not some genteel bootlegger from the island. And he's crazier than Charlie. Come with me now. I can keep you safe." He reached for her hand, holding it out for her until she gently shook her head. "We can drink old-fashioneds and dance to the radio and be happy wherever we are."

The roar of the propellers was at her back, and she knew Max had landed. Her mind was on fire with what Thom had proposed. What he was offering sounded beautiful, but it also frightened her, and she was struck with desire to be far away from all these bloody and complicated entanglements, to have nothing to do with the past.

"I can't," she said simply, and gave him her hand to shake.

When she let go, he bent down and lifted his pant leg. The gun didn't frighten her, because by the time she saw its metallic flank he'd pressed it into her palm.

"It's the gun you came after me with. That night. I've been carrying it around with me; I don't know why. But maybe you'll need it now, more than me," he said.

It was the gun her father had taught her to shoot with at the beginning of the summer, at a time when she'd believed life wouldn't go on if she never saw Thom again. Tears were welling in her eyes, so she slipped the gun into her pocket and turned toward the sea.

Meanwhile the seaplane was bobbing on its floats next to the ship. Max had propped open the door to the cockpit and was extending a long, foot-wide board, which he wedged between the boat's railing and the cockpit. He had barely glanced at Cordelia yet, but she could see how worried he was, how intensely focused on the task at hand.

"Steady that," he commanded Thom, who obeyed though it must have pained him. "Here," Max called to Cordelia, and threw her a rope. Holding tightly to the rope,

Cordelia clambered to the railing and then onto the board. After a few steps, she was within arm's length of Max. He grabbed her and with all his strength pulled her into the cockpit, where he drew her tight against his chest. "I told you not to," he whispered, but it was not a reproach.

"I'm sorry. I had to."

"I know."

Max let go and was once again all business. He kicked the board down into the water and sealed the door to the cockpit without glancing back at Thom. The goggles came down over his eyes as she fastened herself into her seat.

"Thank you," she said. "There's no one I'd rather see right now," she added, and meant it. She knew that Thom was down below, and that if she dared to look at him his eyes would be wide and shiny, silently offering her a future that sounded more real than any she had ever contemplated. But she couldn't take it. She couldn't keep running. She had to be here, with a boy whose motives were pure, who was always reaching for some clean, bright future.

"You're welcome. But mostly I came because I would have gone crazy, not knowing where you were, if you'd come back to shore all right."

She smiled faintly. "I'd better go tell Charlie it's done."

"Don't worry, I talked to Charlie."

"You did?"

Max glanced at her, and for the first time his serious facade cracked open into a grin. "How do you think I found you? After I got your telegram this morning, I was frantic, trying to get hold of Charlie. I told him there was a storm coming. Little exaggeration—it won't hit for some hours. But he told me to do what I had to do to keep you safe. We'll call him from the East End."

"Good," she said. The pale green water rose and fell back on itself below them, and she saw that none of it was so frightening as she had found it before. Nothing was really so bad, if you were brave enough to confront it. Relief washed over her, knowing she had done what she had to do, and as the plane lifted off she rested her hand on his shoulder and whispered to him that everything was going to be all right.

12

"I FEEL SOOOO MUCH BETTER," SOPHIA RAY SAID INTO
her compact. "Don't you feel *soooo* much better?"

"Yes." Letty was gazing into her own compact and was
indeed feeling much improved. Her reflection showed a finely
tuned version of herself—her lashes looked longer somehow,
and her lips more full. The only way to escape the heat with
dignity, Sophia had told her, was to go to Bergdorf. At the
department store's salon Letty had had her hair freshly bobbed
and her nails and toes trimmed and painted. Sophia emerged
with her short hair freshly peroxided, her features dramatically
made up, and her spirits high.

As they stepped onto the sidewalk, she took her protégée

by the arm and led her to their waiting limousine. "Hector, hurry, please, we haven't much time, especially with traffic like this."

As they pulled away from the curb, Letty noticed a group of young girls gathered tightly together under a large umbrella, baldly gawking at Sophia Ray and her friend. They did not live in the neighborhood—Letty could tell by their clothes—and they weren't there for shopping. Letty smiled at them and didn't feel even a little guilty for being so glad not to be one of them anymore.

The limousine was blocked by a tangle of traffic, worsened by the bad weather. Drivers berated one another with bleating horns and fists thrust through open windows. Meanwhile, in the back of the beige town car, all the surfaces were soft and fine, and the hurly-burly of the street seemed like another world.

"You know I'm going to need your friendship more than ever when I'm away."

"Tell me why you're going away again?" Letty sunk against the soft leather upholstery. Although Letty had more or less decided not to think about the incident at Jack Montrose's party, she couldn't help but feel a little curious about Sophia's unexpected departure.

"To lose five pounds, dear. Seven, if I can possibly manage. Three days of mountain air and interminable walks and a ghastly amount of celery! We're going to start filming the picture on Monday, you see. I want my cheekbones to cut right through the screen."

"But you're already so thin."

"Well." Sophia closed her eyes, as if that went without saying. "There *is* another reason I must go." The pause that followed was charged with meaning, and Sophia's eyes traveled back and forth to the front of the car twice. Letty looked, too—Hector was wearing his chauffeur's cap and staring impassively at the street in front of them. The girls bent their heads toward each other. "You remember how we talked about Mr. Montrose, how very important he is? And you know how we had to . . . be alone at his party?"

Sophia's voice went very low and her brows went very high, and Letty was trying hard to return her gaze neutrally. Letty sensed what she going to say, and wished she wouldn't, and tried to prepare herself not to appear scandalized by the revelation.

"Well, you see . . . Mr. Montrose is *escorting* me to the spa." Sophia's eyes widened significantly when she said this, and the corners of her mouth flickered. A current of excitement flowed from her toward Letty, and though Letty felt a little sickened by the thrill her mentor derived from her deviance, she tried to grin back in response. "You won't tell, will you?"

"Of course not!" Letty winked, hoping this would disguise the sorrow she felt for sweet, true Valentine. "It's our secret," she added earnestly.

"Good. And Letty?"

"Yes?"

"Take care of Valentine for me while I'm gone, all right?"

"I'll try," Letty promised with an earnest nod.

"Keep the motor running, won't you, Hector?" The green awning of The Apollonian filled the car window, and the liveried doorman was rushing to open the door, wielding an umbrella to protect the ladies from the drizzle now making the sidewalk slick. Sophia had leaned forward to address the chauffeur, and only half turned when she spoke to Letty. "Letty, hon, you'll take the bags up, won't you?" The girlish intimacy of the previous moments had been replaced by Sophia's more customary brisk assertiveness. "And tell Val how bad the traffic was, and explain to him that I *would* have come up to kiss him good-bye, but it seemed very likely that I'd miss my train if I did . . ."

A few moments later, the elevator doors drew back, and Letty stepped into the penthouse, weighed down by the shopping bags she carried in both hands. An involuntary smile sprang to her lips at the tranquil scene in the sunken living room. Under a purring ceiling fan sat Valentine, wearing a white dress shirt tucked into white slacks over brown loafers, his face half obscured by the *New York Star-Courier* that he held aloft.

"Hello, beautiful." There were a few wondrous seconds when Letty believed that this had been directed at her, but when Valentine moved the paper and his smile shrank away, she realized he'd assumed it was Sophia who had just disembarked from the elevator. Though she wished it wouldn't, her stomach twisted in disappointment. "Oh. Hello, Letty. Where's my missus?"

"There was—traffic," Letty mumbled. Then she heard herself say *train* and *spa* and *celery*.

She watched Valentine, to see if he was wounded by his wife's failure to say good-bye, but his face remained blank, his eyes focused somewhere in the distance. For a few seconds he continued staring into space, and then his gaze slowly traveled around the room, over buckskin-colored carpets and elaborately framed portraits, eventually settling on Letty. His face was the face he often wore in the second half of his pictures, during the part of the story when everything seems impossible but he nonetheless continues to be winning and brave.

"Are you lonely when she goes away?" Letty asked.

"Lonely!" he exclaimed. "How could I be lonely with you here? And of course, Sophia needs these little retreats." With his next breath he puffed his chest out, as though he had just ingested a great deal of fresh mountain air himself. "And

I need my escapes, too. We begin shooting the new picture on Monday, and it will be much easier to learn my lines without her here . . ."

"Doesn't Sophia need to learn her lines, too?" Letty set the shopping bags to one side of the brass elevator doors and stepped down into the living room. "I mean, she's in the picture, too."

"Yes, of course! O'Dell and Ray, we're a team!" Valentine laughed from the back of his throat and waved his hand in the air as Letty perched on the edge of the sofa opposite him. "Sophia is the reason we got as big as we did, you know. She was the one who had the ambition, the stomach for the whole game of it. Sometimes I think she even loves it. But she doesn't care about the things I hold most dear. She doesn't love the craft, as I do."

Letty rested her elbow on the sofa's arm and her cheek against her palm. She thought of the house on Main Street, where her mother had taught her how to dance, and where she used to put on plays starring herself and her older siblings. Her mother had always said that there was something sacred about artists, and Letty believed that still, and she was happy to discover that Valentine O'Dell, whose face on screen had always given her chills, felt just the same way she did.

"Say . . ." Valentine turned to face her again, and she saw

that his smile was strong and true now. "Perhaps you'd help me? With my lines, I mean. You could read Sophia's part."

"I—I'd be honored."

"Good!" Valentine clapped his hands together, punctuating the decision. "I'll go get the scripts. Put on a fresh pot of coffee, will you? This might take all night . . ."

The smell of coffee was strong when Valentine returned, and Letty took the script from him and sat down at the kitchen table. Folding her legs underneath her, she began to flip the pages. She had never seen a script before, and it gave her a chill to think that this sheaf of papers was the real thing, what genuine motion pictures were made out of. "Miss Ray" was printed on the first page, and Letty's index finger rested there a few seconds.

"You don't think she'll mind?"

"No, no—Sophia usually only does one take, anyway. It annoys her how I obsess over getting every tiny thing exactly right. You'll be doing her a favor, as I will be much better prepared and not need quite so many takes as usual!"

Valentine poured them each a cup of coffee, and they got to work. At first Letty said Sophia's lines as though she were just a secretary helping him memorize his part. But when she came to understand the story and Marie, the heroine, she delivered every word with emotion. Soon she was stopping in places, as Valentine did, when she thought a line was false or didn't

suit her character. This was precisely how she'd imagined artists spent their evenings, back when she was trapped in Union
on one of those interminably boring nights after Mother died
and Father became so strict. It didn't matter that they were
in an apartment house on Park Avenue. The room could have
been any hole in the wall, down in the Village or in faraway
Paris, and everything they said was full of energy and punc-
tuated with impassioned hand gestures and laughter. Several
times, Valentine interrupted their recitation to tell her a story
about movie sets he had been on, times when he had changed
a script or used a costume choice to convey something about
his character.

She liked picturing how the scenes they were reading would play on a screen. It would be embarrassing to tell
Valentine as much, but this was the most exciting night she'd
yet had in New York. She felt more alive here than she had in
any nightclub, more alive than that night at The Vault when
she'd been discovered.

"I was a broken man when the war ended," Valentine
began a new scene, his brows riven with feeling. He was standing, as though on the edge of a woods looking down on a valley,
with his chin raised and one arm resting behind his back. "I
thought my life was over, and wished I *had* died in that ditch
along with my men . . ."

"But you have done so much for our village." Letty moved

ahead of him, turning one cheek to rest against her shoulder as though the emotion was too strong for her to bear. She let her eyes sink gently closed and almost murmured her next line. "Much more than we will ever do for you."

"I am gratified to see the village coming back to life, after so much death and dying . . . But you cannot think I did it for them." Valentine had taken another purposeful step across the tiled kitchen floor, and Letty cracked an eye to check her next line. But there was no next line, only a stage direction that made her heart go thump.

Kiss. Her face went numb, and she could no longer feel her fingertips. *Are we really supposed to kiss?*

"I don't believe it," Letty heard herself say. Now she was making up lines that were not in the script, and though she didn't know where they were coming from, she felt she had to stall. Perhaps this was what she had been hoping for when she winked at Sophia and promised to take care of Valentine. But now, alone with Valentine, holding a piece of paper that said she should kiss him, it all seemed too frighteningly wild. "I don't believe you weren't thinking of us when you—"

Before she could say any more, Valentine had put both his hands around her small waist. His eyes had closed, and his mouth was lowering toward hers. She let her eyelids sink, afraid she might faint.

The kiss, when it came, was so soft it might almost not have happened, except that the featherweight of his lips against hers was a weight she could feel all over, in her knees and way down in her toes.

When she opened her eyes, she saw that he was already looking at her. The muscles around his eyes contracted, and a sparkle passed over his dark irises. His hands were still on her waist, and she was sure he could feel how her heart pulsed.

"Oh, my," he said, and she knew it was not "The Lieutenant" speaking now but Valentine himself. "That—that was incredible."

Out on Long Island, the bad weather was gathering again, obscuring the stars and their strange magic. Perhaps this dampened their ability to cross lovers, because, in a nook off the Sound's coastline, where the water was still and reflective in calm weather, two young people recently and famously married were together, on a proper date, he in a fine suit of caramel-colored linen and she in a sleeveless white lace dress that seemed calculated to remind everyone that she had recently been a blushing bride.

In fact, Astrid had forgotten until they had arrived at the White Cove Yacht Club that she had once thought of having her wedding there. The spur-of-the-moment way her nuptials had happened in the end was a point of pride with her, and now she wouldn't have it any other way. But when she saw the twinkling lights strung up along the edges of the outdoor dining area, and remembered where she had thought about positioning the altar on that wooden plank deck, she wondered if everything could have turned out differently, had they done it the right way.

Not that anything was so rotten, she reminded herself. That kiss with Victor after billiards earlier hadn't really meant anything, and certainly Charlie deserved it, after all the things he had done. Except it was difficult to pretend that it hadn't happened, with that hangdog expression Victor kept giving her when she came down in her evening clothes, and the way the skin over her cheekbones got toasty warm when she thought of him now.

"Baby?" Charlie was holding the door for her expectantly, and Astrid realized how lost in thought she must have been.

"Thanks, darling!" She forced her most brilliant smile and put one high heel in front of the other. But whatever foreboding she had felt before dissipated when she stepped into the dining room of the yacht club. She registered the envy in the eyes of the women who moments ago had been so proud of the fortunes they had married into, but now saw how their husbands suffered in comparison with brash and handsome Charlie.

Smiling privately to herself, she thought how long a girl's

walk can be, just from the front door of a joint to her table, and all the things that can be made clear along the way. She knew she was a very rare bird—special and free—and it was only natural that she should feel a little caged, what with the suddenness of her marriage and all. Because she and Charlie were not like other people—they were bolder and more adventurous, and they did things that provoked the judgments and jealousies of others. But this was no reason for her to chafe at him. Perhaps it was darker, this far inside his world, but it was more interesting than any other place and would only take a little getting used to, and anyway, she wouldn't want to be anywhere else.

"A bottle of champagne, the nice stuff I sold you yesterday," Charlie told the man as they were seated. "Marco'll know what I'm talking about."

"Yes, sir." The host nodded in that subtle, deferential manner practiced by people who were trained young to serve the upper classes. But she smiled privately and knew that he respected men like Charlie, who didn't bother with niceties.

While Charlie lit a cigarette, Astrid took a long time in crossing her legs, allowing the dramatically scalloped hem of her dress to ride up and show off the girlish shape of her calves.

"Nice night," she said.

"Just wait."

The champagne came then, and Charlie, cigarette still

wedged beneath his teeth, waved away the waiter and opened the bottle himself. He was too rough, and the bubbly liquid overflowed the thin green neck and their wide-brimmed glasses when he filled them. But Astrid didn't mind—she knew there was plenty more where that came from, and she liked the festive way the pale liquid refused to stay in its place.

"To us." Charlie cocked his head back and raised his glass.

"To us," she repeated with a coy wink.

"Everything's gonna be better, now that Cord settled it with the Hales. We can stop worrying about the body-guards so much. And I decided we should have a big party for your birthday next week. I already called Dad's favorite caterers, and I already told Milly to ring everyone with the date . . ."

"Oh, Charlie!" Astrid bit her lower lip. "I was sure you'd forget."

"Will you dance?" But he was already standing, and it wasn't really a question.

Even so, Astrid stalled. She removed her compact and checked the candy red of her lips. She fluffed her hair. She turned her chin right and left—but by then Charlie had had enough, and he took her by the elbow and pulled her toward the dance floor.

"Why play silly games like that?" He dropped his ciga-rette, and they fell into a loose Charleston. The music was still mellow, and they moved easily toward and away from each other. "You know you're the best-looking girly in the room."

"Am I?"

"Don't be stupid."

"How about her?" Astrid jutted her chin in the direction of Willa Herring, an occasional friend who had been a few years ahead of her at Miss Porter's.

Charlie shrugged. "Her teeth are too big."

"Well, what about her?" Astrid indicated a tall blonde who had just come through the door wearing Chanel black that looked fresh from the department store.

"Do I look like the kind who has to buy himself a woman?"

"No." Astrid's eyes rolled toward a girl sitting at the table next to theirs, who was only twenty or twenty-one but already on her second husband. "Tell me I'm prettier than *that* number."

Charlie didn't bother to look. "You know you are," he said, and brought her closer and kept on dancing. "They're all dogs compared to you."

After that the music changed. It got louder and faster, and she and Charlie kept pace with it. They did a more manic Charleston, kicking their legs back and then making their knees wobbly and duck-walking around each other. They did the Lindy and the Black Bottom. They swung their arms and let their feet be light, always keeping their eyes on each other. Nobody could dance like Charlie—another thing she had forgotten. He could keep up with her like nobody else, and he always taught her a few new tricks. They were still dancing while couples who had arrived after them ate and left, and by the time they themselves sat back down again her thirst for champagne was real and her appetite was big and true.

"I think I'll order steak!" she said, wiping the sweat off her forehead.

"You order whatever you want."

For a moment, the earnest way Victor looked at her sprung into her memory, so she said her husband's name quickly to distract herself. "Charlie?"

"Yes?"

"Let's do this every night."

Charlie's face was flushed, and there was sweat on his brow, too. He leaned across the table, and his lips made a smacking noise against her cheek. "All right," he said, and poured more champagne.

It was a long time they had been standing facing each other in the kitchen. Hours, maybe, or lifetimes. Their lips were parted and their eyes were dewy, and in those suspended moments they were any girl and boy who have just kissed for the first time and, in the process, felt the ground shift beneath them.

Then, all of a sudden, he was Valentine O'Dell again, which meant that she must be Letty Larkspur. If he was Valentine, then he was married, and if she was Letty, then she must be his wife's friend.

"Unbelievable," he repeated in that booming and self-assured voice. "That was unbelievable."

"Oh, *God*," she wailed, and sat down heavily at the table with her face in her hands. But the touch of her hands did not help, because they were soft and recently manicured, and it was Sophia who had paid for that, and instructed the girls exactly how they should do it, and watched to be sure that they weren't lazy and didn't scuff the polish or mar Letty's cuticles. Earlier, she had allowed herself to think that Sophia might be an adulterer and didn't deserve Valentine. But now Letty saw that she had only been tricking herself, and in fact she was the one who was guilty.

"I know." Valentine was behind her, and he lay his palm against her shoulder, which only made her feel worse. She sensed his pulse through his palm and wanted to be kissed by him again and thus knew for certain that she was a damned, no-good kind of girl.

"Oh, oh, oh!"

Letty twisted suddenly, so that he was forced to remove his hand from her shoulder. Her knees wobbled, and her hands found each other. They were clasped the way she used to clasp them when she and her sisters knelt to say their prayers before bedtime. "I'm sorry," she whispered.

He was gazing down at her with those beautiful brown eyes, the sight of which made her heart swell with longing. They were so beautiful that she wanted to erase any knowledge of right and wrong.

But she couldn't, so she forced her eyelids shut. "I'm sorry. So very sorry. It was my fault, of course, and I won't tell her. I promise, it will be our secret, and we'll never tell her, and I'm sorry. You mustn't think—I wasn't brought up this way. I'm really not that sort of girl. I wouldn't dream of—of—of . . . with a *married* man. And especially when that man's wife has been so *kind* to me. So good to me. Like my sister, really—and, you mustn't worry, I won't tell her, I would never tell her."

When he didn't say anything she cracked an eye. He was staring at her, but differently now, more calmly, so she unclasped her hands and waited for him to speak.

"Ah, my sweet Letty." He chuckled softly and pulled one of the chairs away from the table to sit on. "Me oh my."

In the ensuing silence, she realized what he was going to say, and her stomach dropped. He was going to say: *When I kissed you, the earth moved.* He was going to say: *Let's go away together, you are the most beautiful girl I've ever seen, I have been searching for you my whole life without knowing it* and

all of that lovely, movie-house stuff. And she was half terrified of everything he was about to tell her, everything he was
going to propose, and half dying for it, and she bit her lip and
couldn't wait.

"Letty, darling," he said.

"Yes?" she whispered.

"What lies did they tell you out there? What stories of hell-
fire and brimstone did they lord over you to keep you in line?"
His voice had changed. It had grown low, calm and knowing,
reminding her how much older he was, that he had been working since he was a child. "You've done nothing wrong, sweet girl."

"I haven't?"

"What have you done except what you do best? You put
all your emotion into a scene, into playing a character. When
you closed your eyes and received my kiss, it was Marie receiv-
ing a kiss from the Lieutenant. The kiss was incredible because
it was the perfect performance of incredible yearning between
a broken soldier and a war widow who are coming to life again
for the first time in a long time, and . . ."

As Valentine carefully put words together Letty's shame
faded away, but a new fear had replaced it, and she had to take
hold of the table for balance. The patient manner in which
Valentine was talking to her was nice, but it had nothing of the
epic romanticism of their kiss. She had yearned for him, and he
had seen it, and surely the extent of her yearning was still quite

plain on her simple, stupid face. And he was trying to tell her in the gentlest way possible that it had only been acting and that she was a confused little girl.

"You see, you are a fine actress—you pulled me into the scene as I didn't know I could be pulled in, and—" Valentine's voice became hoarse and he broke off. He lowered his head, and in the silence that followed, Letty contemplated the thick mahogany brush of his hair and thought that if she could just have one more kiss from him, she would give up on wanting any glory for herself and be forever contented with whatever fate life handed her, whatever punishment it meted out. Without raising his eyes to hers, he reached for her hands, and when he went on, she had to remind herself to breathe. "Well, how could either of us have seen a kiss like that coming? Who would place a blame for something as good as that?"

Breath came in and out of Letty's lungs. Mist glazed her eyes. A tingling sensation spread from the skin of her cheeks over her throat. "You mean . . . that kiss was real?"

"If that wasn't real I've never known anything real my whole life. I don't think I'd even want to."

She knew just what he meant. Sitting in Valentine O'Dell's kitchen, barefoot, with the imprint of his lips still on hers, was in fact the most vividly real moment she'd ever experienced. She'd only been kissed twice before—once by a horrible man who had used her, and once by a sweet boy who had been kind—but never like this. It was just like her mother always told her when explaining why Letty was special: The third time is a charm. "Kiss me again?" she whispered, and waited as he squeezed her hand and brought his face to hers.

13

"LET'S GO HOME AND GET BUSY."

Astrid let out a little gasp, and her mouth puckered. On the other side of Charlie sat Narcissa Phipps, a friend and rival of her mother's whose second advantageous marriage had joined her to Alfred Henderson Phipps, of the coal-money Phippses, and Astrid could tell that she had heard what Charlie said by the slight turn of her head and the clatter of her dessert fork against the porcelain plate. By then it was late, and the dining room had thinned out, and there was no din to cover up small noises.

Giggling, Astrid put her elbows against the table, leaned forward, and replied quietly (though not so quietly that Mrs. Phipps wouldn't hear): "Whatever you say, hubby dearest."

Charlie grinned and pushed back his chair as he stood up, making a rude noise and slightly bumping Mrs. Phipps. He ripped his jacket from the back of his chair and produced a fat billfold from its pocket before draping the jacket over Astrid's shoulders. As they moved toward the door, Astrid glanced back and noticed the hundred-dollar bill on the tabletop.

"Oh, darling, don't you need change?"

Charlie nuzzled her ear and kept them moving. "Why bother? I'm in a hurry."

This extravagance made Astrid burn with delight, and she strode toward the door with gusto. "Good night!" she trilled to anyone who was listening while Charlie held the door for her, and with hair flouncing she forged on, not glancing back to acknowledge the chorus of *good nights* and *thank yous* that followed.

As the door swung closed, Charlie grabbed for her hand, pulling her backward, and though she resisted at first, he was stronger. He twirled her around and pinned her to the door. The plate glass was surprisingly cool against her shoulder blades, and she knew that everyone inside saw how he took a fistful of her hair and pressed himself against her.

"Why, Charlie!" she exclaimed and dropped her bottom lip in fake shock at this public display of passion. This time she pulled him by the hand, giggling as they hurried down the plank toward the dirt lot where cars were parked.

The night smelled salty and sultry. While they were inside, the moisture in the air had gathered strength. They were both laughing now, and she was all warm inside, and suddenly she realized how much champagne they'd had and that they were both probably a little drunk. He leaned against her more than she did against him, and this reminded her how big and unwieldy Charlie was, which for some reason made her laugh even harder. In the darkness it took her a few moments to see straight and determine which car was Charlie's. Once she spotted his shiny new blue sedan, she emitted a happy little "Aha!" But then she saw the man in the shiny blue suit step away from it and come toward them.

"Charlie Grey," he said.

Before she got a good look at the man, Charlie had moved to shield her with his body. A moment before his limbs had been loose and heavy, but now he was rigid, his back straight and his shoulders flared. "Get in the car," he whispered tensely.

Astrid peeked around Charlie and saw that though the man had a big scar across one cheek, he was not particularly mean-seeming. His suit was expensive, and he had an expensive way about him to match—that unhurried manner of people who know themselves, or have enough money not to care.

He wasn't a friend of Charlie's—that was plain enough—but he seemed like a worthy adversary.

"Go." This time there was no resisting Charlie's tone.

With a *harrumph*, she went around the car and got in from the passenger side, but she leaned over the driver's seat to listen.

"What do you want?" That was Charlie, sounding awfully tough.

"I represent Coyle Mink's outfit," the man replied. He spoke casually, but the way he pronounced "Coyle Mink," it was like saying "the Big Time."

"Oh, yeah?"

"Yeah."

"Well." Charlie paused to light a cigarette—Astrid could tell by the three strikes it took him to get the match lit that he must be nervous, although there was nothing of that in his voice when he went on. "What does Coyle Mink want with me?"

"Nothing." The man made an unpleasant, sneering sound. "Nothing at all. He just thinks you're getting too big for your britches."

"I don't wear britches," Charlie replied coolly, and Astrid wished that she was next to him, hanging on his shoulder, so she could look the man in the eye and say "That's right, mister," just like a real gangster's moll.

"Mink doesn't give a rat what you wear, so long as you stay out of his territory."

"You tell him to stay out of *my* territory! My territory is wherever I sell, and nobody can tell me otherwise, not Mink, not nobody."

Astrid's eyes were bright with excitement as she watched the action. The man in the blue suit didn't say anything at first. He just stepped away and smiled mysteriously. "It's a warning, Charlie. What you do with it is your business."

"Hey, I'm not done talking to you!" Charlie shouted.

The man shrugged and retreated unhurriedly toward his car.

"You can't threaten me and run away like that!"

"I'm just a messenger, Charlie, sent to give you fair warning. If you don't back off Mr. Mink's territories, it won't be such a friendly visit next time."

"Friendly? You call this friendly? Threatening me when I'm out with my wife?" Now Charlie was really yelling, but the man in the blue suit appeared as unruffled as ever as he slid into his own car and started it up. Quick, before Astrid knew what was happening, Charlie was in the driver's seat.

"Wowie!" Astrid gasped as she sat back in her own seat.

The engine was ignited, and the car was shaking. When the man in the blue suit pulled out, Charlie followed him, careening around the corner and down the dark country lane.

As their headlights swung through the darkness, illuminating the rain that was falling again, Astrid braced herself against the dash and smiled at her husband adoringly.

But the big slabs of Charlie's face were hard and white from the taillights, and his eyes were large with fury. He didn't look at Astrid or acknowledge her, and his knuckles bulged where he gripped the wheel. She would have liked him to say something, but she was glad he was concentrating on driving, which he had probably drunk too much to really be doing properly otherwise.

The car ahead of them turned on Sandy Point Drive, and Charlie followed him, making a wide turn to avoid the overgrown oak tree roots that spread into the road there. The man in the blue suit didn't know about those roots. He went right into them, and they cut his speed in half. That was what did him in. Afterward, Charlie was right on him, and he rammed into the back of the man's car. Astrid felt the impact in every bone of her body, and her sense of fun seeped away. She closed her eyes before the second impact, but she felt it, and opened them again in time to see the blue car go flying off the road into a big abandoned field that the headlights of both cars revealed to be full of knee-high weeds and yellow wildflowers.

The other car seemed briefly like it might break away, but then it began to weave wildly back and forth before suddenly hitting a ditch and flipping over, like a toy automobile thrown by a naughty child.

"Oh, dear!" Astrid's hands flew to her face. By then her mind was ticking with fear. The sight of that car upside down with its top bashed in made her insides go quiet.

Before she could peel her hands away from her gaping mouth, Charlie was out of the car, charging toward the wreck. She thought he must be going to see if the man was all right, and that she had better help, too. But as she came to the upside-down car, she knew that Charlie wasn't going to help him. Charlie was waving a pistol in the air.

"Charlie—"

But he wasn't listening. "You threaten me in front of my wife?" he shouted. "In front of my wife?" he repeated like a skipping record. "In front of my wife?"

The man's reply was just a low, agonized groan. Astrid heard him before she saw him, and when she saw him her stomach did a flip. He was trying to crawl through the shattered window. The brawny confidence he'd exhibited in the parking lot was gone. His teeth were clenched, and his eyes were wild. The rain that had been off and on all day was a downpour now, and he slipped when he reached the overgrown grass.

"I'm just a messenger," the man wheezed. He was having a hard time getting the words out, as though his ribs had been knocked into his lungs. He was reaching under his lapel, but he was too slow to get a good grip on the gun.

"A messenger?" Charlie kicked the gun away. His arm drew a long, furious arc through the still night air before the butt of his own pistol met the man's temple. Blood spurted from the man's forehead, and Astrid instinctively covered her face with her hands. The next time Charlie spoke, an uncommon ferocity had taken over his voice. "*That's* what I think of your message."

After that Charlie started kicking him. She knew because of the way Charlie grunted and the sound of his hard shoes against the man's soft body and the way the man groaned. Finally she couldn't stand the groaning anymore, so she forced her hands away from her face and rushed forward. "Charlie, stop it!" she wailed.

"Stop it?" Charlie was kicking the man more savagely now. Strands of hair had come unglued and were hanging in his eyes as he went on swinging his leg with full force. "They thought they could humiliate me! They thought they could humiliate me in front of my wife!"

The man's eyes had closed, and though he was still groaning he seemed to have gone beyond pain somehow.

"You're going to kill him!"

She reached for Charlie's arm, but he spun around before she got hold of him. When he was facing her he seemed magnified, like a giant. His eyes were as shiny as an animal's, and his face was sleek with rain.

"Charlie," she whispered, but she knew that somehow it wasn't really him. "Charlie, if you don't stop, you're going to kill him."

"You want me to kill him? You want me to kill him?" he shrieked. His eyes were fixed on her when he took the first shot. Though he hadn't looked where the gun was pointing, the bullet hit the man in the middle of his blue suit jacket. The man screamed, and the smell of burning gunpowder mingled with the metallic odor of blood.

"No, Charlie, *don't* kill him." Astrid used as much force as she could muster to get the words out, and still it was the voice of a small, frightened child.

"Now I *have* to kill him," Charlie replied, almost irritably, as though he were talking about a workhorse ruined by a broken leg. She stepped toward him, but it was too late. Charlie's back was to her when he fired the second shot, but she was close, and when the man's head erupted, blood splattered all over her white lace dress. She couldn't breathe, and she couldn't hear anything, couldn't even remember what it was like to hear.

Neither she nor Charlie said anything as they got back in the car. Charlie was driving fast, but she knew it wasn't possible to go as fast as they seemed to be going. It was like in the pictures, when the action gets sped up and everyone does everything in double time. But that was usually for comic effect, and Astrid couldn't imagine ever laughing again. The blood was seeping through her dress, and she was afraid to glance down for fear of what she might see there.

They came through the gates of Dogwood at a reckless speed, and the wheels shrieked and sputtered against the wet grass as they came up the hill. Already the lawn was beginning to flood. Charlie put his hand against the car's horn, three long insistent blasts, as Astrid tumbled out the passenger-side door.

She could hear again. She could hear, but she wished she couldn't, because that just meant the awful sound of Charlie's voice speaking urgently and callously to his goons about what they were going to do with that man. Her hands clung to each other as she moved up the switchbacking flights of stone steps, into the pooling yellow light of the house. Her hair and clothes were soaked, but this didn't seem to matter very much. It occurred to her, as she went up the main indoor stairwell, that she might be a ghost, so little did she feel and so barely did her feet touch the ground. But when she reached the second-floor landing, she knew that she was alive because her stomach turned inside out and the steak she had eaten for dinner was all over the floor in tiny, revolting, half-masticated pieces.

14

THE STORM MADE LANDFALL AFTER MIDNIGHT, although by then most people were indoors. On the east end of the island, windows had been boarded up and the electricity shut down. The old two-lane road that ran back toward the city was impassable, and many of the houses that had been built close to the shore or in low-lying areas were flooded. Trees had been ripped out and tossed around and woke up in new positions with their roots exposed. Very little business was done in the places that made a nightly mint selling illegal liquor, although there were a few, in Manhattan, where people were forced to stay all night and the reserve stocks were completely wiped out, and everyone present left with shameful smiles and forever after asked new acquaintances where they'd been during the hurricane of '29.

The famous pilot Max Darby and the bootlegger's daughter Cordelia Gray watched the storm come and go from the mostly empty ballroom of the Grand Marina Lodge out at Montauk, whose seaplane Max had borrowed to scoop her up. He had done aerial exhibitions for them when they first opened, he explained, and the manager had remained a friend, even after Max's patron dropped him. That, plus the fact that they still owed him for the last time he had scrawled a marriage proposal for one of their important visitors in the sky, had gotten him the use of the plane—plus a dinner of fried clams, which they'd eaten off red-and-white paper plates on the beach before the real rain arrived. Most of the guests got out in time, before the electricity was shut off and the last ice shipment started to melt. The staff were forced to eat the oysters, which otherwise would have gone bad; they did it with a cheerful sense of duty and brought out old stores of white wine to wash them down.

The band had stayed, and their playing got louder as night gave in to morning and the chambermaids started dancing with napkins on their heads. They could see the waves beating against the rocky shore, and the dark clouds charging toward them from the south, but to Max and Cordelia none of it seemed to hold any real threat. They sat side by side in low-slung canvas chairs that usually lived on the deck, and they held hands through the storm and drank cola. Later, the staff of the lodge grew sentimental and began telling each other sweet lies. The band played slow, and Cordelia convinced Max to stand up with her.

"I can't dance at all," he told her four or five times, before she put his hands in place and rested her head against his shoulder. He couldn't, that much was true, but she didn't mind. She liked just moving vaguely to the music in his arms.

By dawn the storm had passed. The shore was strewn with wreckage, but the sky was a delicate pink where the sun nudged against the pale gray. The staff of the Grand Marina were sleeping on tables, those who had not returned to their own quarters, and Max and Cordelia drowsily watched the colors change out on the horizon.

They talked to each other in quiet, honeyed tones. Max's voice was slow, and for a few moments she thought he must be on the verge of sleep. She put her hand up to his chest, to comfort him. That was when she felt the tension in his muscles, and her eyes opened again.

"Before I met you, all I ever thought about was flying. It's really the only thing I've ever liked."

"It's a nice thing to like," Cordelia murmured.

"I don't think I've ever cared about someone's good opinion as much as I care about having your good opinion."

"You have it."

The sun was really up now. The big glass windows magnified its rays, and she could feel the heat on her skin and through her eyelids, and she was smiling vaguely to herself.

"Cordelia . . . ," he began, but his voice was like a car that won't turn on. He shifted in his seat and exhaled hard through his nose. "When we leave, when we drive back to the North Shore . . . when I drop you at Dogwood." He exhaled again and swung his head away from her. "I want to know for sure I'm going to see you again."

Cordelia remained very still. Her legs stayed languidly crossed, and she left her hand where it was, just above Max's heart. His words had been perfectly ordinary, but she knew that he was telling her something he hadn't told her before, that it was a kind of declaration. She couldn't look at him. Suddenly she knew how badly she'd been wanting him to make a declaration like that all along, and she was afraid that if she saw his face when he did it she'd burst into tears.

"I'll never find another girl I want to talk to as much as you, and I know that for sure." He was talking fast, as though he was afraid she might say no to him if he paused long enough for her to speak. "Flying is all I've ever wanted. I want to be the best at what I do. I want everybody to know I'm the best. I think I've been afraid that if you were my girl

I'd be thinking about you all the time, that my mind would get hooked on you, and I'd lose everything I've worked for. But now I *have* lost everything, and I know I'm going to get it back anyway, so I'm not scared anymore. Not of being distracted by you, nor what anybody will say about you being my girl . . ." His voice had grown hoarse again, but he pushed through: "Will you be my girl? For real, so that everybody knows?"

"I'm your girl already, Max, and I don't care who knows it."

When she heard herself saying those words an involuntary smile bloomed on her lips. Over on the other side of the ballroom people were waking up, talking to each other, making coffee. She could smell the coffee, and she knew the day was advancing. She was excited for the future days in which she would be known as Max's girl, but she wasn't ready for this private moment—alone with Max in a faraway corner of Long Island that was drenched in new-day sunlight—to end. "Only sit with me like this a while longer."

"All right," he said, and laid his hand on his chest over hers.

"How did your mother know to call you Valentine?"

"What do you mean?" He was standing before the mirror in his dressing room, off the cream-and-gold master bedroom he shared with Sophia, adjusting the high collar of the knee-length gray coat that was to be his costume for *The Good Lieutenant.* It was Sophia's room, and Sophia's husband—Letty had not totally forgotten these facts. But she kept thinking of what Valentine had said, that something that felt this good couldn't possibly be wrong, and anyway, since Sophia was off with Montrose, wasn't Letty really in the position to do something quite selfless, by saving him from a loveless marriage?

The studio had sent the costume over that morning, although neither Valentine nor Letty saw it until the afternoon, when Hector stepped off the elevator carrying it over one arm. They had fallen asleep late last night, curled on opposing couches in the sunken living room. The last thing Letty remembered was that Valentine had said he wanted to sketch her, just as she was, and asked her to stay still. She had tried hard to keep her eyes open, but her eyelids had been so heavy. On the radio they reported that there had been a storm in the night, but they had slept through all that. Now, sitting on the edge of the red velvet settee, all she could think was that he looked like the human embodiment of romance. That was what she meant, but when she realized it her cheeks flushed and she began to fidget with the hem of her skirt.

"It's such a *perfect* name for you," she murmured. After

the words came out she realized how fawning she had sounded, and a dark thought occurred to her. Perhaps their kiss didn't mean much, perhaps they'd just gotten carried away in the moment, in which case she ought not to be so starry-eyed now. "That's all I meant."

"But you've never known me by any other!" He was absorbed with correcting the arch of his left eyebrow with his right pinkie. "If you'd known me as Herman all these years, I would seem the perfect Herman!"

"Herman!" Letty repeated, half laughing, half snorting. "You could never be *Herman*."

"You don't think I'd be handsome if my name was Herman?"

After he spoke he went on watching her in this hopeful way, which for some reason reminded Letty of Good Egg, how she gazed up at her mistress for approval, and when she saw that, she felt not so shy anymore and went over to him.

"Letty." He pronounced her name as though it were some beautiful, mythical land, which he was just glimpsing for the first time. With his index finger he traced the line of her chin. "Letty, what a lucky thing it was to meet you."

"You really think so?"

"Yes." His fingertip traveled from the tip of her chin down her neck and along her arm, until he had her small hand in his larger one. "Will you have dinner with me?"

The idea of sitting across a restaurant table with a man like Valentine, who had seen his name in the newspaper and traveled to Europe, whom women all over the world thought of when they were drifting off to sleep, was so overwhelming to Letty that she almost felt she should say no. Except she didn't want to say no. She took a deep breath and told herself that last night had been real.

"Yes."

"We'll go separately, just so it doesn't look strange to Hector . . . or any fans of mine. Is that all right?"

She nodded. In fact, she wasn't sure why this mattered, and she knew in some vague way that if she thought hard about it, she might come to the conclusion that she was doing something wrong. But mostly it sounded exciting—that they would be out in the world, around all kinds of people, but only they two would know of the feelings they harbored for each other.

"Good—now go get dressed. And Letty?"

She was on the threshold of the bedroom by then and had to look back at him over her shoulder. "Yes?"

"Will you wear that dress you wore the other night?" Suddenly he was grinning at her like a boy. "The red one."

This sent a shudder of happy pride through Letty, and though she was tempted to respond with an enthusiastic affirmation, she first asked herself what Sophia would have done, and so it was with nothing more than a vague smile that she drifted away toward her own room to make herself pretty enough for a date with the star of *The Hobo and the Heiress*.

15

THE SKY WAS THAT WEAK BLUE THAT COMES AFTER A rain, and the fields below them were dark and waterlogged from the weather that had passed over Long Island in the night. It was cool high above the fields, even though Cordelia had replaced the yellow slicker with a leather jacket like the one Max always wore in his publicity photos. The Grand Marina Lodge's little green-and-white biplane roared so that they would have had to almost shout to hear each other, but there was no need. Since their conversation in the ballroom of the lodge, they were easy in each other's silence.

Then, all of a sudden, New York City was before them. The sun was on the water, as well as on the skyscrapers, which jutted up from the island of Manhattan like the points of a particularly chaotic crown, pink with the morning. She glanced at Max and was glad that she had not blinked, that day in Union, when the urge to run was strong enough in her to pack a suitcase.

It was about the time she saw Roosevelt Island—a narrow slip of land splitting the broad river in half—that Max brought the plane down quickly. At first she was sure that something was wrong with the engine, or that he had made a terrible mistake, and her insides flooded with fear. The water, which was busy with boats at that hour, came at them fast. But when she glanced at him she saw he was not afraid. In fact, a hint of a smile lingered on his face. She looked straight ahead of her and held her breath as they went swooping down, close enough that she saw the green-and-white fuselage reflected on the glassy surface as they whisked by. Over their heads went the span of the Queensboro; to their left were the stern white buildings of the Roosevelt Island insane asylum; to their right was the road that circumnavigated Manhattan's east side, where perhaps one of the passengers in one of those miniature cars was turning his head at exactly the right moment to see the airplane emerging improbably from under the bridge and ascending back toward the clouds.

Cordelia's heart lifted as they climbed higher. She wanted to say something clever and quippy, something like "I've been over the Queensboro, but only you could take me under it," but before she could form the right phrase, she saw the Williamsburg Bridge growing large in the windshield. A little figure on the bridge waved, and the space began to fall away beneath them.

"Woohoo!" she whooped, when she comprehended Max's audacious plan, flattered that she was in on it. Her smile held until she heard the long, rude drone of the foghorn and saw the big barge that lay like a beached whale on the water, directly in their path.

"Oh, God," she muttered and closed her eyes.

But the impact never came, and instead she felt her body turning sideways with the plane. Cracking one lid, she saw that Max had maneuvered so that they whipped by the barge, just barely, and then they were up again, watching the river curve along the bottom of Manhattan. As soon as her breath returned she realized that she trusted Max to take her anywhere. Anyway, she already knew where he was going, and when the plane dipped down under the Manhattan Bridge, scattering seagulls, she was neither surprised nor particularly afraid. She was smiling broadly by the time they came upon the Brooklyn Bridge, the fine spiderwebs of its cables rosy with the rising sun and its two proud towers urging them onward. They seemed to say: "Come on in." Down went the plane, through the shadow of the span, and there was New York Harbor, gaping wide in the direction of the sea.

Max looked at her and returned her smile. "I hope I didn't scare you."

"Only a little," she answered, eyes sparkling. "Nothing I couldn't handle."

"Yes, that's what I thought."

The harbor was littered with boats of every size—pleasure cruisers and tugs and the kinds of ships that carry rich people across the oceans and the kinds that carry freight. As Max pulled the plane higher they erupted, blowing their horns in loud celebration, as though they had heard the news already of Max's feat and knew what they were witnessing. Of course that wasn't possible, and Cordelia was happy with the knowledge that she was the one with him when he piloted his aircraft under all four East River bridges.

"You know, it's funny," she said, once they were turned back in the direction of White Cove.

"What is?"

"All this time I thought you were such a serious, secretive sort, but now I see you're just a showoff, really!"

"I don't have any secrets anymore." He glanced at her and shrugged. "I guess I don't have much to hide now."

Cordelia nodded and sighed. It seemed to her at that moment that nothing could go wrong, ever. "I hope you don't regret it. Asking me to be your girl, I mean. I know you want to be the greatest. And I know you are. I just—I'd hate it if I were the reason you don't become what you most want to be."

"Don't say that." Max was quiet a minute, but then he turned to her and his face was open and soft with understanding. "Anyway, you want to be the greatest, too."

"Yes, I guess that's true."

Below them the packed grid of streets had given way to greenery, and they were quiet, listening to the roar of the engine slowly sinking through the clouds. When Cordelia saw the hangar squatting on the vast airfield, her stomach felt woozy and she wished she didn't have to come back down to Earth yet. She wanted to keep going, out over Long Island, toward the ocean, or wherever Max would take her. Up in the air it was easy to feel that everything was clean and perfect. But that notion faltered when she saw the crowd that had formed near the hangar. Shiny black automobiles were parked at all angles, more than on any normal Sunday. They touched down—the ground meeting them with sudden impact—and sped across the grass. She watched through the glass as the crowd by the cars grew larger, and she began to make out the details of their clothing and to see that some of them were holding cameras.

"Oh, dear," she said as they rocked to a stop.

Max's jaw was set in a hard line. Cordelia's eyes darted from him to the crowd and back again. She knew he was thinking of all the things that had been taken from him, the harsh words written. She remembered what he had said—that they would eat him alive for being a black boy with a white girl, and she was afraid that despite all he'd said to the contrary, he would regret this public coming out. But when she let her eyes rest on his, he gave her his brilliant smile, and she knew for sure that the public wouldn't be able to stay out of love with him, even if they wanted to. "If I hadn't been trying to impress you, all those people wouldn't be here now."

"You were trying to impress me?"

"Yes."

She flushed with pleasure at this admission. Max pushed his flying goggles back away on his forehead, showing her his eyes before he pressed his lips to hers.

"Consider me impressed," she whispered when he drew back.

The crowd was coming toward them now, cameras aloft. "Ready?" Max said, grabbing for her hand.

She undid the strap of her leather flying cap and shook out her waves of tawny hair. The crease of a smile appeared on one side of her face. "Ready."

Max nodded and turned. He undid a latch and pushed on the door so that it opened upward, letting in the humid air as well as the clamor of the crowd. She watched him, heart aflutter. He was the same Max, serious and taut, but there was something new about him, too. His movements were freer, and his eyes didn't avoid contact. Then he pushed open the door on her side, and she felt the breeze in her hair and the exhilaration of a great many people inching in her direction.

She didn't look at them. She looked at Max as he raised his arms to catch her. They shared one quick, private wink before turning and moving forward so that the wall of bodies had to part for them. The sight of Max and Cordelia so confidently and publicly together momentarily stunned the crowd, but once they believed what they were seeing they turned and followed them in a herd. She wasn't sure where she was going until she recognized one of the Greys' Daimlers and her bodyguard Anthony standing at the edge of the embankment of cars.

"Miss Grey, were you in Max Darby's plane when he flew under all four bridges?" It was a dry male voice, scratchy from cigarettes, and when she turned toward it she recognized Claude Carrion.

"You're up awfully early, Mr. Carrion."

"Boy pulls off a thing like that, I'll drag myself out of bed. Anyway, sleeping isn't my thing."

He was hurrying along next to them, wheezing a little in the humidity, and Cordelia was secretly thrilled to think that the famous columnist was chasing her.

"Yes, I was with him." By then Cordelia was close enough—she gave Anthony a significant expression, and he jumped from the front seat and opened the back door for her like a proper chauffeur. "That's how we celebrate," she said as she slid into the backseat of the Daimler.

"Celebrate what?" she heard Claude Carrion shouting.

"What does it look like?" Max replied before climbing in next to her.

By the time Letty was ensconced in the backseat of a taxicab, her shyness was gone and her eyes had begun to glitter. She had used every one of Sophia's tricks as she got dressed and made herself up, and in every movement of her fingers, every pigment of makeup, was a whispered *Valentine*.

"It's here," she told the driver outside the little Italian place. Through the windows she could see the white tablecloths and the candlelight and knew it was the spot Valentine had chosen for their first real date. It was the perfect set for a romance. He had said that Frankie's was out of the way enough that they wouldn't have to worry about people speculating on their being out together. Some part of Letty knew that this ought to make her ashamed, but by then everything unfurling between her and Valentine had come to seem so entirely right that she didn't want to think too much about his wife, whether or not this made her his mistress. Through the taxi window she gazed at the scene and let her heart open with happy expectation.

"You sure?" the driver asked her. He had one of those peculiar accents that add two extra syllables to even simple words.

"Yes." For once in her life, there wasn't a doubt in her mind, and her voice was loud and clear. She handed him a bill and told him to keep the change.

With drama and confidence she stepped onto the sidewalk. Her chin was lowered, her eyebrows raised, her hair still. She had slicked it with oil so that it looked almost like a glossy headpiece, short enough to reveal her earlobes.

Just outside the restaurant, Letty caught a glimpse of Valentine through the glass. He was sitting at one of the small round tables off to the side, a lit candle in a tall brass candleholder and an untouched bread basket before him. She was gratified to see that the red dress didn't make her *over*dressed—he was wearing a tuxedo, just as she had hoped he would. He was staring off and his hand was tense on the table, and she realized that despite all his charisma and success, he was nervous to be meeting her, alone, like this. The straight, strong line of his nose was illuminated by the candlelight, and she could see the beautiful skin of his neck underneath the high white collar of his dress shirt. Her bottom lip dropped, and her knees went weak. She forgot the practiced, elegant walk she had learned over the last few weeks and went rushing in toward him.

When he saw her, he blinked, and a smile overtook his face. Standing, he opened his arms. She fell into them and turned her face up for a kiss, but his eyes were closed and he only pulled her against his chest, pressing her closer as though he had just crossed an ocean in the hope of seeing her and could not quite believe she was real.

"Letty," he whispered, and released her.

They sat down, smiling moonily at each other.

"Doesn't it feel like absolute ages?"

"Yes!" She bit her lip. In her old life she might have blushed at this moment, but she didn't feel at all embarrassed by what was transpiring between them. "It was almost . . . *painful* . . . wasn't it?"

"Yes, isn't that peculiar?"

They stared at each other a few moments, and then he had to look away, as though overwhelmed by his good fortune.

"It *is*." Letty took in a sharp breath. She wished that she had words for all the explosive color inside her, but it frightened her a little, too, trying to articulate such wild emotion. But she was feeling brave, and she decided to try. "I think it's that everything just seems perfect when I am with you, so that even an hour away is a dreary, too-long time before I am with you again and all is as it should be."

"I know just what you mean," Valentine said simply as he lifted her hands and began to kiss her knuckles.

If there were other people in the restaurant, Letty had forgotten them. It was like the movies, when the camera shows you first the whole room, and then the man's face, and then the woman's, and then the man's again, and then the woman's, until you have forgotten that they are in a room at all.

The candle between Letty and Valentine flickered, and the spell was briefly interrupted by the appearance of a waiter at their table. He was wearing a long white apron, which hung below his knees, and his dark hair was parted down the middle and polished to his ears in the old-fashioned way.

"A bottle of mineral water for the table?" His arm was folded elegantly behind his back.

"Yes, please." When he was gone, Valentine leaned back in his chair and sighed. The mahogany disks of his eyes blazed as he gazed at Letty. "Where did you come from?" he asked eventually.

Letty set her elbows down on the white tablecloth and rested her chin against her hands. With Valentine's eyes upon her, she knew what she was—all red dress and white skin and thick eyelashes. Union, Ohio, seemed like a faintly remembered children's story. "It was called Union, and they had plenty of churches but no movie theater. There wasn't much to do, so I lived for the movie theater the next town over, and used to save all my money so that I could go there whenever I had time off from the dairy farm. The theater was in a town called Defiance, which sort of makes sense, because Father hated the movies and told me I was losing faith with God, going to them so much. Father had very strict rules, and he made all of us wear black, even after our year of mourning Mother was over, and we girls always had to wear buns, and my brothers always had to wear jackets, even in the summertime . . ."

"You miss them, don't you?"

Letty had been telling her story in a sparkling voice, but now when she saw how sympathetically Valentine was regarding her, her smile wobbled and her light manner began to dissolve.

"I don't know why." Her eyes darted away from Valentine's. "They hardly knew I was there! It's only my little sister, really. She didn't know yet how mean the world can be sometimes, and I was the only one who tried to protect her from it . . ." Suddenly her throat was chalky, and she had to draw her hands to her lap and clasp them. She told herself she must not cry. Here she was, in the great metropolis, in a little Italian place with candles dripping wax down the brass holder toward the white linen tablecloth, on a date with a movie star she had dreamed of her whole life, and she was teary over a long-gone place! "It's so *silly* . . ." she began, and though she had tried to sound light, her voice broke over the words.

"Oh, Letty." His hands were gentle against her forehead as he tucked strands of hair behind her ears. "Most of us are like you, you know—we didn't really leave because we wanted to. It was more that we had to. I was eight years old when I ran away from home. But you're one of us now, and I promise you, your talent will save you."

"I'm not crying because I'm sad." The saltiness of her tears had reached her lips, and she could taste it, but she wasn't ashamed of crying anymore. "It's just that I'm so happy."

Even the reappearance of their waiter at the table didn't make her feel ashamed over her outburst, although she was grateful to Valentine for ordering swiftly for both of them and then taking up her hands again.

"But it can't all have been so grim," he went on, when the waiter was gone. "Otherwise, how would you have known how to dance, to sing?"

Using the white dinner napkin, Letty dried her cheeks. The sadness had passed, and she enjoyed telling him about Mother and the big house on Main, and how they used to practice ballet and fox-trot and put on little musicales for the family, and how Mother always told her that she was born with extra luster. Valentine listened intently, as great oval platters of fragrant food came and went. Many of the dishes were made up of ingredients she had never heard of before, and he explained what everything was, and it tasted better to her because of this. As customers arrived and ate and departed around them, he began to tell her the story of why he ran away and how he came to work in vaudeville, and though she had read much of this story in the movie magazines, the version he told her now was more heartbreaking, and more true, than the one she knew.

It was many hours later that they stepped back onto the sidewalk, and this time Valentine didn't seem to think secrecy was necessary. His arm was draped loosely around her shoulders. Above them the sky was that dark velvet of midnight, and though the stars were not so dense as they would have been in Ohio, where some of the houses did not even have electricity yet, those that she could make out twinkled through a romantic mist.

"You see those?" he said as he gestured heavenward. "That's what you're going to be."

16

WHEN SHE PULLED ON HER WHITE SWIMMING COSTUME
her hands trembled, but Astrid was still convinced that Sunday
was the day she was finally going to get out of bed. Saturday had
been a sad, silent nothing, but today was going to be just like
any other day. She donned a thin kimono, which she tied loosely
at the waist, and fluffed her hair and put on a wide straw hat
with the crown cut out. In the hallway, she turned up her nose
and threw back her shoulders and walked the way her mother
had taught her to walk. As she floated through the ballroom she
saw Charlie from behind, and for a moment she thought everything was normal. She could just pretend that the last moment
they had shared was that kiss outside the yacht club. After all,

he was still Charlie, and he was sitting on the verandah of their big house, enjoying their view.

At the edge of the verandah she spread her arms wide above her head, saying hello to the day and the lawns rolling outward from the house. The pool did in fact look inviting, and the air, even though it was so hot, felt comforting, like a nice, warm bath. Virginia had always joked that Astrid must be part lizard, because her blood ran so cold—she was cold when nobody else was—and she was happiest baking in the sun. The other night, when everything had felt so scraped out inside her, happiness would not have been something she'd thought of ever having for herself again. But in the light of day she remembered that happiness was the one thing she was chiefly good at, and she decided there was no reason she shouldn't make herself as happy as possible that afternoon.

But all that fell apart when Charlie didn't even look at her. His eyes were focused, if that was the word, on something far away. He pushed back his chair, its iron feet wailing against the large gray stones, and brought himself to his full height. Then she remembered how he had been the night of the storm—so big, as though magnified. Without acknowledging her he went back inside. Astrid's eyelids fluttered, and for a moment her vision was full of spots. She blinked and saw a figure coming toward her across the grass.

"Victor!" she called out, waving one long thin arm above

her head. Then the landscape drained of color, and all she saw was white. She could feel her heart, because its beat was so ragged. But she could no longer feel her toes.

"Where am I?"

"Is she awake?"

Astrid pushed herself up on her elbows and blinked. There was Cordelia, sitting on the window seat, and when she saw that Astrid had come to, she put away her newspaper. The curtains were drawn, and a standing fan was blowing at her. On the other side of the bed, sitting on a chair, was Victor. He was looking at her as though he had been looking at her for a long time already, and when she saw those dark, pensive eyes with their long lashes she had a flash of him staring at her as he carried her up the stairs.

"Oh . . ." Astrid groaned as she fell back into the pillows.

"You're at Dogwood." That was Cordelia, speaking in a clipped but assuring manner. "I'm here with you. The heat was too much, that's all, and you fainted."

"How do you feel?" Victor asked softly.

"Like I lost a lot of blood." After she spoke she remembered that it was someone else who had lost all that blood, and regretted her words.

Cordelia bent to kiss Astrid's forehead. "Are you thirsty?"

As soon as she gave the faintest nod, Victor was up and

moving across the room to pour her a glass of lemonade. The ice rattled in the silver pitcher before he returned and sank down beside Cordelia. They both hovered over her as she drank, and afterward she wiped the sugary lemonade from her lips with the back of her hand. "Really, what a lot of fuss!" Astrid was trying to sound brave and careless, but her voice was halting, and she knew that she was failing by the way Cordelia's long, thin lips made a wavy line.

"I should tell Charlie you're awake." Cordelia took the glass away and stood up to go. "He told me to tell him as soon as there was news."

As soon as Cordelia mentioned Charlie, Astrid couldn't help it, her thoughts returned to that man. How blood had gushed out of him, his life leaking into a field at night where no one could help him. How it was Charlie who had finished him there, and how scared he'd looked in his final moments, just like a frightened animal.

"Cord?"

Cordelia was nearly out of the room, but she paused and revolved in the open doorway. "Yes?"

"I think . . ." Astrid closed her eyes and swallowed. "I think it would be best if I could get away for a while."

The room was very quiet, and some seconds passed before Cordelia replied, "Let me see what Charlie says," and then her footsteps grew faint as she moved down the hall.

Astrid turned her head against the pillow and fixed her gaze on Victor. "It's not the heat," she said after a while.

"I know," he replied.

For a while she stared at the expanse of bedding in front of her and imagined that those white peaks and valleys were a snow-covered slope she could ski down. At the bottom there would be a little chalet, with a fire in a pit and hot chocolate, and Victor would be there, in a thick turtleneck sweater. She thought about how in the coldest part of winter everything gets so peaceful and quiet, and all you can hear is your own breath. But she knew she didn't deserve an escape like that.

"Victor . . ."

His face twitched as he glanced up at her, the corners of his mouth twisting down. "Yes?"

She extended her hand across the bedspread, working her fingers as though grasping for something just out of reach. "Hold it, just for a few seconds."

The worry in his face didn't go away. It just darkened a few shades. His eyes went to the door and out the window and up at the ceiling. But Astrid knew that he would do as she wished. She flipped her palm open, showing him the soft flesh, and let her eyes close. The bed went up when he rose, and back down when he sat, closer to her, and interlaced his fingers through hers. The warmth of his skin relaxed her mind, but this comfort was short-lived. He heard footsteps returning before she did and stood up abruptly when Cordelia burst through the door.

"Enough moping!" Cordelia declared with a clap of her hands. She was smiling broadly and had suddenly acquired a sunny disposition that was not native to her. "Charlie agrees we ought to get out of Dogwood. And I've called Letty and told her to be ready to cheer you up. Let's pack you a bag. We're going to the St. Regis."

"It's Letty Larkspur." Victor leaned his shoulder against the door frame that separated the big bedroom from the sitting room of the suite that Charlie had rented for the girls, waiting for instructions.

"Yes, Letty's one of us; let her in right away!"

When Victor had gone, Astrid sank back into the uphol-stered headboard and smiled at Cordelia, who was sprawled next to her on the bedspread, a half dozen plates of half-eaten sweets strewn between them. As soon as they had arrived they had ordered every item on the room-service dessert menu, which included chocolate fondant cake, macaroons, profiter-oles, pear-shaped marzipans, strawberries in cream, and several brightly colored delicacies that they had not yet had the chance to try. It wasn't Astrid's usual careless smile, but Cordelia was glad to see her at least attempting a happy expression, which was more than she'd been capable of that morning. "This was a good idea, Cord. I'm feeling much better."

"Good," Cordelia replied, putting her fork into a slice of yellow cake with thick vanilla frosting. Ever since her big coming out with Max she had been feeling quite ready for anything, and everything tasted delicious to her, and she knew that whatever it was that was plaguing Astrid couldn't last long.

"Darling, what's the matter?"

The girls on the bed turned as Letty rushed in carrying a huge cone of peonies wrapped in brown paper. A little private smile played on Cordelia's lips. Letty had always been a notch more vivid than those around her—she had charm, and she knew how to move, and her eyes had an extra light in them. But in all the years of their friendship, Cordelia had never seen Letty so brimming with confidence and life. It was as though something had switched on inside of her. She was wearing a smart dress that Cordelia had never seen before—sleeveless navy with white polka dots that swished around her legs—and bright red lipstick. Without meeting Victor's eye, she handed the flowers off to him—the way one hands something off to a servant—and climbed on the bed next to Astrid. "Tell me *everything*."

"You'd better have some cake first."

Astrid handed one of the plates to Letty, and though Letty dutifully took a bite, she seemed mostly indifferent. After a second bite she pushed it aside and curled into the great heap of pillows at the head of the bed, turning her face up to Astrid expectantly.

"I was on my way to the pool when I fainted . . . the world just went dark, darling, and the next thing I knew I was in my bed and everyone was fussing over me!"

"Ever since the storm passed, the heat's back, almost worse than before." Cordelia propped herself up on her elbow, her temple against her fist, and gave Letty a knowing look. "I told her, where we're from, people know to stay indoors when the summer gets bad."

"But it wasn't just the heat." Astrid paused, and her round, green eyes sank toward her lap. A moment ago she had been telling her story in that blithe, careless manner she employed at lawn parties and in limousines, but now that tone disappeared, and she seemed again like the stunned girl Victor had carried up the stairs of Dogwood. "Something happened the—the night of the storm."

"What?" Letty whispered. She was listening with her entire body.

"There was a man . . ." Astrid's voice faltered, and her hands shot up to cover her face. A curl of yellow hair fell over her fingers, and her shoulders shook with her silent sobs.

Alarm traveled down Cordelia's spine, and she sat up straight. She'd seen Astrid angry at times, but she'd never seen her like this—stunned and confused and at a loss for words. Letty's eyes darted to Cordelia and then back to Astrid.

"We were having such a good time," she wailed. "And

then there was a man. One of Coyle Mink's men. He didn't seem to mean us any real harm, but Charlie was so angry. And then we were driving so fast. And then we were off the road and . . ."

The name Coyle Mink made Cordelia stiffen. Ever since she had successfully negotiated with the Hales, ever since Max had appeared on the horizon and whisked her away, ever since he'd told her, once and for all, that he wanted her to be his girl, she had felt so settled and sure that all the days to come would be wonderful. But now she remembered what Thom had said about Coyle Mink. At the time she thought he had only been saying things were going to be bad to get her to go away with him, but she couldn't help the sense of foreboding his name stirred in her now. "And what happened?" she demanded, not quite so gently as she meant to.

"It was awful! The blood. The way the blood *smelled*. Those pathetic eyes when he looked at me right before he— right before Charlie—" The sobs were audible now, and Letty began to stroke Astrid's shoulder, although it was hard to tell whether she registered the touch. "And then there was the way Charlie's face got, right before he shot him. It was so stony and mean, and though he looked at me, he didn't seem to see me at all. He was kicking that man, and I just wanted him to *stop*." She paused to gulp air, pulling her hands off her face and nervously spreading them over her knees. When she went on, her words were slow and faraway. "I said, 'Charlie, don't kill him,' and he said, 'You want me to kill him?' and before I could reply the gun had gone off and he made that terrible sound and there was blood everywhere." She pressed her eyelids closed, the black lashes fanning against her wet cheeks. "Oh, God, do you think it's my fault?" she whispered.

"No." Giving a firm shake of her head, Cordelia reached out and rubbed her friend's ankle. She wanted to say more, but she couldn't think of what. She was too stunned, and too angry. Now it made sense why Charlie had so readily agreed to let them go into the city—he had agreed because it wasn't safe for them to be at Dogwood. Anger burbled inside her to think that just when she had secured an element of tranquility for her family, he had put them in danger again. And she was furious that, after everything, he would keep the whole story from her. "No, it's Charlie's fault" was all she could say.

"What a horrible, awful, no-good thing for you to see," Letty was saying in a gentle way.

But Cordelia's thoughts were full of Coyle Mink and what was coming to the Greys now that they had stolen his business and killed one of his men. Her teeth were set hard against each other, and she wished that she was alone so she could pace the room. Her gaze drifted away from her two best friends, and that was when she caught sight of something else to worry about.

In the door frame stood Victor, holding a tall vase of

peonies. His dark eyes were soft with concern, and he was watching Astrid as though he had been watching a long time already. For a moment Cordelia thought that he must be pre-occupied with the same thing she was—that he was thinking about Coyle Mink, and how he would surely seek revenge. But then she recognized a special agony in his gaze—she'd seen it in John Field's eyes—and knew that he was consumed with something else entirely.

As though we don't have enough problems without the men falling in love with Astrid, she thought, and pushed herself off the bed. With brisk movements she made her way across the room and took the vase out of Victor's hands.

"We can't stay in here all day."

Letty and Astrid glanced up from their huddle and blinked at her, and she realized how heartless and perfunctory she had sounded.

"I only meant that the best thing is to forget about it until there's something we can do," she went on, more softly, lower-ing the peonies to her waist.

"Right you are, darling." Astrid smiled bravely and wiped both cheeks dry. "There's nothing to be done about that man now, and we're in the best city in the world, and together, and the only thing the living can do is have a little fun, don't you think?"

"Yes, that's just what I meant."

"Yes." Astrid nodded, as though she might thus convince herself out of her bleak mood. "I'm going to put on my dancing shoes and have a little fun. Victor," she called out flirtatiously. "You don't think I'm so old and sad and married that no one will want to dance with me, do you?"

The way Astrid pronounced Victor's name sent realization like a hard winter gale through Cordelia's mind. However she wished she could be rid of this knowledge, it was coming at her from every direction. There was something between Astrid and Victor, something more than a one-sided crush, and whatever it was meant yet more trouble for her family.

Shooting Victor a warning look, Cordelia stepped forward, planting herself between the bed and the door frame and blocking Astrid's view of the bodyguard. "I'll dance with you, darling," she said. "But let's get pretty first."

17

IN THE WEEKS THAT ASTRID HAD SPENT AWAY FROM Manhattan, the glittery world had moved on without her. At the St. Regis roof she saw that new couples had formed while she was off honeymooning, and they were doing dances that she didn't recognize. The hole-in-the-wall places that people used to go to after midnight were no longer mentioned, and while new places were mentioned in their place, she wouldn't know the passwords necessary to get into them. Of course she was still a person of interest, but the glances she got were some-what askance, although Cordelia assured her that in fact those glances were for her—they didn't like that a boy from a very different part of the city had passed himself off as a hoity-toity flyboy, she said, and they weren't sure what to think now that the papers were reporting that she and Max really were an item. But none of this mattered particularly. Astrid was in no mood to put on any kind of show. She was simply glad to be in her favorite company, and far from Dogwood and Charlie and men with guns.

"There's really nothing a good dress can't fix," Astrid said, draping a slender arm over the back of her chair and leaning away from the round table. A bowl full of orchids sat at the center, and next to it a gold bucket filled with ice was chilling a bottle of champagne. "*This* one is awfully good on you, Letty darling."

"Valentine bought it for me," she replied, in a voice dusted with sugar.

"You know, before you two darlings came into my life— and this is not a brag—I was the most talked-about girl this side of the Mississippi. Well, one girl can only hold the torch so long without getting burned. Cordelia came along and carried it for a while, but now I think it's Letty." Astrid sipped her champagne and enjoyed watching a touch of the old blush come into Letty's cheeks. "Cord, don't you think so?"

The band was at a high swagger just then, and Cordelia had to turn away from the saxophone player to reply. A subtle smile came over her face. "Yes, I think it's Letty's turn."

"To Letty," Astrid said, and they all clinked glasses and

nodded in satisfaction at everything the petite girl from Ohio had become.

The song ended with a gleeful eruption of horns, and the couples on the dance floor stopped to clap. They were the boys and girls Astrid had grown up with—the children of the best families, home from boarding school for the summer to play and spend money and get in minor scrapes before returning, unscathed by their bad behavior, for tranquil seasons of football games and midnight picnics in the quad and sneaking in and out of dormitories. It wasn't very long ago that she had been as careless and reckless as any of them. Ordinarily, the habits of her peers charmed her, but for some reason she couldn't grasp, the sight of them laughing away up high above the city made her stomach tight.

The last song had ended, and the applause died down. Astrid turned away from the scene, toward her friends, grateful that she was here with them and not at the center of activity. That was when she heard the sound.

A pop like a gun.

She wheeled around in time to hear a shriek of hilarity and saw Beau Ridley at the next table over, wielding a champagne bottle. Pale liquid flowed from its narrow mouth. The cork had flown across the room, to a table whose occupants were bemusedly fishing it out of the flower arrangement. But knowing where the sound had come from did nothing to quiet the ringing in her ears. Her eyes darted across the room, over chiffon party dresses and tables littered with drinks and flower arrangements and discarded bow ties.

They settled on Victor, who had been standing against the wall. He was watching her, with that same steady gaze, and she remembered that if there was danger, he would protect her. Her shoulders relaxed, but she knew she was no longer going to be able to sit still while the party reached a fever pitch. She searched for a distraction and found one.

Had it always been there? She'd spent so many nights at the St. Regis roof. Coming-out parties and wedding celebrations, fetes for spring and fetes for fall. Never on any of those nights had she noticed the small, arched door frame on the far side of the room, nor the hand-painted sign above it. She murmured an excuse to her friends and glided through the shaking bodies. As she left the circle of chandelier light, she began to make out the letters. PHILOMENA, the sign read, CLAIRVOYANT. PARTICULARLY PROPHETIC IN MATTERS OF THE HEART & STOCK MARKET.

"You probably weren't expecting anybody tonight," Astrid said as she pushed through the thick purple curtain and into a dimly lit room that smelled of incense and cigarettes. "Not with things so fizzy out there."

"On the contrary—I was expecting *you*." The accent was vaguely European but impossible to place. Slowly Astrid's eyes began to adjust to the darkness, and she made out a woman sitting cross-legged amid many tasseled pillows. Her body was wrapped in layers of Oriental-patterned fabrics, and her hair was done up impressively, a winding structure of braids and beads. With a mercurial smile she announced, "I am Philomena," and gestured for Astrid to sit. Then she quickly added: "Four dollars for the reading."

"Oh, yes, right, of course . . ." Astrid plucked a bill from her garter and handed the clairvoyant a five.

"Thank you." Having tucked the bill away, Philomena returned to her lyrical manner. "Close your eyes, dear, and take a breath."

Astrid did as she was told.

"I want you to forget your troubles and open yourself to the mysteries."

"All right." Though Astrid wasn't quite sure what this meant, she tried to sound cheerfully obedient.

"Give me your hand."

When she offered up her palm, Astrid cracked one eye and saw the furious concentration with which Philomena immediately began attending to the lines of her flesh.

"Ah," she began. "I see you are already a lucky one. You have traveled far. You have been much admired. You have married a wealthy man."

"Yes." Astrid couldn't help but slump a little at this reference to Charlie.

"It is a great love . . ." Philomena traced a line along Astrid's palm. "But also a rocky one, no?"

"Yes."

"He is brash and ambitious but sometimes seems incapable of correctly handling a delicate flower like yourself."

"Yes." This time it sounded almost like a whimper.

"It is never easy to love a powerful man." Philomena chuckled. "Believe me, child, I know."

"No." Astrid swallowed. "It isn't."

Now the clairvoyant's tone changed. "But what's this?"

"What's what?" Astrid's eyes got big. "What is it?"

"You will have *two* great loves."

"I will?"

"Yes . . . But only one will do you good. The other, harm."

"Which one? I mean, my husband or—or—the other one?"

Philomena's eyelids fluttered shut, and she curled Astrid's fingers back over her palm. Several seconds passed like this, with her lids rising occasionally to reveal that her irises had rolled back. Out in the main room the bass drum sounded, shaking the floorboards. Suddenly she released Astrid's hand, and her head drooped forward.

"It has not yet been written," Philomena pronounced wearily. She rose from the pillows and walked across the room, where she poured herself a glass of water from a pewter pitcher and drank it in one swift gulp. "Either way," she went on in a distant voice as she gazed off at nothing, "your life will be a storm."

"But what should I do?"

Philomena took two languorous steps toward Astrid and sank down beside her. "You'll need money. Do you have money?"

Astrid was about to protest that she didn't have any of her own, but then she remembered Grandmother Donal's gift and smiled. How silly of her to have forgotten the gift, but how perfect that it should be there, waiting, for just this moment. "A little."

"Good. For another dollar, I give you stock tip!"

Hurriedly, Astrid produced another bill. Philomena took up both her hands and closed her eyes, and Astrid did likewise. "Put everything you can in the Marietta Phonograph Company, guaranteed to triple in three months!"

"Really?"

"Yes, my dear. Philomena knows all."

"Oh, thank you!" Astrid kissed the woman exuberantly on either cheek. "How *lucky* I was to find you."

When she stepped back into the party, she was met with the same chaotic swirl. The psychic's dark room and soothing cadence seemed like a dream, but they had lifted Astrid's spirits. She knew what Charlie would say about psychics—that they were a lot of hokum—and she wasn't sure she believed it herself. But the woman's advice was like a pretty bedtime story, the moral of which was that she was not so trapped as she had felt before. Her life would be a storm, the woman had said, and there would be too much love rather than too little. Well, would she want it any other way?

Earlier in the evening the soirée on the St. Regis roof had been to celebrate the arrival from Europe of Franklin Otis, whom everyone called Junior—the youngest son of the oil-fortune Otises and, as it happened, Astrid's second cousin—but by two A.M. the party had doubled in size, and nobody could remember why they had come in the first place. When Cordelia returned from her suite, the wrought-iron elevator stopped for a moment and she remembered that she shouldn't have left the roof without Victor. She had been missing Max and wanted to ring White Cove to see if there had been any messages. But there hadn't been any messages, and now she was caught in the elevator alone, with nowhere to go and a stranger about to get in with her.

The doors drew back, and her shoulders relaxed. Claude Carrion's wasn't the most welcome face she could imagine at that moment, but she knew he wasn't an agent of Coyle Mink.

"Well, Miss Grey." As he ambled into the elevator, he finished tying his tie and his crooked smile shot up to the left.

"Mr. Carrion." Though she returned the smile, she tried to keep her voice cool and detached. "Where are you coming from?"

"Would you believe I find stories in the strangest places?" he drawled.

"Yes." Cordelia kept her shoulders back and her eyes on the elevator doors as they slid shut. "I'll bet you do."

"In fact, I just heard a story that pertains to you, my dear, and I think congratulations are in order."

"Oh?" The skin of her ears prickled. She knew right away it was going to be about Max, and though some part of her didn't want to trust Carrion or show him what she was feeling, how much pleasure she would derive just from hearing Max's name in *any* story, she couldn't wait for him to tell her whatever it might be.

"Yes. Everyone's talking about that li'l stunt Max pulled this morning."

"And?"

"And it seems one of those people is rich. Somebody has agreed to be his new patron. They are putting a lot of money behind him. He resumes training at the airfield tomorrow. Seems your boy won't be kept down, no matter what's said of 'im."

Cordelia sucked in breath. "It's a lot of money, then?"

"Rumored to be quite handsome. If I told you the figure, you wouldn't believe me."

"Who is it?"

Carrion shook his head. "Anonymous."

"Oh, *tell* me."

The columnist laughed—two big blasts of hilarity—and shook his head faintly. "No, I mean the donor is anonymous. Perhaps they don't like the idea of sponsoring a Negro, but they certainly like the idea of sponsoring Max."

Before she could make him tell her more, the elevator doors opened onto the roof, and the sound of a horn section in an uproar met her ears. Anyway, all her teeth were showing between her freshly painted red lips, and she wasn't sure she was capable of saying anything very sensible. "Thank you, Mr. Carrion!" she gushed, a little stupidly, as though he had done it.

"You're welcome," he replied grandly, as though he, too, felt responsible for the change in Max's fortune.

"Cor*delia!*" They both turned to a happily shrieking voice, rushing at the elevator. Letty was still wearing the polka-dotted dress, but her shoes had disappeared. She was already reaching out for Cordelia's arm as she dashed toward her. "Where have you been?"

"Just placed a call to Charlie. Have I missed anything?"

"No, but it's not as fun without you." She covered her giggle with the back of her hand and caught her breath. "I hope you're being nice to Claude," she said, shifting flirtatiously on her bare feet. "We must *always* be nice to Claude."

"Any complaints?" Cordelia arched an eyebrow in the columnist's direction.

He picked up her hand and kissed her wrist. "It has been a pleasure."

"Good-bye, then," Cordelia said.

"Good-bye!" Letty echoed happily. The night had gotten to her, and Cordelia was almost surprised by her petite friend's strength as she pulled her back to the dance floor, where they found Astrid in the midst of trying to teach Victor how to quick-step. His expression seemed to indicate that he wasn't sure he ought to be dancing with his charge, but his arms and legs were following her instructions.

"Come on, darling, you've never shown *me* how to quick-step!" Cordelia quipped, cutting in.

With an apologetic nod, Victor withdrew to a nearby wall, and Astrid—who seemed to have had a good deal of champagne—laughed a bubbly little laugh and hiccupped and replied: "At least now I'll get to teach someone who isn't *utterly* hopeless!" Astrid rested her arm along Cordelia's back and lifted her opposite hand and issued a lazy wink. "You be the boy, but I'm going to lead, all right?"

"All right."

By the time they went gliding onto the dance floor, Letty had been taken up by Junior Otis, who'd been following her with his eyes for some hours already. He was grinning, now that he finally had her in his arms, and though Letty was answering his questions with a sweet expression on her face, Cordelia could tell, even at a distance, that she was hanging back from him. Like Cordelia, her thoughts were half-elsewhere, though she was content to spend some hours amid music and happy, shouting people. Outside there was danger and uncertainty, and Cordelia—and Letty and Astrid, too, it seemed—had learned to want things that were complicated and came at a high price. But in the meantime, before the check came due, there were far worse places to be than the St. Regis after midnight with your best friends.

18

WHEN THE CONCIERGE RANG TO TELL CORDELIA THAT
she had a visitor, her friends were already snoring lightly in the
big hotel bed. Even the sound of the telephone didn't wake
them. Cordelia kissed each girl on the forehead, left them
a note, and draped a thin, silken wrap over her shoulders as
she hurried through the darkened sitting room. The elevator
seemed to take forever, but she experienced its floor falling
away beneath her feet like a thrilling amusement park ride.
Then there was Max, waiting for her in the lobby. He reached
out his hand for hers, wordlessly leading her outside. Like that,
they were once again a society of two.

"That's mine." They were standing under the hotel awning

between two great topiaries, and it took her a few moments to realize that he was talking about the gleaming white-and-tan automobile parked halfway down the block. Its headlights stood up alertly on either side of its long snout, and its flanks curved exuberantly over the gold hubcaps. "It's a Studebaker President," he said, and she could hear the pride in his voice. "The stock-car drivers can get it to go almost sixty-five miles an hour!"

"It's awfully pretty."

"Can I take you for a drive?"

"Why, yes, Mr. Darby, I think I'd like that."

The air was dense with mist as they ambled down the indigo sidewalk with their arms loosely attached. She could see the white drops hanging above the road when a car sailed by. There weren't many cars or many people out at that hour—just silhouettes keeping close to the wall of buildings, in and out of the orange light of the street lamps, figures as wrapped up in themselves as Cordelia and Max were in each other. The skin of her arms was almost sleek with the moisture, but neither of them was in any particular hurry to get out of the weather.

"Where did it come from?" Cordelia asked as Max opened the passenger-side door for her.

"I have a new patron—"

"I *heard*," Cordelia interrupted with a smile.

Max grinned and closed the door. His eyes shone at her

through the open car window. "You see? I knew you knew everything. Anyway, he gave it to me."

"He?" she asked, once he'd come around the front of the car and started up the motor.

"I guess I don't know that. I just assumed. He—or she—can't tell me their name. So far, they've only dealt with me through a lawyer."

"They must have a lot of money, to give you this."

"Yes," Max acknowledged.

"I'm glad."

"Wait till you see my new apartment. They've set it all up for me, Cordelia. I'm going to be able to fly every day again."

She didn't know how to congratulate him for this good fortune, so she just leaned across the front seat and placed a kiss on his cheek.

"I just couldn't wait to tell you. Are you hungry? Can I take you for a bite?"

"I'm starving."

They continued to the all-night diner on the corner of Fifty-first and Broadway, where the glass windows curved and all those seated inside had a view of the whole intersection. The place was so illuminated from within that Cordelia could already see the pies in the pie case on the counter and the dyed red hair of the woman making change at the register. They crossed Broadway arm in arm. Only about half the booths were occupied at that early stage of the morning; girls in evening gowns were awaiting stacks of pancakes with gleaming eyes, while a few less-well-dressed souls gratefully accepted plates heaped with pastrami on rye.

A waitress wearing a yellow uniform and a placid face led them to a table. If she recognized either of her customers she didn't let on. She took their order—apple pie with cheese for Cordelia, eggs and bacon for Max—as though she were listening to a husband she no longer loved reading aloud from the sports page.

Cordelia pulled a few pins from the back of her head and let waves of honey- and bark-colored hair fall around her shoulders. Propping her elbow against the table, she put the heel of her palm against her temple and pushed her fingers through the thick strands.

"Where I come from," she murmured, "you can't order breakfast past nine or dinner past six, and if you go out at night past ten you would think the whole town had died. They might actually have arrested you if you were out this late. They certainly wouldn't make you eggs."

Shrugging at the wonder of it all, she closed her eyes. Being here, with Max, felt like a confirmation of the dim suspicion she'd held since way back in Union, on nights when the lights had been shut off but she could not yet sleep: that she was destined to be remarkable.

When she opened her eyes, he was still there. The brave and expert character the papers wrote about, with his pale blue eyes and taut, sure posture.

"I just can't believe it," she said simply, meaning the scene and him and being there together and the fact that he was getting another chance, all of it. "Tonight I think I could go almost anywhere and no one would stop me."

"I know just what you mean."

Cordelia put the mug down and fixed him with an amused gaze. "But you always could go anywhere! You know how to fly."

"Me?" He shook his head as he stirred his coffee. "That was nothing, just what I did before. This is a whole new beginning. I don't want to spend my life entertaining people with silly tricks, you know."

"No? What then?"

"I want to fly solo to Alaska. Or Patagonia. I want to be the first person under twenty to fly from New York to Paris."

"New York to Paris?" She smiled at the way the two silky syllables that represented a city across the big ocean flowed into each other. There was a time when that place would have sounded impossibly distant to her, but now it seemed just within her grasp.

"Yes—I'll need the right plane, of course." His brow gathered over his broad, flat nose, and his fingers tensed around his coffee cup as he stared off into some vague, future place. He didn't even notice when the waitress arrived at their table and let their plates clatter down against the tabletop.

"Anybody home?" Cordelia singsonged when she realized that he still hadn't noticed the food right in front of him.

"I'm sorry. I'm boring you." Max drew his knife through the fried eggs, and the yolk spilled out over the hash brown potatoes. "I just—I can't wait."

"Boring me!" Cordelia smiled over the rim of her coffee cup. "You think boys where I come from use words like *Patagonia*?"

"I don't want to know about boys where you're from," Max said quickly without looking up from his plate as he put a bite of egg and potato in his mouth.

"Oh." The spell that had been over them broke, and Cordelia's eyes went down to her pie and she found she didn't want it as much as she had before. There was only one boy where she was from to speak of, and she had left him as surely and irrevocably as she'd left the town. Until that moment she hadn't thought that there was anything to tell Max about him. But ever since she'd learned Max's secret, she must have half thought he would eventually come to know hers, which was that the day she left Union she had promised to be John Field's wife forever, in the church on Main Street, with her aunt and uncle and his whole family watching. But it wasn't really John she was worried about. She thought of the way Thom had kissed her on the boat, and hoped that Max never learned of it. She wanted nothing but to be in Max's company, but now she knew how easily her desire for Thom could be stirred up, and she hoped that it would stay away forever.

While Max went on cleaning his plate of eggs, Cordelia's attention drifted to the window. Outside the mists had intensified to true rain. A downpour gusted across the wide intersection, and a rogue wind brought the onslaught against the glass as loud as pebbles.

The door opened, and a mixed group came through the door screaming with laughter. Although the air that followed them was not remotely cold, Cordelia shivered and put her hands around her coffee cup. The newcomers were abuzz over the state of their clothes and the torrent they'd been caught in. The girls' dresses were drenched and clinging to their skin, and Cordelia could see the boys' undershirts through their wet dress shirts. They were holding newspapers over their heads, which had done little to protect them.

Outside the rain continued, so loud and beautiful that Cordelia couldn't help but smile. As the drenched group went past their booth, a petite girl with a muddied hem dropped her newspaper on the ground. Her slicker must have protected it from the rain, because it was dry, unlike the others, which had been abandoned in gray wet clumps by the door, and Cordelia was perfectly able to read the type on the far right corner, which proclaimed it Monday morning, the 19th of August, 1929. Max must have noticed the paper, too, because he reached to pick it up, but when he moved as though to return it to the girl, Cordelia gave him a quick, subtle shake of the head and flashed her eyes so that he would know to keep it. "It's the morning edition," she whispered.

Max handed it over and went back to his eggs.

But her good mood was replaced with a quickening dread when she saw the headline. LARAMIE SAYS NO NEGRO COULD BEST HIM, it read, CHALLENGES DARBY TO RACE.

In a few seconds, her eyes had absorbed the rest of the article—a young pilot from Queens had said that Max must be chicken because of his color, and all kinds of other nasty things, and though he wanted to prove it by racing Max from one tip of Long Island to the other, he doubted that Max would have the courage to accept.

"Eddie. He's a big jock," Max explained. "Hangs around the airfield but he's got no discipline. Nativist type. Thinks because his granddad was born there, that makes him more righteous than somebody who just got off the boat. Or somebody whose people were forced over on boats. I guess he doesn't like me very much anymore."

"He sounds like a moron." Cordelia was trying to be reassuring, but she couldn't really tell what Max was feeling. He was gazing off as he had been before. If Eddie Laramie's words had hurt him, she couldn't tell.

"He is. And not much of a flyer, either, though he can get off the ground."

The wedge of pie sat between them, the orange slice of cheese hardened and shiny on top, a few brown crumbs scattered around the table. The silence lasted until Max cracked his knuckles. He cast a worried glance around the diner as though the world's benevolence toward him was slipping then and there, and he might be able to prevent its fall, if only he were quick enough. Cordelia reached out for his hand, but before she had a chance to squeeze it, a grin broke across his face.

"You're not going to do it?" she said.

"Of course I am. I could beat that boy with a blindfold over my eyes." He put his elbows on the table and smiled until she had to smile back, too. "I'll beat that boy easy, and then everyone will have to take me seriously again. *You'll* see."

Lowering her chin and holding his gaze, she replied: "I believe in you."

"Good." Max pulled a bill from his pocket and dropped it on the table. "Now come on, I want to show you my new apartment."

"It's going to rain again." Astrid was standing so close to the glass that her words formed a misty screen that blurred the greenery.

"Doubt it." Victor was sitting on a folding chair just outside the door of her bedroom, where he had stood watch since they returned from the city. When Charlie had called the St. Regis first thing that morning, wanting to talk to Cordelia, they had discovered that she'd disappeared to see Max in the night. He'd insisted that Astrid come home immediately, despite her protestations that Cordelia would be back soon. Of course Charlie was nowhere to be found since she had returned. Now her suitcase was splayed open on the bed, the clothes that she had thought she would wear during her city escape spilling across the bedclothes, disappointing reminders of the fun she'd thought she was going to have. "It was on and off all last night, but I think it's over."

"Well, just in case, I think I had better take a walk now, before it gets so bad I can't be outside. Ever since we drove back through those gates I've felt like a caged bird!" Astrid spoke just as carelessly and irreverently as she always used to, but Victor didn't laugh or even smile. He'd heard her, though. She knew because he stood up when she walked past him, and followed her down the stairs at a respectful distance.

"Don't you think you had better put some shoes on?"

They had reached the front entryway, and Astrid paused on the threshold. The motorcars that were usually parked down the hill, in front of the garage, were all gone or put away, and

the lindens that flanked the gravel driveway bowed in her direction. Overhead, the clouds were heavy and dark. Without the
cars the landscape looked timeless; it might have been a scene
from any old Victorian novel, the kind where a tortured heroine
makes the mistake of walking on a moody heath to clear her
mind and comes back with a fatal cold.

"No," Astrid replied as she stepped into the stone porch
and began down the switchback of carved stone steps. She was
wearing white linen pajama pants and a white linen blouse—
which was exactly what she was wearing when Charlie had gone
ballistic and ordered her home—and she couldn't think of any
shoes suitable to such a costume. "I don't think so."

By the time she reached the grass, he had caught up to
her, and they walked out across it side by side. She wondered if
Victor knew where Charlie was, and what he'd say if she asked
him to tell her.

"Have you ever killed anyone?"

A long pause followed. "Why would you ask me that?"

They were coming up to the hedge maze, its plant walls
rising, bluish, over the trim lawn, with the two stone sphinxes
that sat on either side of the entry like the sentries of some lost
civilization. It had never occurred to Astrid what a lonely thing
a country estate was, how underpopulated and far away from
the rest of life. "I mean, is it a very normal kind of thing? Does

one get used to it? Do you think I'm a very pampered, silly girl to be so shocked by it all?"

Victor clasped his hands behind his back and sighed as they glided past the topiary flourishes and into the maze. "No, you shouldn't have seen it, that's all."

"But I *did* see it. I'm married to a man who—who does that sort of thing, so why shouldn't I see it?"

"If you were my girl—" Victor broke off. The maze had turned, and they were standing in an empty corner, and it was suddenly very quiet. Neither moved, and though Astrid turned her heart-shaped face up in his direction, he wouldn't meet her eyes. His gaze went up to the sky in a tortured arc and back down to his feet. "Then it wouldn't have happened like that," he concluded, his voice breaking a little over the words.

"But I'm not your girl." She said it simply, as though this were neither a good nor a bad thing. There was no invitation in her voice, but even so he moved in her direction and put his hand against her hip.

"No," he replied, with equal simplicity. Then his eyes flicked up to meet hers.

"You shouldn't—"

"I know." He withdrew his hand and fitted his thumb in his belt buckle. She had thought this would be a relief and was unprepared for how overwhelming the disappointment was when his touch was taken away. "I know I shouldn't. But I keep thinking about that kiss and . . ."

Before he could finish Astrid began walking farther into the maze. "Well, don't," she said, putting on a careless tone, even though she was now thinking about that kiss, too. How much she had wanted it; how airy and wonderful it had felt. "I don't imagine your odds would be very good if you decided to play that game."

"It's not a game." She was walking fast now, but he kept pace with her as the path curved and took them deeper in. "I kept thinking—"

"Nobody saw, Victor." Her eyebrows swung together and away as she went, and her words got faster and her heart kept ticking ever more rapidly. Her feet were moving so quickly she was almost running. "You'd be dead already if anybody knew."

"Oh, believe me, I know. I've thought about all that. But that's not what worries me. I'm not worried for myself. I'm worried that—"

"Damn!" Astrid exclaimed with a furious stomp of her foot. She had come around a corner and found herself staring up at a dead end, its high wall overgrown with vines. A vein in her forehead twitched, and she glared at that wall, as though if it were only a little more accommodating, she might be able to climb over it and into some other life. With a slow shake of her head she turned around. "I'm sorry I kissed you, Victor, I'm a selfish, impulsive girl, and I oughtn't to have put you at risk like that and—"

"Don't do that. Don't take it back."

She wished he wouldn't stare at her that way, with those serious, shrouded dark eyes, like a peasant boy who has just seen the queen for the first time and can't quite believe her splendor. "Oh, Victor, what? What would you have me do?"

"Listen to me."

"All right."

"I'm not worried about what could happen to me. I'm worried because I keep thinking about that kiss, and I don't know that I'll be able to stop myself from kissing you again. I'm worried because Charlie Grey is a violent man, and I'm in love with Charlie Grey's girl."

"Love?" Her insides felt woozy and her throat itched. She wanted to reach for him, but he was too far away. He was just standing there on the grass, so tall and slender. When she compared him to Charlie in her mind he looked almost feminine, and she thought about what Charlie had done to that other man and what he could do to Victor, who was slighter of body and so much more thoughtful.

"Do you think you might love me, too?" he said eventually.

"I don't know!" She put her hands over her eyes. "I don't know, I don't know, I don't know."

Neither said anything for a while, but the quiet didn't calm her. Her chest kept heaving and her face felt hot and her heart wouldn't unclench.

"Because either way I'd better go. You see that, don't you? And if you love me, you should come, too."

"Oh, goddamn!" Astrid took her hands off her face and balled them into fists at her side. She gazed at Victor with a washed-out, desperate expression and wished that he would just come toward her. That he would pick her up and press her against the soft, leafy wall, and she could wrap her legs around his waist and run her hands down his spine and pretend she wasn't married, like she wasn't Astrid Grey, that she could still do anything and none of it would matter. But he didn't move. "Damn," she said again, this time a low, whispered curse.

"Do you?"

"I don't know, Victor. I don't know anything. It all sounds so crazy." She took a step toward him, but her legs were as unsteady as a fawn's, and she knew that he would have to come forward to catch her. Already his watchful gaze had registered something wrong with her. "I might," she went on as she sank against his chest and looped her arms around his neck. "The only thing I know is that I want to be held. Could you hold me? Just for a little while? Please?"

It couldn't have been the answer he hoped for, but he put

a delicate kiss on her hairline anyway. "All right," he said as she rested her whole weight against him.

The dream that she came out of was a pleasant one, but Cordelia's brain began to tick as soon as she realized that the room around her was unfamiliar. She lurched up, pushing the covers aside, and saw that she was still wearing clothes. A simple black dress with a long, slender tank bodice and a scalloped hem that fell just below the knee in the front, and slightly longer in back. Then she remembered: She had put it on to go dancing on the St. Regis roof, and later she'd worn it to the all-night diner with Max, and he had driven her out to Long Island as the sun was coming up. He had seemed so happy and proud of himself, and he had wanted to show her his apartment. Try as she might, she couldn't recall arriving at the apartment—he must have carried her in. With a sigh, she closed her tired lids and fell back into the pillows. Sooner or later, she and Max were going to have to learn to get to bed at a reasonable hour.

But she didn't fall back asleep, and after a few moments passed she climbed out of the narrow bed—which, besides a three-drawer chest, was the only piece of furniture in the room—and tiptoed through the open door. The second, larger room was nearly as spare. Two chairs were pulled up to a square table in the center; a gas-station calendar hung from the wall. The floorboards were wood, but they had been painted a light grayish blue that had been worn thin in places. Under the window was a basin sink and next to it a small stove, and that was the whole kitchen. But it was impressive, for all that. Though Cordelia had run away to live in a mansion, she knew that even a room like this would have felt like a castle after she left her aunt Ida's, so long as it was really and truly hers.

Twisting her hair over her shoulder, she stepped around the table to the sink. She wondered where Max had gone, but it didn't trouble her particularly. Perhaps he had gone out for the newspaper, to see if Eddie Laramie had made any new public insults, or maybe to get them breakfast. She might have gone on smiling privately to herself had a voice not whispered in her ear: *Cordelia, look up.* She twirled around, but there was no one in the room with her. Was she still asleep, or was she hearing things? But when she turned back to the window, she knew that she was wide awake, and she was grateful to whatever strange magic had called out for attention.

The view was of the airfield, a great expanse of half-ruined grass, and though the bad weather appeared likely to return before long, there was a patch of blue above the hangar. It was big enough to highlight the red biplane making loops in the sky, leaving behind puffy white lettering that she was coming to recognize. The plane had completed the *C* and *O* and was beginning on the *R*, and then the *D*.

By the time he completed the *A* she felt that she was

beaming with her whole body, with every inch of skin. She could hardly believe that Max—who had been so stoic and resistant when she first met him—was capable of this grand gesture. It was as though he'd climbed to the tallest mountain he could find just to shout her name into the clear, thin air. Even with no one there to see her she blushed a little, and she couldn't wait until he came down so that she could throw her arms around his neck and tell him she felt the exact same way.

19

"PERFECT! PERFECT!" MR. BRANCH EXCLAIMED AS HE
scurried into the brilliantly lit center of the vast studio. From
her place in the shadows, Letty had determined that the little
man wearing the panama hat was the famous director Lucien
Branch.

It had taken her some time to wind her way through
the vast studio and find the enclosed stage where *The Good
Lieutenant* was filming. But once she arrived she stood still,
watching intently as Valentine did take after take. He was positioned on a fake hill next to a fake tree in front of a painted back-
drop of a countryside populated by windblown orchards and
houses with thatched roofs. After he finished his lines, a pack

of people would descend upon him—adjusting his coat, fixing his makeup, moving the big camera around. He would remain composed through this routine, and then when they fell away, his shoulders would draw back and he would gaze off into the distance, exactly like a man haunted by the sorrows of war. To Letty, observing the goings-on with a swiftly beating heart, that bright, busy set was just how she'd always imagined heaven would be.

Now Valentine stepped down off the artificial turf-covered mound and in so doing shrank back to human size.

"Perfect!" Mr. Branch repeated. "I've got my shot."

"Do you really think so?" Valentine asked.

"You were a man without hope. A man without *joy*. It was fantastic!" Mr. Branch enthused as he led Valentine away from the set to the high folding chair with the name MR. O'DELL stenciled on the back.

She might have stood there forever, quietly taking it all in, had Valentine's polished head not rotated in her direction. "Oh, Letty!" he almost shouted. "Come over here."

"Hello!" she called as she came darting forward from behind a giant plaster cannon. "I'm right here."

A warm shade spread across Valentine's face, and she was gratified that he didn't try to hide how happy he was to see her, even now that they were in public. "Mr. Branch, here's the young lady I told you about—Letty Larkspur. Sophia and I have taken her under wing. She is a magnificent talent."

"How do you do?" Letty gave the director a shy smile and curtsied.

"Ah, very lovely!" Mr. Branch's shiny cheeks bulged indulgently. "What a beauty you are! I saw you perform, you know, the night The Vault opened. You are even more incandescent up close."

Letty wasn't sure what *incandescent* meant, but she thought it sounded nice, and glanced at Valentine to see if he had heard the compliment.

"Letty, did you think the scene was good?"

"Good! I thought you were *marvelous.*" *Marvelous* was a word Sophia used frequently, and Letty was pleased by how sophisticated she sounded as it rolled off her tongue. "Really marvelous."

"A chair!" Mr. Branch squawked. "Will someone get Miss Larkspur a chair?"

In seconds a man appeared with a chair. It was just an ordinary kitchen chair, hard and without the superior vantage of the director's and star's thrones, but Letty couldn't help but thrill to the deferential way her seat was presented to her.

"Did you think I was too much?"

"No, I thought you did it just right. Why, you made me cry a little." Letty was gazing up at Valentine and didn't think to hide the look.

Valentine beamed at this proclamation and then accepted a goblet of water from one of the many assistants scurrying around them. "She's a wonderful actress, you know. We've been training her."

"Have you?"

The two men glanced at each other and then down on the petite girl sitting before them. Valentine placed a thoughtful index finger over his lips and turned his head to one side. "Yes, singing, dancing, elocution. All with our own coaches. Sophia has taken *such* a liking to her."

"Yes, yes, I can see why. Well, we'll have to find a little role for her, don't you think?" Mr. Branch crossed his legs and clasped his hands over the higher knee and regarded Letty, as one might a prize pony at a state fair. "Will you do me the honor of auditioning for me, my dear?"

Letty's eyes popped at this suggestion. "I'd be honored," she said.

"You won't be disappointed. *Wait* till you see what my Letty can do."

A thought clouded Mr. Branch's eyes, and he shook his head, and Letty tried to keep her shoulders back even though she sensed that the dangled role was about to be taken away from her. "It's a pity, really," he began musingly. "You are so like my idea of Marie. So much more *gamine* than Sophia . . . Ah, well. Stay around, my dear, while we film the next scene?

And perhaps if there is time afterward, you can read something for me."

When he turned back to Valentine, she was overcome by a tingling sensation, the same sensation she'd experienced that first night at The Vault as she hovered on the margin of the stage and knew that she already had within her everything she needed to succeed. All that was required was the courage to step into the spotlight. But now she saw that her moment of opportunity was slipping away from her—Mr. Branch's attention had moved on and might not return—and she stood up, sending the chair away from her with a squeak, determined not to miss the moment.

"The other night I helped Valentine with his lines," she announced. Mr. Branch's eyes returned to her, and though they gleamed with interest, he didn't quite seem to follow. "I read Marie's lines," she charged on. "It's a wonderful script—I mean, I really enjoyed it—I mean—"

"What *do* you mean, Miss Larkpsur?"

The way Mr. Branch stared at her, she wasn't sure what she'd meant at all. She briefly experienced her body as though it were floating in a tank and she were speaking through water. But she reminded herself of her feet and felt them touching the ground. She lowered her chin, took a breath, and knew precisely what she'd meant. "Well, you said I looked just like your idea of Marie. I thought perhaps you'd like to see me and Val do a scene."

"It's true." A moment ago, Valentine's face had been rigid with surprise, but now his words tumbled out. "She was exquisite as Marie. Why don't we do the scene where the Lieutenant and she finally confess what they really mean to each other? If you get good closeups of me, you may even be able to use them later."

Mr. Branch hesitated for several seconds, during which anticipation built to a boil within Letty. But when he addressed her, it was solicitously. "My child, would you do us the honor?" He extended his hand in her direction, and she stepped toward him, allowing him to kiss her hand. "Would you perform for us?"

"I'll try," she whispered.

"Fantastic!" Mr. Branch let go of her and clapped. Then he began shouting commands. "Change of plan!" he cried. "I need the makeup girls to do up Miss Larkspur as Marie. Lighting—this is an afternoon scene, so you'll have to . . ."

There was more, but Letty was hardly listening. She was being ushered toward the dressing rooms by a woman in a formless black dress and a severe bun who didn't appear to share in Letty's delight over her miraculous break. Everybody was moving again, more frantically this time. She glanced back once and saw that the only person not hustling was Valentine. He was gazing at her, and there was such a mix of pride and adoration in his face that she almost couldn't stand being led away from him.

Was this all a little too perfect, or was it exactly what life had planned for her? She didn't know, and she wasn't sure she cared. All she could think was that she was going to say those beautiful lines for the camera. She was going to audition for Lucien Branch, with Valentine O'Dell at her side.

"I was a broken man when the war ended." Valentine turned his profile to the camera, and a ripple of feeling passed over his features. "I thought my life was over, and wished I *had* died in that ditch along with my men . . ."

"But you have done so much for our village." Letty stepped toward him and lifted her chin in his direction. She was wearing a wig with a long heavy braid that rested on her shoulder and hung down over her chest. The dozens of lights pointing at her from every direction were hot on her skin, and the makeup was thick on her face. But she scarcely felt any of that. Mostly she felt the emotion between Marie and the Lieutenant. Her lips trembled with it. "Much more than we will ever do for you."

"I am gratified to see the village coming back to life, after so much death and dying . . ." Valentine's gaze focused suddenly on her. "But you cannot think I did it for them." He gripped her shoulders with both hands. "Everything I have done, I have done for you, Marie . . ."

"I don't believe it," Letty protested as she gazed up at him in adoration. "I don't believe you weren't thinking of all of us when you—"

She broke off and they stared at each other for a few seconds. Then the kiss came, bending her backward like a strong gale. It went on and on, until Letty was weak with it. This was a lengthier kiss than the one they had rehearsed that night in the kitchen, and she supposed it was for Mr. Branch, to show him Letty wasn't just a kid and could do the really passionate stuff. But she knew that some part of it was Valentine, wanting to kiss her again. When he drew back, his eyes were misted over.

"Do you think you could ever love a man like me?"

It wasn't in the script, but Letty knew how to answer. "Yes. Oh, *yes*. I love you as I could never love any other man."

"More even than you loved your husband?"

"Don't ask me about him." Letty threw herself against Valentine's chest and closed her eyes. "Let's never talk about the past. Let's only look to the future."

They held still like that, a tableau for the camera, Letty with her eyes shut softly and Valentine holding her. Then Mr. Branch yelled "Cut," and she waited for him to release her. The stage lights were hot against her back as she lingered in the embrace a few more seconds. Somebody coughed, and she remembered that she was Letty, not Marie, and she stepped away from Valentine.

"Incredible! Unbelievable! Amazing!"

When she came off the set, her eyes had to adjust, and she squinted at Mr. Branch as he came forward. "It was magical, my dear little darling. Magical! Did you feel the magic?"

"Yes," Letty whispered as she was ushered back into the unilluminated world of snaking black cords and huge, mysterious gadgets.

"Ha, ha! Look at you, my boy. You are drained by what you have given."

Letty glanced back at Valentine and saw him smile in rueful acknowledgment.

Mr. Branch was moving about in circles, his pudgy hands fluttering just above his head. "I have had a vision. A vision of the picture I always wanted to make. You two understand, you share my vision, I know you do. You were living it there! We hardly needed *words*—you have intuited everything I wanted from your performances. I can see the whole work of art. I have had a glimpse of the divine. It is all at my fingertips."

As if to demonstrate, he took two handfuls of air and drew them into his chest. Letty was watching breathlessly and holding on to her long braid as though that might steady her. She knew she had been good, but the approval of Mr. Lucien Branch was so beyond anything that she had ever hoped for that her legs trembled.

"I can't allow this vision to vanish. We can do the scenes between the Lieutenant and Marie in a few days and finish the rest afterward. Only I don't want to stop. I must keep that glimpse in my sights. Are you with me?"

"Of course," Valentine said, flashing that rakish smile he had used so often on screen.

"And you, my exquisite child?"

"Yes," Letty whispered. Then, to her regret, she heard herself say: "But what about Sophia?"

"What about art?" Mr. Branch exclaimed. In a more subdued voice he added: "Perhaps she can play your mother. Would that satisfy you?"

Letty thought for a minute about how if Sophia were here and not traipsing around with Jack Montrose, there would have been no question of the part going to Letty, and none of this would have happened. So she nodded, and felt how her luck had changed forever.

In Valentine's dressing room, he threw himself down on the couch, crossed his ankles against the armrest, and opened his arms wide, beckoning her into his embrace. She slipped the wig off her head and tiptoed toward him, hovering uncertainly. Did he mean for her to perch beside him on the edge of the couch, or sit next to him on the ground? But then he drew her in, so that she was lying on top of him, her legs against his legs and her chest against his chest and her nose almost brushing his nose. They had kissed, and they had talked into the night, and they had shared plates of spaghetti with red sauce, but they'd never been in so terribly familiar a position as this. Yet it felt natural, after what they had been through in that scene. Performers and artists did things differently; she saw that now. They were affectionate and free, and they didn't obey the rigid rules of places like Union.

"Letty," he said softly, letting his index finger draw the line of her chin. "You know those words I said in that scene, the ones that weren't in the script?"

"You mean: 'Could you ever love a man like me?' That bit?"

Valentine put his arms around her middle, hugging her to him. "I really meant them."

"You did?" Her body felt weak, like it might disintegrate into tiny motes and blow away on the wind.

"It's all a sham between me and Sophia; you can see that, can't you? We haven't understood each other for a long time, and everybody knows about her and Jack Montrose."

Letty averted her eyes in shame. She had protected Sophia, because she thought Sophia could teach her how to be a star. "I know," she began haltingly. "That night at his party, I saw them . . ."

"Hush." Valentine kissed each of her temples. "It doesn't matter. I don't love her anymore. How could I, when all she cares about is fame? When she would do anything for it? And with that great greasy ape, Jack Montrose . . ."

"I'm so sorry."

"No . . . no. Don't be. I've despaired of meeting a woman who could understand me, who could understand what I do. Now I have. That is all that matters."

"You don't mean . . . me?"

Valentine's hands slid up her back, holding the back of her head as he brought his lips to hers. Any resistance she had felt before, any lingering guilt over Sophia, any offended sense of decorum evaporated. Living with the O'Dells had at first seemed extraordinary. Almost *too* lucky. But now, when she was being handed so much more—cradled in the arms of the dreamiest man she'd ever known, about to star in a real motion picture—nothing felt wrong. All the pieces fit together so neatly; she could see the scheme of the whole puzzle. Valentine had been here waiting for her all this time, and his image on screen had been some cosmic message, beamed to her in that faraway town. They *were* two halves of the same soul, after all—a more perfect team than O'Dell and Ray had ever been.

"Yes, I could love you," she said, and let him kiss her again.

20

"YOU'VE BEEN NEGLECTING ME, DARLING, AND WHEN it's raining, too." Despite her age, Virginia Donal de Gruyter Marsh put on a pouting face as her daughter approached from the far side of Marsh Hall's airy sitting room. The lady of the house was dressed impeccably in white chiffon dotted with small green circles, and her dark hair was pinned away from her face, but she slouched against the sofa as if she hadn't changed out of pajamas in several days. The frown remained even after Astrid kissed her mother hello and sat down next to her on the ivory cushion. "*Summer* rain," the older woman muttered, as of some pestilence for which there was no cure.

"It doesn't seem to keep Billie in," Astrid replied as she

arranged the skirt of her coral-colored tank dress over her crossed legs and cast her gaze through the large glass windows. Her stepsister was out on the grounds, practicing archery despite the intermittent downpours of the last few days. The skin of Billie's bare arms appeared damp, it was true, and her instructor had removed his shirt. But she was concentrating furiously on her stance, and her arrows seemed to be hitting their mark with fair accuracy.

Virginia's head lolled toward Astrid. "But my dear, Billie is not like you or me."

"No." Astrid exhaled in faint amusement. "I can't argue with you there."

"So tell me everything. Who is going around with whom, and who is giving the best parties, and who is hosting flops. About the liquor biz, and how much money your husband is making, and all of that."

"Ohhhh . . ." Astrid's hand waved gracefully so that her collection of tennis bracelets clinked lightly against each other. "It's all the same faces, Mother, you know how it is. But Charlie—well, that's what I wanted to talk to you about."

Despite her facade of careless indifference, Astrid must have conveyed something of the confusion that she had discovered married life to be, because her mother sat up straight, and the light of calculating intelligence returned to her eyes. "Oh, dear," she murmured. "Trouble in paradise."

"Oh, no, nothing like that," Astrid replied quickly. "Only—I thought since you are so much *older* and more *experienced* than I am, you might be able to give me some advice."

Ignoring the insult, Virginia patted her daughter's knee. "Of course, my darling. But go make your old mummy a bourbon and soda first, won't you?"

As Astrid slid across the room to the well-stocked bar, she thought how strange it was that a few months ago she had wanted nothing more than to be out of her mother and stepfather's house, with its constant fighting and ever-changing rules of propriety. But now her mother's decadence seemed amusing, like an occasional irritant one could nonetheless depend upon. The well-kept rooms of the Tudor-style house smelled of hyacinths, and as she mixed the drink (nice and strong, the way her mother liked it) she realized that Dogwood was badly in need of a cleaning woman to dust and mop and do probably a dozen other tasks she never thought about.

"Now, my dear," her mother said, as Astrid handed the drink over. "All men cheat; you cannot go to pieces over a little infidelity."

"It's not that," Astrid said with a sigh. In fact, this assertion did make her think of the time, before they were engaged, when she'd found Charlie in bed with Gracie Northrup, a rather full-faced girl a few classes ahead of her at Miss Porter's.

The memory made her heart sore. "Everything is peachy, really it is. We're rich and we throw wonderful little parties and everyone wants to be just like us. Only, every *now* and then, forever sounds like an awfully long time, do you know what I mean?"

"*Do* I," Virginia replied, rolling her eyes and sipping loudly from her highball. "I can't tell you, sometimes I wake up in the morning and see Harrison there snoring into his pillow and I think—"

"Mother," Astrid interrupted delicately. "Really, I thought you and Harrison were getting along so well."

"Splendidly!" Virginia slurped again, muffling her tone with the sound of clinking ice cubes, so that Astrid wasn't sure whether she was being sarcastic or not. "You know, Narcissa Phipps told me she saw you at the Yacht Club. The night of that big storm, when all the trees got uprooted. She said you two were making a real spectacle."

"Who cares what that old bore says. I know *you* don't."

"Darling! Of course I don't. Only . . . people do talk, you know. And once a girl has made herself very obvious, there is no going back. Now, you ought to do whatever you like and have as much fun as you possibly can. Lord knows *that* doesn't last. But women like us . . . we always have at least one practice marriage early on. Maybe two or three." Virginia sighed and cupped her daughter's chin. "My dear, I have no idea what is happening between you and Charlie. Perhaps it is some quarrel that will seem absurd to you in a week or two. But you must not forget that if it does fall apart, well, a youthful divorce is nothing a few seasons in Europe and a new wardrobe won't fix. You'd come out of that one fine. So long as you are not too far gone, that is."

For a moment Astrid forgot that she was playing the sophisticated and careless married lady, and her voice became low and childlike. "Do you really think so?"

"Of course! Look at your mother. I know life seems dark at times, and a girl can feel awfully trapped. But something always comes up." Virginia winked over the rim of her highball. "You'll see."

Astrid's instinct was to throw her arms around her mother and kiss her on the cheek like a child, and she was saved from this only by the opening of the door onto the main hallway.

"Sorry to interrupt." Both women turned to see Victor, slim in his denim shirt and pants, standing all the way across the room on the edge of the Persian carpet. At the Greys', Victor never looked out of place—there were always rough men dressed in work clothes there. But at Marsh Hall, where people did not enter social rooms without the assistance of the butler and where the art was old but the furniture was replaced every year by an interior decorator, he was like someone from another world.

"That's all right." Virginia's tone waxed seductive. "How can I help you?"

"I just wanted to tell Mrs. Grey that Jones called. He said that—well, that we should go back to Dogwood as soon as possible."

"All right." Astrid's shoulders sank away from her neck with a disappointed sigh that was only half disingenuous, and when she stood to go she bent immediately to kiss her mother good-bye. "Thank you, Mummy, I'll come back soon," she said.

"He looks good enough to eat," her mother whispered in her ear.

When Astrid drew away, she knew her mother was right. It was a long walk across the Marsh Hall parlor, and the closer she got to Victor, the more delighted she was to find him standing there looking good enough to eat, just as her mother said. Virginia's advice had made her feel bold, and she let her hips rock as she traveled between tall marble lamps and soft sitting areas. Why had she wanted so badly to prove that she was nothing like her mother? Suddenly it seemed rather lovely for a girl to be a little fickle and change her mind now and then, if the result is more happiness.

At the threshold she didn't say anything, but a dimple was obvious on one side of her face, and she gave Victor an audacious wink as she passed into the hallway. "Don't forget: I turn

eighteen Friday!" she called back to her mother, before leaving
the house.

The world as viewed from the backseat of a Daimler, chauffeured by a slim, pretty-eyed boy who happened to know how
to kiss, was incredibly full. Astrid didn't have to look at Victor
to feel the wild electrical charge between them. *Victor, my par-
amour*, she thought to herself. *Victor, my lover*. Even in her
thoughts the sentences made her lips curl and her spine shiver
with delight.

When the car rolled to a stop, she lifted her drowsy lids
and leaned forward and put her hand on the back of the driver's
seat. "Victor, you know I love you, don't you?"

That was when she saw the tension in his neck. His head
went to the left, the beginning of a shake, and their eyes met in
the rearview mirror. But he didn't shake his head. He winced,
and she realized she had made a mistake. During the drive,
while she had been lounging in the backseat of the car, he had
not, contrary to all her fantasizing, been sharing her sense of
elation. Before she could ask him what his worry was about,
she noticed something else—they were not in Dogwood but
parked on Main Street, in front of a square brick building
with the words POLICE DEPARTMENT OF WHITE COVE carved in the
lintel.

"I love you, too," he said.

"Victor, what are we doing here?" she started to say.

But before he could answer, she knew. Jones and Charlie had emerged from the brick building and were getting into the car. The intimacy of the Daimler in the previous moment—the four walls containing her and Victor and everything lovely in the whole universe—was like a distant memory. As soon as Charlie slammed the door behind him, she felt the world close in on her as surely as she had felt it open when she floated across the vast parlor of Marsh Hall toward Victor. Her husband didn't look at her—his eyes were smaller than she remembered them, and they burned above a tightly constricted mouth. Once Jones was situated in the front passenger seat, he gave the order that they should drive.

Twilight was turning the lawns of Dogwood a sweet orange hue by the time they arrived home, and still nobody had said anything. Victor stopped the car in front of the house, and they all got out and started to walk toward it. Jones reached the first steps up to the front door, with Victor just behind him. She was almost there when Charlie grabbed her arm, spinning her around so she saw how fixedly he was staring at her.

"Ouch!" She returned his glare with an indignant grimace of her own, but he only dug his fingertips deeper into her flesh. For several seconds neither said a word, and his face got more stern and clouded. "What were you doing at the police station?" she asked eventually.

He let go of her arm, as though it disgusted him, and half turned away from her, snarling.

"Nothing. They got nothing on me. No body, nothing."

"Well, if it was truly nothing, you should take that ugly mug off!" She was attempting her usual gay, breezy manner, but she could hear the strain in her voice and was sure he could, too. He had said *body*, which meant it was that man.

"They wanted to talk to me about Coyle Mink's man, but they don't care about him, not really." Charlie's eyes darted to the south. Someone was in the pool, splashing, but he seemed to make a quick calculation and determine that it was not a threat.

"They don't?" Astrid dared a glance up and down Charlie's back. "Well, that's lucky, isn't it?"

"They don't want to hang me for murder; they want to get me for bootlegging, take down the whole operation."

"How do you figure that?"

"Because it wasn't just them policemen. It was the Feds in there, too, in their suits. They were all talking nonsense. They got nothing 'cept our reputation to go on."

"Well, that's wonderful, Charlie, let's have a little drink and forget about this icky business."

He kept facing away from her, his big back a broad rebuke. In the silence Astrid heard all the other noises of Dogwood and also the swimmer climbing out of the pool. It was Cordelia, she felt certain, dripping on the patio. That she was there, not so far away, was the only fact that Astrid could think of.

"But they did know things."

Astrid's stomach turned over. "What things?"

"They knew where the car went off the road, which it's possible they discovered by poking around themselves, or maybe it was a lucky guess. They knew the man's name, which they coulda got from gossip in Coyle Mink's operation." Charlie paused to light a cigarette. The smell of that cigarette intruding on the fragrant night air made her feel a little sick. Meanwhile, she could see the shadows of the boys moving around on the second floor. She wondered if Victor was there, and if he was thinking of her, and she wished that she could just close her eyes and fall against him. "The thing I can't figure is how they knew what I said to you right before I shot that man."

"What you said to *me*?" Astrid attempted a laugh. "Who can remember what anybody says in a moment like that?"

"You did. And you told somebody. And that somebody told the Feds. Maybe there's one more somebody in the equation, or maybe there's one less. Tell me, Mrs. Grey, have you ever talked to a federal agent?"

"No!" Astrid snorted.

"Then who'd you tell?"

"Who'd I tell what?" she snapped back.

"Who'd you tell how it happened, who said what to whom, right before that man ate it?"

"Nobody!" she screamed.

He brought his hand up and smacked her across the face. It wasn't a hard slap, but he'd never touched her like that before, and the sting spread from her cheeks down to her chest.

"Oh!" she cried, and put her hand over the place he'd struck her.

His face contorted when he saw her pain. For a moment his eyes softened, and she knew he was confused and remorseful. That he loved her and regretted talking to her that way and wished he could undo the hurt. She looked up at him, trying to make her own eyes as wide and innocent as possible, hoping that his love would overcome him and he would forget his anger. But no such luck—in the next minute, his features had hardened.

"All right. Make it tough. But don't think I won't find out. In the meantime you speak to nobody but Cordelia or me. You don't leave your room. You're on house arrest, and I'm watching everything you do, you hear me?"

There was nothing to say. *How could I help but hear you?* she might have sassed, but her face was still sore. She stared back at him hatefully until she realized that Cordelia was there too—that she had come over from the pool and had been watching them for some time already.

"Take her to her room!" Charlie shouted, at neither girl in particular. Just loudly into the night.

Astrid turned toward Cordelia expectantly, but she wasn't looking at Astrid the way she usually did. Not with the usual friendliness—she gazed at Astrid as though at a stranger. She hesitated on the grass, her wet hair tucked behind her ears, taking in the scene. It was as though she'd been watching Astrid a while already, fierce as a hawk. Her eyes had none of the heat of Charlie's, but they frightened Astrid anyway, because they seemed capable of clear vision.

Cordelia glanced at Charlie, and then her eyes rolled back to Astrid. "All right," she said, sounding like herself again as she came and put an arm around Astrid's waist.

In those seconds she felt that Cordelia had gleaned all that had passed between her and Victor, every word exchanged. What else could cause her to regard Astrid with such cold distance? And with a drop of her stomach, Astrid knew that her friend was deciding whose side to take.

21

TWO DAYS BEFORE THE LARAMIE–DARBY RACE, AND
no one was fooled by the official line that it was "a friendly
exhibition of skill between respectful fellow aviators." Bets
were being placed all over Long Island, with the odds in Max's
favor—although not so heavily as one might think, given his
wider celebrity and greater experience as a pilot. Everyone
had a proclaimed favorite, which often revealed a person's true
feelings about the modern world. But Max, for one, did not
seem perturbed in the least by all the talk. In fact, he seemed
to thrive on it—he had been uniquely focused over the last few
days—and Cordelia, lying on the patchy grass on the far side
of the airfield with her head in his lap, felt briefly calm as well.

"You think this weather will hold?" she asked, idly tapping the toes of her brown oxfords together. Streaky clouds obscured the blue sky, but there had been no rain since early yesterday.

Max, who had been scribbling in a notebook, paused and sniffed the air. "The newspaper said it might not, but I don't believe it. I think it's going to be clear and fine by race day."

"I'll have to take your word for it," Cordelia replied, for she'd sworn off reading newspapers. They were full of bile about Max and his mother, which only made her angry, and she was additionally frightened that she'd come across some story about one of Coyle Mink's former associates who'd been found floating in the river without his face. One way or another, trouble was coming to her family—she'd realized as much last night when she came up from the pool and saw Charlie and Astrid standing there looking so wrecked. But she'd have to leave the airfield soon enough—she could think about all those messes then.

"After you beat Laramie, I'm taking you for oysters at the St. Regis, and you're going to ask me to dance in public." She had spun this fantasy mostly to herself, but when he didn't answer she sat up and faced him. "Max?"

"What?"

When she saw that he'd been contemplating the patterns in the sky and hadn't really heard her, she slapped him lightly on the shoulder. "Is my hour up?" she asked, smiling.

Gently he placed his fingers around her wrist. "I don't want you to go."

"But you had better get back to work. *I* know when your mind is elsewhere, Mr. Darby."

"I'm sorry, Cord, I—"

"Don't be silly! I know what you're thinking about, and I don't blame you, and after you win the race we will have lots of time to talk about whatever I like. But just now I'll go and let you concentrate." She stood up and began to stuff the remnants of their lunch—wax-paper wrappers and the crusts of sandwiches—into their empty potato chip bag. But Max took them from her and pulled her to him by the waist with unexpected strength.

"What was that for?" she asked, smiling, when the kiss was over. He took her chin with his hand and gazed at her as though he were trying to memorize the architecture of her face.

"Just because." With his arm still on her waist they began to amble toward the place near the hangar where Anthony had parked the Daimler and remained waiting at a respectful distance. As they approached, she could hear the blare of a radio, discussing the upcoming race, and couldn't help but feel excited for Max, who seemed so sure that once he won nobody would ever question his capabilities as a pilot again.

"You know what I think would make an even better story?" she said, resting her head against his shoulder.

"What?"

"If you brought me with you. In the airplane, I mean. I'd be very good and quiet, and when we landed I'd—"

"No!" His answer was so forceful that it felt like a rebuke, and she had to step away from him.

"I'm sorry." She blinked and glanced down at her shoes. "It was only an idea."

"I can't have you with me," Max replied in a softer tone. "It might be dangerous, and I know Charlie won't allow that."

"When did you ever care what Charlie said! Anyway, you yourself said you've done this flight a dozen times, and it will only go to show how little Eddie Laramie knows about aviation. Didn't you?"

"Yes, but . . ." Max trailed off and turned toward the south. "This flight—I just can't take you on this flight, all right?"

"All right." He was still looking away from her, so she drifted toward the car, feeling confused and hurt for reasons she couldn't quite figure. When Anthony saw her, he came around and opened the back door.

"Cord!" She turned to Max. The arc of his shoulders was rigid under his white T-shirt, and his hands were balled into fists at his olive work pants. His brow was tensed, and she realized that he must be nervous about the race after all. "Will you come bring me lunch tomorrow, too?"

"I guess you'll have to just wait and see," she replied with a wink. His shoulders relaxed a little when he heard the lightness in her voice. Then he returned her wink and headed in the direction of his airplane, just outside the yawning door of the hangar. By the time she was situated in the backseat, however, her sense of lightness had vanished, and she was instead beset with the notion that a heavy thing had gone unsaid between them.

The way to Dogwood was blocked by another vehicle; when Cordelia thought of all the things this might mean, her heart skidded. But then she recognized the driver—he was one of the caterers from the days when Darius was alive and threw parties—and saw that the bed of his truck was full of crates of oranges and lemons. He waved and drove ahead of them through the gates, up the gravel path that was lined on either side with lindens. In fact, the workers moving busily about the lawn on the south side of the house seemed to be in the process of re-creating Dogwood as she had first glimpsed it—they were erecting a white tent, the kind under which an epic summer party might be held.

"What's all this?" she demanded of the guard who was standing at a remove, watching the goings-on with a rifle slung over his shoulder. He turned, and she saw it was Victor and remembered what she had seen in his face that night at the St. Regis.

"Preparations for Mrs. Grey's birthday party." The skin under his eyes was bruised, as though he hadn't slept very much, and she disliked the way he'd said *Mrs. Grey*—it sounded strange, and she realized she'd never heard him, or anyone at Dogwood, call her that before.

"Does Charlie know about this?"

"It was Charlie's idea."

"You can't be serious."

Victor's eyes flickered in her direction and away. "Afraid so. It's a bad idea, if you ask me—"

"But I didn't ask you," she snapped.

"My mistake." He didn't meet her eye, but neither did he sound contrite, which only made her angrier. Until just that moment, she had been thinking of him rather pityingly as a lovesick boy who was going to learn sooner or later that the object of his desire was dangerous. But when she thought of him, standing there in the hotel room of the St. Regis, holding a vase of peonies while he gazed adoringly at Astrid, she remembered something else, which was what Astrid had been saying as he walked in.

Cordelia stepped decisively in his direction. "It was you who told the police."

"What?" His head swiveled in her direction, and his eyes narrowed.

"Or maybe you told the Feds. What Charlie said right

before he killed Coyle Mink's man. You overhead her telling us at the St. Regis, and you passed it on."

He turned so that he was facing her straight on and fixed his gaze on her.

"Who are you?" she demanded with what shallow breath she could summon. "What kind of make-believe have you been filling Astrid's head with?"

At first he didn't say anything, only scanned the surrounding area to make sure there was no one within earshot. "You know it's a lunatic idea, to throw a big party right now."

"That's not what I asked, is it?" Cordelia crossed her arms over her chest. "Who are you?"

He sighed and after a long while said: "I'm not going to tell you that. It's better this way. All you need to know is this: I love your friend, she loves me, and I can keep her safe. She's already seen too much. The attention this party will bring, and the strangers it will allow onto the property—that's not good for *any* of us. It's going to blow up, Cordelia. Talk Charlie out of it. You can do that. If you don't, well—he's a bomb that's going to go off sooner or later."

She turned her chin at a sharp angle. "How do you know it will blow up?" she demanded.

His sigh was heavier this time, and without any denials he stepped back from her and turned his eyes on the busy scene under the tent. "Talk to Charlie."

"That's exactly what I'm going to do," she replied hotly. As she moved toward the house she passed him too close, letting her shoulder knock into his without apology. By the time she reached the verandah, she was mouthing angry words to herself. Who was this person who had wormed his way into her family's house and told lies and spilled their secrets and seduced her brother's girl? Her anger had reached such a pitch that when Charlie came through the ballroom at a fierce gait she almost didn't recognize him. "Charlie!" she exclaimed.

"What?" he shot back as he passed her by.

"Charlie," she went on, twirling so that she could follow after him. "This is no time for a party! What's gotten into you?"

"Why not?" He was almost shouting, and when he paused on the lowest step and turned around to look at her she saw that the whites of his eyes were tinged with red, as though he'd drank too much coffee and stayed up two nights in a row.

There were about ten reasons that she could think of why not, but the most obvious reason, the neatest one, was that Victor—who was new to the operation but nonetheless knew plenty—was working for someone else. But the mania in his face recalled Victor's words—her brother was a bomb, and sooner or later he was going to go off.

"Have you had a conversation with Astrid recently?" Cordelia asked softly. "I don't think she's in any mood for a birthday party."

"If you think that, you don't know Astrid very well," Charlie shot back.

Then he spat on the grass and strode off in the direction of the tent, leaving Cordelia standing on the top step by herself. A wind picked up, pressing her skirt against her legs and sending an anxious current up her spine. For a while she remained there, wondering why she hadn't told Charlie what she suspected about Victor. Maybe it was because of the sincerity with which he'd said he loved Astrid and that Astrid loved him. Still, she wasn't sure she could trust Victor—but if she exposed him, it would be the end of Astrid, and as she turned back to the house she knew she couldn't tell her brother about his duplicity. Not yet.

22

LETTY HEARD SOPHIA A WHILE BEFORE SHE SAW HER, but the sound caused no immediate distress. She and Valentine had filmed all day, and she was blissfully lounging in her dressing room at the studio, on a pink suede couch, gazing at the costume she'd worn for Marie's final scenes. A good deal more had to be shot to finish the picture, but her part was complete. The eye mask she had been napping in was pushed back on her forehead. Lucien Branch himself had said that her reading of Marie was the most promising he had ever seen, and Letty knew from the way Valentine watched her, from the steady light in his eyes, that he was impressed by everything she did.

"Where is she?" Sophia's voice was closer now, just outside the door. "Where is the little brat?"

Letty ripped the eye mask from her face when she realized that Sophia's yelling was not benign at all and had everything to do with her. The reality of what she'd done, and all the ways that it should make her feel ashamed rather than proud, rushed over her. She was wearing a terry-cloth robe belted at the waist, which somehow enhanced her guiltiness. Furtively she moved back and forth across the room, without any clear idea of what she should do. The vanity mirror caught her reflection, and this gave her some confidence. The heavy makeup they had put on for filming was still highlighting her best features; she looked like a movie star now herself.

"Narcissus at his pond." Sophia's words were quieter now, but no less wrathful. When the door slammed shut behind her, Letty stiffened and waited. But Sophia didn't say anything for several seconds, and the tension in the room became stifling.

"He told you, then?" Letty, who sang with such power, could barely give breath to these words as she slowly revolved to face the woman who had taught her how to pose on a red carpet. Sophia was still wearing her trench coat—the belt was undone, as though she'd begun to take it off but had been too overcome with fury to finish the job. Her cheeks were gaunter now than before she had gone away, but this somehow detracted from her prettiness. For the first time, Letty saw the flaws in her mentor's beauty. That nose, which was so adorable on a child star, looked piggish on the face of a woman; and her eyes, which had winked adorably in her early pictures, were too small to convey real emotion.

Suddenly it was all so obvious why Lucien Branch had wanted to recast his Marie, and the obviousness made her pity Sophia even more. But then Sophia started toward her across the floor, her nostrils flared and her hand raised as though she might strike Letty, and Letty felt herself shrink inside. "I'm sorry," she said with as much dignity as she could muster. "I'm so sorry."

"Sorry?" Sophia enunciated the word as though she were interrogating it. "You planned this all along."

"I didn't! I *swear* I didn't."

"To think I trusted you. And you betray me—like *this*. Me, who taught you everything!"

"But you see, it all happened so naturally . . ." The satisfaction that Letty had been basking in earlier was completely doused. It was impossible to go on feeling proud about her love for Valentine when the woman who was wronged by that love was standing right in front of her, especially when the whites of that woman's eyes were tinged red. "And I thought that perhaps it wouldn't matter so much to you in the end."

"Matter to me? How dare you presume to know *what matters to me*."

The anger that pulled at Sophia's features aged her, too, and Letty remembered how many years were between them. That Sophia and Valentine had been married some time already, and that marriage was something that she herself knew nothing about. Letty tried to picture Valentine's handsome face. She reminded herself that in a few hours she was going to meet him, at Frankie's—*their* place. If she could conjure the sweetness that had bloomed between her and Valentine over the last few days, she thought, it would protect her from the mess she was now in. Even a whiff of that would do. But she couldn't conjure it, not with Sophia looming over her.

"You see, since you and Jack Montrose have your, uh, arrangement, I guess I thought perhaps it would be all right— that you might even be happy about—about me and Valentine."

"You and Valentine!" Sophia exclaimed contemptuously. Then she stepped back, exhaling like a bucking mare and lengthening her neck. "You and Valentine, an item?"

"Yes—I mean—" Letty's cheeks had begun to burn, and she was afraid Sophia's gaze might actually harm her. It was so lancing that Letty longed to crawl behind the couch and hide. "I mean—I assumed he told you."

Slowly Sophia withdrew a cigarette from the pocket of her coat and lit it. Taking a first drag, she shrugged the coat off her shoulders and threw it over the couch. All the while she went on looking at Letty in that same excruciating way. "Yes, I suppose in his way he did," she said eventually as she strutted over to the couch and sat down, crossing her legs with lady-like precision. "Letty, you little drip, you don't really think I'm angry about that, do you?"

"You're not angry?"

"Oh, yes." Sophia nodded vigorously. "Very angry. Though *angry* doesn't even really begin to describe it."

"But you just said—"

"You nitwit! Not angry about Valentine. I don't care what Valentine does. I haven't since we were children. In fact, I'm always quite relieved when a little nothing like you comes along and distracts him for a while so that I won't have to be always attending to his *feelings*." Sophia hissed this final word and rolled her eyes as she put her cigarette out, into the couch cushion. "Oh, well, what's this? You thought you were the first?"

Letty hoped the tears would hold back just a few minutes. But of course that was a foolish wish. Another moment passed, and she realized that what she really should have prayed for was that Sophia would say no more on that topic.

"Did he tell you he loved you?" she sneered. "Did he take you to Frankie's?"

This final bit was hurled with special bitterness, and Letty winced at its force. Meanwhile the notion of her and Valentine began to crumble. Slowly, at first, but once she began to think that way the whole structure looked flimsy, and she knew that

Sophia was telling the truth: Valentine had done this before. He had swept girls off their feet by promising them the whole world; she had been a sucker for a story that was too good to be true. As she wiped the wetness away from her nose with the back of her wrist, she realized that she had been unbearably stupid.

"No, my darling ingénue." Sophia's eyes softened, as though she knew she had struck the fatal blow and no longer saw any reason to tire herself out. "You can have Valentine if you want him. But he won't want *you* long. He never does. He just likes a distraction now and then, and if there's an opportunity for him to hurt me in the bargain, all the sweeter for him."

"I wasn't the first." Letty squeezed her eyes shut.

"No. Not even the first this *summer*." Sophia turned down the corners of her lips in an exaggerated frown. "But you know, unlike Valentine, I actually thought you were special. I knew you were better than the others. I was going to see that you didn't get the usual bad treatment when his affection moved on."

Timidly Letty raised her eyes to meet Sophia's, but she immediately regretted this act of courage. Sophia leaned forward, eyes narrowed, her sharp elbows propped against her thighs.

"I was going to teach you to be a star," she spat. "But you

couldn't wait! You had to have it all right now. You took my *part*, sugarplum. That's what has me in such a temper."

"Oh."

"Yes—*oh*. Oh, my. Oh, dear. Oh, no. That's what I care about. That's what I lay down on those casting couches for. That's why I go to the parties. That's why I laugh at all those tedious jokes the moneymen tell. It's because the thing I most want, have always wanted, was to be in the pictures, and stay in them, forever. You. Took. My. Part." She laughed, but there was no humor in the sound, and she drew back her upper lip so that Letty could see her teeth.

The terrible smile Sophia was wearing made Letty feel precisely three inches tall. In the handful of beautiful days when she had existed only in Valentine's adoring gaze and in an imaginary future where he brought her roses every night, and they lived in charming garrets and read each other poems before they fell asleep, she had forgotten that she could feel this way. But that sense of her own insignificance had never really gone away. It had just been lurking, waiting for the right moment to remind her that she was nobody.

When Sophia stood up, she did so in a slow, showy manner, making her way to the door with exaggerated elegance. On her way to the door she snatched her coat by the neck like a naughty kitten. Letty remained as she had been, frozen in one spot, watching Sophia's mannered movements. At the door she paused and let her eyes pan up and down Letty's figure, and Letty realized how ghost-like she must have appeared in her white robe and with her pale skin.

"You see," Sophia went on grandly, "I'm a real star; my light will never go out. Watch your step, honey."

Then abruptly she was gone. Letty was quaking like a mouse the cat has got in a corner. The room was the same—there was only that burned spot on the pink suede, and what did that matter? The costume was still hers. But she no longer felt proud about any of it, and the idea of standing in front of a camera, with dozens of people breathing around her in the dark, seemed frightening rather than exciting. She had gotten the part of Marie by playing opposite Valentine, the man she was in love with. But they hadn't been in love. That had just been a lie too lovely for her to see through.

At first she thought she was imagining the laughter. But when she peeked her head out of the dressing room, she saw that it was real—Sophia was standing with a cluster of women Letty had met briefly while she was being fitted for her costume. They were from the hair and makeup department, and though they had been mostly kind, Letty had not bothered to learn any of their names. She had been too overwhelmed with her new life to think about much at all, and she'd acted under the vague belief that a star should not interact with the staff. But Sophia was smiling and talking to them like old friends. Then the woman in the formless black dress and the tight bun glanced up and saw Letty, and her laughter got louder, so that it was obvious what they were all laughing about.

23

THE SKY WAS A PERFECT ROBIN'S EGG BLUE; THE
clouds hung in it like cotton balls and the air smelled of fresh-
mown grass. Astrid drove with a sure hand, and her magenta
silk scarf billowed in the breeze. She realized how well she
was driving and knew that it was a dream—in waking life she
required a chauffeur. *No*, she told herself, *don't wake up*. But it
was too late—she had realized the fiction of her dream, and by
now she could hear the rain.

By the time she lurched forward from her bed she knew
that the rain wasn't real, either. It was the drumming of fingertips against the windowpane, soft enough that it might have
been one of nature's midnight noises. But it wasn't. A fearful

light passed over her eyes as her mind came out of sleep and she comprehended the unknown presence outside her window. Then she realized that it was Victor, come to save her.

Her white nightgown billowed around her body as she tiptoed to the window, and she couldn't wait to pull back the curtain so that she could see him clearly. There he was, stock still and returning her stare with a steady, open gaze. Just looking at him was a better escape than her dream.

"Are you crazy?" There were so many other things she might have said, but she wasn't accustomed to making big, romantic pronouncements. Usually boys made them to her. The fact that she could still quip made her feel that her life wasn't quite so desperate as it seemed. She placed her cheek against the window's frame, to cool her skin.

He blinked, reminding her how beautiful his lashes were. "It's possible."

"They'll kill you." She shook her head. "Really, it's a wonder they haven't already."

"Charlie doesn't know. I wouldn't be here to talk if he knew. For some reason, though, he reassigned me—I'm not your bodyguard anymore."

"I know." She rolled her eyes toward the far side of the room, indicating the door and the man who waited on its other side. They both thought about that man and what he would do if he found them here, like this, and drew closer, although she kept part of the window firmly between them. She could see that out beyond his shoulder the world was dark and velvety, and for a moment she allowed herself to believe that she could go anywhere in it. "How did you get up here?"

He glanced ruefully at the long fall to the grass below. "I guess love makes a man do some dumb things."

"Charlie hit me."

Victor winced as though he himself had been hit. "Are you all right?"

She shook her head and went on in a hushed, pitiable tone. "Whatever happened at the police station—he actually thinks it's *my* fault. He says I told a Fed what happened the night he killed Coyle Mink's man. He says they know something only I could know. And I didn't tell *anybody* about that."

"You told Letty and Cordelia." He said this quickly, and it was so out of place in their conversation that she stepped away from him. It hadn't occurred to Astrid that Charlie might be right about there being a rat—that it could have anything to do with her—and the notion that Letty or Cordelia might pass on information about her was ridiculous. When he saw her blanch, Victor went on: "That night. At the hotel. You told them. I was coming back from putting the flowers in a vase, and . . ."

The night teemed with insects, but they could not

compete with the sudden buzz of apprehension at her temples. "I didn't know you heard that."

Her voice had risen—was it because he'd kept something from her? Because he was acting strange?—and he placed his hand over her mouth. The gesture put her spirit in revolt. A man had already hit her once that day, and in retaliation she sunk her teeth into his palm. He kept on staring into her eyes just as steadily, as though he didn't feel the pain. "I'm sorry," he mouthed.

"Why are *you* sorry?" She exhaled sharply through her nose and turned her cheek to him. "I'm the one who bit you," she acknowledged, without a hint of apology.

"I'm sorry I didn't protect you from seeing something so awful. I'm sorry to put you in danger. I'm sorry I can't keep away." He pushed strands of dark hair back from his forehead. "But I love you."

She frowned and stared over his shoulder. The sky over the Sound had a mauve lining—light from bootleggers' boats, probably. Maybe Charlie's own people. After several silent seconds, she came to the same conclusion he had. "All right, you love me," she admitted, with a bitter toss of her head. "What is there to do about it?"

"I want you to come with me."

"What?"

"Now."

Her body relaxed away from the window. For a moment she hesitated there between his pretty words and the room behind her, which was the way back to everything she knew. "I can't come with you," she said as she stepped forward into his arms. Her eyes sank closed and she breathed in the smell of him, his skin and the soap he shaved with, which had already come to seem nice and familiar to her. All day she had longed for this smell, and known it would muck up her whole life.

"Because you don't love me?" For the first time a crack emerged in his steadiness.

"I do," she murmured.

"Then we have to go, right now. It's too dangerous to stay. If Charlie suspects any little thing—if he caught the slightest whiff of my being here now . . ." His heart had begun to beat erratically; she could feel it through his shirt. In the same rushed way, he continued: "If you come with me now, I can make you safe. I will keep you safe forever and never lie to you again."

"Lie to me?" She drew back, covering her sheer nightgown with her arms. "What lie?"

"Astrid, don't you see? *I* told the Feds. I'm an agent of the Federal Bureau of Investigation."

"What?" Before she could help herself she was throwing up her hands, hitting his chest. It was a good thing he got his hand over her mouth again, otherwise surely she would have screamed to wake the whole house. She struggled against him a long time. It was only when she felt the energy seeping out of her limbs that she stopped. His hand remained over her mouth until she turned her wounded eyes up at him. "Is that why you told me you loved me?"

"God, no." Victor shook his head. "This is the worst thing for the investigation, for my career. I can't help it that I love you." He shrugged. "I just do."

"Oh." She drew a little back from him, thinking. "How could I go away with you? Charlie would find us, wouldn't he? And then . . ."

"Trust me. I can protect you. But it's too dangerous for you here, and for me, too. I thought they'd keep him for longer, and it would give us a chance to get away. I was wrong, and—I've only made it worse. Please, Astrid, let's go now."

"I can't go without saying good-bye to the girls! Anyway, you're right, if Charlie hasn't killed you yet, he doesn't know . . ."

"But Cordelia does. She's figured it out. And it's only a matter of time till she tells her brother."

Astrid's eyes darkened. "Cordelia wouldn't do that." Once she'd said it out loud, she knew that it was true.

"Are you sure?"

As she became aware of Victor's nervousness, his sense

of their precarious position, she herself grew calm. With all the tumult of the afternoon, she had forgotten the good advice she'd been collecting, the map she'd been making of her many options. Anyway, it was rather more interesting now that she knew her secret lover had a badge. "I'll come with you, Victor, but not yet. I have a little money of my own, you know—my father's mother gave it to me when I married. And that woman, Madame Philomena, at the St. Regis—she told me where I could put it, in the stock market, to make it bigger. She said it would triple in three months."

"That doesn't matter, money; it's—"

"It matters to *me*, darling! You don't know how much I love pretty things, and I'd hate to think what a strain it would be for you, trying to get them on a policeman's salary."

Victor took a breath, and from the sound of it, she would have thought the air was full of icicles. "I'm not sure. If he knows the things you've said to me, the things we've done—" He broke off, and she knew that he couldn't bear to think what her fate would be if Charlie knew that she had been kissing another man.

"Don't worry." She gazed up at him and let her fingernails graze his shoulder. "I can control Charlie. He's angry now, but he never stays angry long. I have him wrapped around my finger, you see, and I'm a really top-notch liar when I want to be."

For the first time that evening, Victor looked away from her. Strands of his black hair fell down over his eyes, and he cursed, too low for her to discern the actual word, only loud enough that she knew he was angry and he didn't like what she had suggested.

"That wouldn't be wise."

"Trust me."

He cursed low again. "I had better get out of here."

"Yes, you had."

With his index finger he traced the line of her chin. "Happy birthday."

"Oh! You're right! It must be past midnight by now . . ." She giggled faintly at how unlikely it was for her, of all people, to forget her birthday. "I guess I'm a grown-up now."

"Well."

"Well." She released him and stepped back. As soon as she was no longer touching him, however, her fear returned. An emptiness crept through her, and she wished she hadn't insisted on staying here another day. She wished she was with him, any place but here, and that she could curl against his chest. "But Victor?"

"Yes?"

"Will you still be here tomorrow?"

His brows worked together sorrowfully, and his lips parted. Then his hands were on her neck and her face, his fingers pushed through the yellow strands of her hair, and his mouth was hovering near hers. Not kissing, but in that moment of resistance, she felt all the force of his being. Her eyes rolled up, meeting his at close range, and then he covered her mouth with his. The heat of the kiss was catching; it spread to her toes swift as wildfire.

24

"WHAT IS IT?" CORDELIA DEMANDED, HOLDING THE door to the Calla Lily Suite open only a few inches.

Keller, lingering in the third-floor hall, pressed up on his toes as though that might allow him a vantage of Letty and Astrid, dressing within. "There's a man who wants to speak with you."

Cordelia cleared her throat, and Keller lowered his heels and met her eyes. "You know Charlie said no guests in the house."

"That's why I came to get you. He's at the front door."

"Why didn't you just ask him what it's about?" she went on impatiently.

Keller returned her gaze, a slow grin spreading across the lower half of his face. "I could've," he replied. "But he's awfully insistent. Anyway, I checked him out; he's not armed."

Behind her, Milly was trying to help ready Astrid and Letty, both of whom were out of sorts—Astrid kept chastising the maid for things she hadn't done, and Letty had just dropped a hairbrush, an eye shadow tin, and a pitcher of water in rapid succession. Down below, under the white tent that had gone up yesterday afternoon despite Jones's protestations and her own, men in bow ties were circulating with cocktails, and girls who had despaired of ever being at one of Dogwood's epic fetes were already squealing and demanding that their dates trot with them on the dance floor. Every time a squeal was loud enough to carry to the third-floor balcony, Cordelia had to press her fingertips to her forehead, just between the brows; her nerves were rather frayed, as well, and she closed her eyes for a moment and wished that all the people downstairs would disappear so that she could get some rest and be up early for Max's big race. He had been strange when she'd brought him sandwiches at the airfield that afternoon, and she longed for tomorrow, when she'd watch him beat Eddie Laramie and they could go on as before.

"All right," she said, when she realized that being cross with Keller wasn't going to fix anything.

"Where are you going?" Astrid called, leaning away from the vanity. Her narrow, arced brows quivered together anxiously.

"I'll be right back. Put some music on! We're all going to have to go to a party, whether we feel like it or not."

The first strains of Kate Smith warbling "Maybe, Who Knows" wafted from Cordelia's bedroom as she rounded the first flight of stairs. Outside of that room, the dress she wore seemed unjustifiably white—it was silk, and its neck cut a straight horizontal line across her chest, interrupted only by the inch-thick black straps. The hem brushed loosely against her mid-calf; she had bought it at the beginning of the season, before so much had happened and before the summer turned her so speckled and brown. Keller was ahead of her, and when they reached the bottom of the staircase, he drew back the heavy front door and assumed a watchful position a few feet behind her. Two more guards hovered outside.

The man was standing on the front porch, facing away. The illuminated white tent was casting the night clouds periwinkle, but there really weren't so many of those. Already the balmy night was blowing them away; by tomorrow, the sky would be clear. As on her first night at Dogwood, guests had been instructed to park along the road, but for all that, Charlie's men had not able to contain the party under the tent—she could see at least one couple, pressed up against one of the trees that lined the gravel drive, which her brother's guards had either missed or chosen to ignore.

"Hello," Cordelia said, when it became obvious that the man wasn't going to turn around.

"Oh!" He rotated the toes of his wingtips in her direction and held out his hand for her to shake. "You're Miss Grey?"

"Yes." Coming down the stairs she had worried that her dress was too innocent for the girl she had recently become. But now, before a stranger, she hoped that her hair, which was braided in a crown around her head, wasn't too feminine and childlike.

"It's a pleasure to meet you." The man assessed her with his shrewd, hooded eyes before nodding, as though he had concluded that she was indeed who she said she was. "Howard Ogilvy, Esquire, executor of the Max Darby Aviation Fund."

"I see." Cordelia brushed her hands against the bodice of her dress, smoothing it, as she brought herself up to her full height. "How can I help you?"

"Mr. Darby sent me. He's trying to rest now, naturally, but he wanted to see that I delivered you this letter." He reached into his breast pocket and withdrew a lined white piece of paper that had been folded in thirds. "And he wanted to make sure you know what it means to him that you'll be at the finish line tomorrow."

"Of course I'll be at the finish line," Cordelia replied,

taking the letter and wondering why that might possibly need saying. "Thank you," she added softly.

"Good night," Mr. Ogilvy announced, quite suddenly, and by the time Cordelia had glanced up he was halfway down the front steps.

"Wait!" With letter still in hand, she hurried down after him.

When he heard her, he paused and turned, resting his hand on the curved stone balustrade and staring back at her expectantly. "Yes?"

"I just wanted to know—" His eyes were so piercing she had to glance down and turn the letter over several times before going on. "Who do you work for?"

"Well, I work for Mr. Darby, of course . . . and also for the man who funds his flight ambitions."

"Yes, that's what I mean. Who is he?"

Mr. Ogilvy smiled subtly, as though this line of questioning amused him. He cleared his throat. "Well, the elder Mr. Hale signs the checks, but I've only ever spoken to Thomas Hale."

The sound of his name, even spoken in that easy, eloquent way, was enough to knock her off balance, and though she reached out for something to hold her she couldn't find the balustrade. Luckily, Thom's lawyer was quick and caught her hand before she lost her footing. "Thank you, Mr. Ogilvy," she said, blinking her eyes to bring them back into focus. "I'm sorry. You surprised me, I guess."

"I think I have."

"Does Max know?"

"No."

When her vision was clear again, she let go of him and backed up a few steps. "Well, thank you, I had better . . ."

"Cordelia, Thomas's instructions to me when we began this whole aviation caper were very specific. I was to tell no one who was funding Max Darby, except you, and only if you asked. Well, that seemed unlikely, so I didn't think much of it. I spoke to him this evening, just before I came over here, and when I told him of my errand, he repeated his instructions."

Her head, nodding, felt so heavy it was a wonder her neck could support it.

"And he added that, if you did ask, I could tell you that his offer still stands. He's in Nova Scotia now, but I know how to reach him." Ogilvy took the letter out of Cordelia's hand, and, using the gold pen that had been in his breast pocket, he scrawled a telephone number. "That's how to reach my office. There's always someone there, day and night; they'll find me if it's urgent, all right?"

"All right."

"Watch out for yourself, dear," he said, and then he was gone.

A sigh several days in the making escaped Cordelia's lips as she stared at the place where Mr. Ogilvy had vanished into the gloaming. He hadn't been gone long, only a matter of seconds, when she saw the red ember of a cigarette appear and start to grow larger. The smoker wasn't moving very fast, and after a few moments of worried speculation, Cordelia recognized Billie Marsh, wearing a men's white dress shirt tucked into loose-fitting yellow trousers.

"Hello, dolly!" she called.

"Am I glad to see *your* face!" Cordelia tucked the folded letter under her neckline and put on a smile. "We're all in shambles."

"Shambles are my specialty," Billie said, as she rose up the steps to meet Cordelia and, putting an easy arm around her shoulders, escorted her back into the house.

"Oh, Billie, thank goodness it's you," Astrid blurted. "We are having an absolute crisis!"

"Hello, Letty," Billie said as she crossed from the entrance of the Calla Lily Suite to the vanity table where Astrid had spent the last quarter hour frowning at her reflection. Placing a hand on her stepsister's shoulders, Billie bent and kissed her cheek. "Absolute, or total? You must be utterly clear on the severity of the crisis, darling, if I am to help you at all."

"Totally, utterly absolute!" Astrid pouted at her stepsister's reflection, and as the dark-haired girl drew back to light a cigarette, she adjusted the diamond tiara perched atop blond waves of hair. "You see, I always planned to wear my grand-mother Donal's tiara when I had my debut, and when I married and realized there was never going to be any debut, I thought I would just wear it when I turned eighteen. But now I *am* eighteen, and I wonder if I'm not a bit too old, really, and a bit too married, to be wearing an accessory meant for a princess . . ."

"Don't tell me you have given up on being a princess," Billie replied as she retreated toward the bed and lounged against its edge. Cordelia, who had come in behind her, perched on the bed as well, placing an ashtray between them. "I will have absolutely no reason left to carry on in this nasty, brutish world."

"Oh, don't be sarcastic!" Astrid stood, so that the ruffles of her long, slim magenta dress flounced around her body as she stepped across the carpet. "And give me one of those."

"That's not very Astrid," Billie replied, although she none-theless extended her pack of cigarettes and, once Astrid had one balanced between her lips, lit it.

Coughing, Astrid lay her hand over her lightly powdered décolletage and let a whitish cloud fill the room. She remembered now why she disliked smoking: Cigarettes hurt your throat, and they tasted awful. But she was rather unhinged with the reckless turn her life had taken, and it reassured her somewhat to have something to do with her hands. Especially when that thing felt tough, and a little ugly. Downstairs Victor was somewhere pretending to be one of Charlie's loyal soldiers, when in fact he was anything but, and meanwhile she was about to have to arrive among a bunch of people she hardly knew anymore and pretend to be the silly, indulgent girl they had come to expect.

"What are you staring at?" Billie had drifted across the room again and come to stand next to Letty, who was absorbed in the scene below.

"A lot of people who believe what they see in the pictures."

"No, they just enjoy pretty faces, darling, same as you." Billie put an arm around her and glanced back at the other two. "You three are a morose bunch! Let's have a nice cold cocktail, shall we, and join the party before one of you gets the bright idea to jump."

As if on cue, Milly appeared from the capacious dressing room, carrying a tray of juleps.

"Very good." Billie took the tray from her and distributed the juleps. Once each girl had a drink, and they were standing in a circle, Billie raised hers and said: "Here's to three beauties I shall never forget. Now, chin-chin, and let's go enjoy this evening, for you never know how long we'll have it this good!"

This toast drifted in and out of Astrid's head as she descended the mahogany switchbacking stairs, her best friends just behind her and diamonds gleaming above her forehead. Of course Billie was right—she always was—there was no sense in being nervous about matters when she wasn't going to be Mrs. Charlie Grey much longer, and it was perfectly obvious that the time would be best spent in enjoying the perks of the job. It wouldn't be so long, really, until she could see Victor's face again, and then she'd wink at him, to let him know who was *really* in her heart. Earlier that afternoon she had managed, amid the chaos, to slip off to the White Cove Savings and Trust and put all of her grandmother Donal's gift into the Marietta Phonograph Company, so now it was only a matter of waiting, really, before she could do away with the dull nervous ache that throbbed between her temples.

That was the happy thought she tried to focus on as she put on a smile and met the crowd.

Letty arrived at the party in the wake of the birthday girl, who had collected an armful of calla lilies from a vase before they came downstairs and then exhibited great delight distributing them to the guests. The second-to-last lily went to Beau Ridley, himself a practitioner of notable scenes, who fell to one knee and kissed her knuckles in homage. The last flower was for Charlie—Astrid paused for a moment at the center of the tent, as the piano player gently tinkled the keys and the drummer beat out a slow march. Everyone began to clap time then, so Letty, however blue she felt, raised her hands and began clapping, too.

Astrid made a flourish with one arm, pointing the flower like a sword, before advancing as a fencer might toward Charlie, where she feigned at stabbing him in the heart. Charlie, wearing a suit of pale gold and a shirt of dark pink, and flanked on either side by his men, crossed both hands over his heart and stumbled forward, as though the lily really had struck him down. By then, the band was into a manic tango, and though neither Astrid nor Charlie knew how to tango, they did a good impression, lunging forward across the tent and then twirling back in the other direction. At the place where they had begun he dipped her low, so that she had to put her hand up to secure her tiara as she winked extravagantly at no one in particular.

The couples retook the floor one at a time, whispering what a perfect match Mr. and Mrs. Grey were, and Letty, still standing on the edge of the grass, sighed at this vision of a boy and girl who really *were* meant to put on a show together. Cordelia and Billie had been absorbed into the crowd as well, and she was left standing there, gazing at a mass of people decked in feathers and beads and brightly colored clothes, who had no doubt already forgotten her name, or that it had recently been called promising.

That the first person Letty saw when her gaze finally settled was Peachy Whitburn did not particularly surprise her; in fact, she might have been amused by this sad, comical symmetry, if it didn't tighten the winch on her heart. Peachy's strong

New England shoulders were revealed by the navy column of her evening gown, and the girls on either side were pressing in to get a look at her left hand. With a wince, Letty apprehended the meaning of this tableau. The ring finger sparkled hatefully, reminding her of what she might have had if she weren't always seeking something better for herself. How easy she had always felt with Grady, and with a flush of sorrow, she thought how she was never to feel that again.

Her eyes widened and rolled to the left. By then she ought to have known who she would see next. There was Grady, standing a few feet from Peachy and her friends, his hands stuffed in his pockets as he rocked on his heels. A rueful smile came over his face when their eyes met. He glanced at Peachy, and once he had determined that she was fully absorbed, he moved through the crowd to the edge of the tent.

"Miss Larkspur," he said, offering his hand. "Direct from the Montrose Filmic Company's studio, I expect."

"Something like that," Letty said. Her voice was soft, but not from shyness, and in the silence that followed she heard all the sounds—loud chatter and low gossip, a swagger of trumpets, the gravel scattering as more young people made their way up from the road.

"Would you dance with me?"

Letty's hesitation was not because she didn't want to dance, only because she had somehow assumed, after Valentine used her and Sophia shamed her, that no one would ever ask her to dance again.

"I'm going away, so it may be your last chance for a while."

"Of course." Letty tried to smile as Grady led her onto the floor. There they moved fluidly, like old friends, to the music. "Is Peachy going with you?"

"Yes." Grady lowered his eyes and his cheeks flushed. "That's how it happened, actually. The engagement, I mean."

Letty nodded. Though she had seen the ring plainly and known what it meant, hearing him say it out loud made her wince again. "Where are you going?"

"To Hollywood. One of the studios out there, they bought a short story of mine for the movies, and they've offered me a job, as well. When Peachy found out, she threw a fit, and my sister told me I had better ask her to marry me. Well—" Grady broke off, as though he was surprised to find himself in the middle of someone else's story, and met Letty's eyes. "She said yes."

"Congratulations, I guess."

"Thank you."

After that they were quiet a while, although Letty moved closer to Grady while they swayed. She could faintly smell the cologne he must have applied some hours ago, and the pomade that set his hair in two smooth ridges over his forehead. Already that week she had felt the sting and humiliation that ensued when you pursued another girl's fellow, and she didn't intend to ever try that again. Yet there was something so familiar and comforting about being with Grady, and she felt too broken down not to enjoy it as long as she could.

"The real reason I'm going is I just couldn't stand New York anymore."

A weak laugh escaped Letty's small mouth, and she was about to tell him that she felt the same way, when she saw the urgency in his features.

"I only mean that I couldn't stand running into you all the time anymore. You're already everywhere here, and it's only going to get worse, now that you're Mr. O'Dell's new costar. So I figured I'd start over somewhere else."

"Oh."

"Peachy's a nice sort of girl, and my family approves," he went on. "And I suppose I know now that I'm not going to feel about another girl the way I do—did—about you. So I might as well make all of those other people happy and try to become as good a writer as I can be, someplace where the winter never comes. But I'm glad I got to see you, before I left; that I have the chance to tell you. Because for me there will never be another you."

"Oh, I—" Letty stopped dancing first, and then Grady stopped, as well. They must have looked strange, with all those bodies moving busily around them, but she couldn't think about that. The feeling inside her was so strong that she wasn't sure she could articulate it, and she stood there for another few seconds, meeting Grady's gaze and feeling the sadness that had kept her features pinched and hard for the last few days begin to thaw.

Before she summoned words, a thunder broke out somewhere to the south. A collective gasp went up under the tent, and everyone turned toward the sound. Screaming followed, and that was when she realized it wasn't thunder at all. Stunned, she stepped in the direction of the gunshots. The first car to speed up the hill didn't bother following the curving path of the gravel drive, and she stared, mesmerized by its blinding headlights. By then her heart was pounding, and she thought what a good thing it was that she and Grady were together, and that he had already told her what he needed to tell her. But when she turned she saw only the black jacket of Keller's suit as he rushed toward her, scooped her up, and carried her into the house.

25

ABOUT THE TIME THE SECOND CAR CAME SCREECHING through the gates of Dogwood, Astrid still had both arms looped around her husband's neck.

Then headlights flashed across his face, and he undid her arms and picked her up by the torso. She would have yelped in pain, but the way he was holding her compressed her lungs so that it was impossible to make noise. With his free arm, he pulled a pistol from its hidden holster and waved it in the air, firing a bullet at the arc of tent above them. At the sound of a gunshot at close range, the nervous murmurs of the guests became a frightened uproar. Couples who had stopped dancing and whose anxious eyes had been darting around to see what other people were doing scattered now, running in every direction. The bass player dropped his instrument, which made a sick, crunching sound when it hit the parquet dance floor.

Astrid, being held sideways at an awkward angle, looked around wildly for Victor, but she didn't see him. It occurred to her that she was simply too panicked to recognize anybody or really know what was happening. But there was Cordelia, being hustled toward the house by Anthony, and Billie kicking over a table—which had been laden with ice and citrus and mint leaves and a great pyramid of crystal glassware—and urging a group of girls whose mouths were wide with fear and whose faces were streaked with tears to get behind it. Meanwhile Charlie was shouting instructions to his men. A third car arrived, blocking another side of the tent. Those who hadn't already fled fell to the dance floor in terror, and boys in white jackets who had never had to fend off anything more dangerous than the judgmental eye of a maître d' threw their arms over their dates protectively.

They had come around to the other side of the house when Astrid realized that her grandmother's tiara had fallen off, and she screamed at Charlie to put her down. But if he heard her, he didn't respond. Right then that tiara seemed to represent her whole life till now.

"Charlie!" she shouted as he carried her up the steps

of the verandah. He had her over his shoulder now, and she kicked her feet to get his attention. "Charlie!"

"What the hell happened?" That was Charlie—she knew because she could feel his body rise and fall with every word—but it wasn't a voice she recognized. They passed a row of Charlie's men, standing with machine guns raised, as they went into the ballroom, where the chandelier blazed against the empty, polished floor.

"Three cars," Jones said. "Joey was coming out of the guardhouse to tell them to park on the side; well, they shot him and drove on through. The boys positioned on the fence, they fired on them—some of theirs must be hit, but I don't know how many. I watched it from the roof—after the first car came through, the others started speeding onto the property."

Charlie cursed. "Who are they?"

"Must be Mink's men."

"Charlie!" Astrid shrieked. His fingers were digging into her side.

"What?" he demanded angrily as he heaved her onto the floor.

His eyes were big and savage, and she was briefly more frightened by the way his chest seethed than by whatever chaos ensued beyond the walls of the house. She stepped away from him. A breeze came through the open French doors, lifting her magenta ruffles, which had felt very soignée earlier but seemed ridiculous now. The men on the verandah were ready and waiting for an attack, but they didn't make a sound.

"What?" Charlie demanded again.

"Where's Victor?"

"What?" Charlie's eyes were furious slits. He grabbed her wrist, bending her arm back terribly. "What does that matter?"

She supposed that she should have counted herself lucky that he didn't persist in this line of questioning, but the way he was pulling on her arm, she was afraid he might wrench it out of its socket. Already he was back to shouting orders—that Keller and Anthony should get Cordelia and Letty to the roof, that the doors should be blockaded—and then he was pulling her through the ballroom, down the hall, to the enclosed porch, where the great glass walls perfectly framed the ruins of her birthday party.

The tent sagged in the middle; Charlie's bullet must have knocked down some of the supports. Or perhaps Coyle Mink's men had done it. Three cars surrounded the tent, their headlights still on, creating pale cones of light in the darkness. The doors of the cars stood open, however—the men who had driven onto Dogwood in those cars had disembarked. Earlier, Astrid had been frightened, but she was beyond that now. Her stomach was tight and her face was cold, and she was no longer afraid something bad might happen, because she knew it would.

Charlie was pulling her across the room, past its worn sofas and potted plants, toward the glass.

"Charlie, don't you think we should—"

"Shut up," he snarled.

That was when she saw the cake. It was resting on a table, between the tent and the wall of the house, where the caterer must have been keeping it until the time came to light candles and sing. She flinched when she realized what the cake was supposed to be—the frosting was yellow and pink and metallic; it was decorated to look like her, wearing a silver dress and golden crown. An Astrid cake. Just as this was sinking in, one of the caterers was hurled through the curtain that obscured the inside of the tent, and his body hit the table with such force that the cake went flying.

"Oh!" Astrid gasped when she saw the red velvet insides burst open against the lawn.

But she didn't have time to mourn the sugar-and-flour version of her, because the curtain was ripped down, and a phalanx of men wearing dark suits and hats and holding machine guns as comfortably as they might hold the kitchen cat advanced toward the house, their faces turned up to the big glass wall of the enclosed porch above them.

"Charlie—what in hell are you doing there?" Jones called from the doorway to the hall.

"Come on, Charlie," Astrid whispered.

But Charlie's grip on her was firm, and he seemed to want to go on staring down the invaders, his face warped with furious challenge, as long as he could. The six-shooter was still in his other hand, but he didn't raise it. He was, apparently, not interested in futile gestures of that kind. He held his stance until the first man fired.

Then, all of sudden, she felt the weight of his body as he pushed her, and they both went flying. The floor came up suddenly beneath her, smacking the side of her body, the fibers of the Persian carpet scratching against her skin. Charlie was half shielding her, half dragging her away from the glass wall, behind the dubious protection of a stuffed armchair, but she managed to shove her hair out of her face in time to see the wall of glass yield to the first hail of bullets, shatter, and come crashing down. She squeezed her eyes shut, but she felt the glass anyway, a sharp pain against her bare calf.

After the glass came down, the machine-gun fire ceased briefly, and she felt Charlie's heart going *ga-dunk ga-dunk ga-dunk* against her back. But the silence wasn't total. A chuckle rose up on air that smelled of gun smoke.

"Hey, Charlie," someone shouted, in a voice that was both hateful and laughing at the same time. "Come out, come out, wherever you are! Coyle Mink wants to say hello."

Astrid's eyes, feral with fear, went to Charlie, but he appeared strangely calm. His large brown irises were directed at her, and the corner of his mouth twitched, giving her a sad, private smile.

"Hey, baby," he whispered. She shook her head, confused but beginning to realize he hadn't had some grand escape plan prepared when he brought her in here. Jones had been in the doorway before, but he wasn't there now. "Till death do us part, right?"

26

"WHERE'S ASTRID AND CHARLIE?"

Anthony, blocking the way into the third-floor hallway, flicked his gaze to meet hers. "You can't go down there," he said.

"But we're trapped up here!"

He glared at her and didn't answer.

A growl of frustration escaped Cordelia's lips as she spun in the other direction. Several of Charlie's other men had ascended to the roof—as though *that* would do them any good if Coyle Mink's army really did lay siege to the house. She was still wearing the white dress, but she had lost her shoes somehow. On the threshold of the balcony stood Keller, and beside him Letty, whom he'd scooped up in those first moments of terror and confusion. Her arms were wrapped around her body, and she trembled as she peered around the corner and down at the scene on the grass. Cordelia was walking toward her when she heard the explosion of gunfire below and knew she couldn't stay cooped up here and wait for Anthony to tell her it was all right to go.

Without looking at Anthony she strode back across the floor, to the bed, where she fell to her knees. She reached underneath the dust ruffle, into a box she had hidden there, and felt around until she encountered the curved handle of her father's revolver. By the time she was standing again the gun was tucked into the folds of her dress, and she pushed through the doorway before anyone could question her actions. Another of Charlie's men was at the top of the stairs, his rifle rested across the railing and pointed down below, but she didn't acknowledge him, either, as she hurried forward on silent feet.

She moved carefully, with her back pressed to the wall. The shooting below had ceased, but the ensuing quiet was charged with danger. She continued to slip down the steps, feeling the weight of the gun now in her hand, telling herself that this time she wouldn't be afraid to shoot. As she put one bare foot and then the other onto the second-floor landing, a jolt of shock traveled through her spine. Someone had reached out and put their hand on her shoulder, and she had to be fierce with herself not to scream out.

"You know how to shoot that thing?" It was Victor, his forehead creased with worry. There were a few agonizing seconds when she wanted to demand of him who he was, really, but then she remembered the way he looked whenever Astrid was in the room, and she knew that all that mattered now was that he would do what was necessary to protect her.

"Yes," she whispered back.

They kept to the shadow by the wall as they continued their descent toward the location of the last round of gunfire. When they reached the first floor Victor motioned to her to get down, and they moved at a crouch from there, to the half-opened door onto the glass-enclosed porch. She put both of her hands around the gun and used her thumb to cock it; Victor lowered his chin at her in silent approval.

At the door, she saw how bullet holes marred the furniture and the wallpaper of the room where she'd first met her father. The room where her father had died. Planters had been knocked over, and smoke wafted from upholstery, the smell of burnt fabric mingling with the loamy spilled dirt. Then she realized that her view of the night sky was much clearer than usual from that vantage, and saw that the whole glass wall was gone. It had been shot out; the shattered remains were scattered across the floor. Nothing seemed to move, and Cordelia experienced a few moments of tranquility. But the calm was short-lived—a dark, shapeless form, halfway between the entrance and the place where the glass used to be, began to shake, and she realized that it was Astrid and her brother in a heap.

Victor saw them, too, but before he could communicate to her what they ought to do, Charlie had leapt to his feet. "Coyle Mink wants to say hello?" His back was to them, his suspenders drawing a large X across his broad shoulders, and he was shouting at someone down below on the grass. "Well, where is he?"

This time Cordelia didn't wait for Victor. She crawled forward, not making a sound, knowing he would follow.

"Oh, I get it!" Charlie went on, his voice twisted with furious irony. "The famous Coyle Mink can't show his face. He gets *you* jokers to do his dirty work."

Until that moment, Cordelia hadn't really known what she would do. But now her course was clear. She prayed. She took a deep breath and asked for a miracle. Just a small one. The men outside wielding machine guns wouldn't disappear, she knew that; and she knew, too, that Charlie wasn't going to come to his senses. So she didn't pray for any of those things. The only miracle she wanted was for Astrid to glance up from the place on the carpet where she lay, and, in the next moment, she did.

"Come here," Cordelia mouthed, scooping the empty space with her hand.

Astrid's eyes were flooded. Black eye makeup was smeared across her face. Her chin quivered when she saw

Cordelia, and she glanced at Charlie and then back again. Was she shaking her head, or just shaking? Cordelia didn't have time to find out. She waved and mouthed, "Come here," again.

Quietly, cautiously, Astrid began to slither across the floor. She was bleeding, but not severely—it seemed only to be from shards of glass, not the kind of big wound that a bullet leaves. Once she was moving, Cordelia became aware of Victor beside her—he was sweating with nervousness over Astrid, and she knew how badly he wanted her to make it to them without Charlie noticing that she was gone.

"Come with us, Charlie," a man somewhere down on the grass yelled. He had a mean, hard, nasal voice, entirely devoid of fear. Though she couldn't see the other men, she knew they were there—she could hear them breathing through their mouths, shifting on their feet. "If you want to meet Mr. Mink so badly. Then you won't have to die in front of your girl."

At the words *your girl* Astrid froze. To Cordelia's great relief Charlie didn't turn around, and Astrid again began her slow journey across the floor.

"Oh, yeah?" Charlie snarled.

As Astrid crawled closer, Cordelia and Victor exchanged a look. Though the worry was still there in his face, she could tell he thought that Astrid would reach them, that they could sneak to safety, that perhaps, despite the desperate twist in her belly, they might leave this room unscathed.

The men below hadn't responded to Charlie, at least not with words. He was staring at them, and they were surely staring back at him, the whites of their eyes huge, their trigger fingers tensed and ready, everybody itching to know how the thing would go down. Then, suddenly, the panic in the atmosphere was given a sound as sirens came wailing onto the property.

Charlie's head snapped in their direction, and he briefly seemed to forget about Coyle Mink's men. Cordelia's heart leapt, and Astrid's must have, too, because she scrambled to her feet as the sirens echoed against the walls. She must have been a bright flash of magenta in Charlie's peripheral vision, because he spun suddenly and stalked after her. It was too late for Victor and Cordelia to hide; they were on their feet, backing to the door.

"Hold up right there." Victor didn't raise his voice much, but it held an authority she'd never observed in him before.

In the corner of her eye, Cordelia saw that he had raised his gun at Charlie. They were all frozen, Astrid hanging like a vision halfway between them. Outside everyone was shouting again. She heard tussling bodies, men ordering other men, wheels against grass, doors being slammed, motors starting up. All that was like a radio playing in the next room—mostly she heard the strained breathing of her brother, his wife, and her lover.

"Astrid, come here," Victor commanded. She did as he said, limping forward and throwing herself into Cordelia's arms, resting her blond head against Cordelia's shoulder. "Charlie, put your gun down."

"What is this?" Charlie barked. The gun was still in his hand, and though it wasn't aimed at Victor as pointedly as Victor's was at him, he showed no interest in letting go of it.

"Put it down, Charlie."

Charlie took two forceful steps toward the door, and the other three shrank back. The whole weight of Astrid was against Cordelia, who glanced worriedly at Victor. His eyes were dark and hard when they met hers, and she knew what he was telling her: that Charlie meant them harm, and Victor was asking her permission to do something about it. She squeezed her eyelids hard and tried to swallow her sorrow, and she clutched Astrid to her. The gun was so loud when it went off that she couldn't even hear her own cry, and Astrid just twitched once in her arms.

"Ouch!" Charlie exclaimed, as though he'd given himself a paper cut.

When she opened her eyes, she was overcome with curious relief. Charlie was bleeding, but from his hand. His gun was knocked across the floor.

"Get her out of here!" This time Victor didn't glance her way. He had cocked his gun again and was aiming it at Charlie just as he had before. "This is between me and Charlie. Go on. Get her upstairs."

By then the sirens were so loud they must have been right up next to the house, and though Cordelia's temper flared briefly to be ordered around that way in her own house, some part of her knew this wasn't her house anymore, that the boy with the bleeding hand over there wasn't really her brother.

"All right," she replied as assertively as possible, and then she laid Astrid's arm over her shoulder and began to assist her on the way back up the stairs.

Whatever was said between Charlie and Victor after that was drowned out by the cacophony of sirens and car engines, of screaming and yelling and the phrase *This is a raid* being repeated through a bullhorn. The man who had been guarding the top of the stairs passed them at a run, a rifle hanging from his shoulder, and she could hear the men on the roof pacing. By now they had seen the foolishness of their position. But Cordelia didn't worry about them. She got Astrid back into the Calla Lily Suite, slipped her father's gun back under the bed, and went over to stand next to Letty, surveying the damage from the balcony.

The cars that Coyle Mink's men had driven in were gone, and ten or so black-and-white police vehicles had taken their place. The tent sagged pathetically, and brightly colored refuse was strewn across the lawn—plates, cocktails, shoes, hats.

Meanwhile drunken party guests were being loaded into a paddy wagon, and policemen were surrounding the house.

"Are you all right?" Letty whispered, wrapping her arms around Cordelia's waist and squeezing her. But they both knew that *all right* was an unlikely proposition at that moment, so they left the window and went over to where Astrid was sitting, on the edge of the bed, her shoulders sloped and her hands cupping her face; urging her to lie back, they began to coax the glass shards from the skin of her arms and legs.

The activity on the ground floor of Dogwood was frantic, but it nonetheless took a long while before it ascended to the Calla Lily Suite. By then Astrid was mostly cleaned up, and the three girls sat in a row, waiting, still wearing evening dresses, their arms woven together. They heard the boots coming up the stairs—a lot of them—and then the door flew open. A current of alarm traveled through their shoulders when they saw the man who'd kicked it in. He was wearing a black brimmed hat, and he chewed on the dead end of a match, and his belly heaved against his white button-down shirt.

"Which one of you girlies is Cordelia Grey?"

"I am." Cordelia lengthened her neck.

"James Kirby, FBI," he reported, staccato, before demanding: "Where are the stores?"

"The what?"

"The liquor stores, sweetheart, where do you keep 'em?"

Cordelia swallowed hard. Her ears were ringing. Somehow, in all her years of dreaming that she'd someday meet her father the famous bootlegger, she had never imagined a man like this one, his worn face as unfeeling as the badge he brandished. "I don't know," she said, as soon as she could manage.

"Arrest her," he shouted, turning away. "Throw her in with her brother."

"You can't arrest her," Victor said, coming up behind him. His clothes were somewhat more rumpled than before, and a badge now glinted from his shirt pocket.

"What did you say to me?" The man put his nose right up to Victor's nose. "I'm the boss; if I say arrest her—"

"They're just girls, they didn't have anything to do with it," Victor replied, not backing down. "They've had enough of a scare. We'll find the stores without her."

"If you'd done your job, we'd already know where the stores were!" The man poked at Victor's chest with his finger, but Victor held steady until the man pulled back and, casting his gaze around the room, sighed. His eyes were small and fidgety, and it took him only a few seconds to change his mind. "Fine. They're your responsibility, then. Get 'em out of here."

"Yes, sir."

The man stomped out of the room, then stopped in the

hall. "Agent Lovo, I want you in my office first thing tomorrow!" he shouted.

"Yes, sir."

"And after I debrief you, you're fired!"

"Yes, sir."

The men who'd followed Agent Kirby up the stairs were tromping down the hall in the other direction, opening up the other rooms. For a moment, Victor hung his head, black blades of hair obscuring his eyes, but when he raised his chin, his features were smooth and blank. "Come on," he said. "They'll be tearing the place up all night. Get what you can quick, and let's get out of here."

"Are you really fired?" Astrid asked, as she lifted herself off the bed and went over to him.

The phrase *Agent Lovo* clanged in Cordelia's brain, and the knowledge that he had lied to them all these months went creeping eerily along the back of her neck. But he hadn't killed Charlie—if Charlie had been arrested, then he was still alive—and she felt grateful to him for that, at least.

"Never mind," Victor said. He removed Astrid's hand from his face and held it. "We'll see about everything tomorrow. Right now, we had better go."

After they had put their things in the back of Charlie's blue sedan, there was an awkward moment, when Astrid hovered by the front passenger door, unsure how it would look for her to sit next to Victor. But Cordelia nodded to her, urging her to go on ahead. "He's good," she whispered. "It's all right."

Astrid bobbed her head thankfully and held the door so Cordelia and Letty could slide into the backseat. No one said anything as Victor ignited the engine and steered the car along the gravel drive, through the row of lindens that had once elegantly ushered guests up to the house. The gate was open, and it was guarded by policemen now—Coyle Mink's men had vanished into the night, and a new authority was manning the entrance. Victor didn't stop the car. He cut his speed and held his badge up, and the policemen waved him on through.

Beyond the property, the way was still lined with abandoned vehicles. Letty's fingers spider-crawled across the tan leather upholstery and picked up Cordelia's hand. They had swung out of the drive, and like that, Dogwood was behind them. *Dogwood*, Cordelia repeated to herself, letting all its connotations reverberate in her thoughts. She had sought it for so long, a fantastical place of endless diversion and permanent summer. It had burned more brightly than she could possibly have imagined, but all the things that she had really wanted from it were dead or gone now, and as the car accelerated up the country road, she didn't bother to look back.

In the front seat, Victor had both hands on the wheel, his gaze focused ahead of them; Astrid had tilted her head and was watching him with wondering eyes. They would be all right,

Cordelia told herself, and with that she relaxed into her seat and put her head against Letty's shoulder. "You know, if you weren't my friend," she whispered sleepily, "I don't know that I'd have had the courage to live at all."

27

THE KNOCK ON THE DOOR WOKE HER, BUT IT WAS THE note on the pillow next to Letty's head that really brought her into the day.

"*Don't forget the race!*" Cordelia had written. "*You're the best friends a girl could have, and it matters to me more than I can say that you be at the finish line.*" But Cordelia herself was gone.

"You sleep all right?" Billie asked, leaning against the door frame.

"What time is it?"

The softness of the bed in one of Marsh Hall's many guest rooms enveloped Letty so sweetly that she thought if she could just stay there forever, the mess she'd made of everything wouldn't hurt so much. Of course, she couldn't stay there forever; it wasn't her home, nor was Dogwood or The Apollonian or any of the other places where she'd spent the night since arriving in New York. Dogwood had been torn up, and Charlie had been taken away bleeding, and it was probably now occupied by policemen. As for The Apollonian, she cringed, imagining the sort of welcome she'd receive if she turned up there. Her heart felt sore at the memory of what she'd allowed herself to yearn for during her brief tenure in its penthouse. But that was precisely the kind of thinking that made her want to bury her face in the pillows and never get up again.

"Almost eight," Billie replied briskly as she arrived at Letty's side. She was wearing a slouchy blue blazer and khaki pants rolled at the ankles, and she appeared not to have slept at all. "Come on, get ready! Max's race begins at noon. With traffic, who knows how long it could take us to get to the East End."

"What's that?"

"Montauk, darling! That's where the finish line is." Billie sat down at the edge of the bed and fixed her dark eyes on Letty. "Oh, dear, you have had a fright."

Of course it was so much more than that—not just the violence of the night before, but the betrayals and double crosses of Manhattan that she'd come to White Cove to escape in the first place—and for a moment Letty was speechless with humiliation, with the knowledge that she was bereft of the dream that had kept her moving forward all these years. Then she remembered about Peachy, and how she was going to have Grady forever, and her spirits sank lower. But she could think about all that tomorrow.

"Everyone did." Letty put on a smile and pushed back the covers. "Just let me throw something on, and we'll go!"

A week of rain had cleared away the extreme heat, and when they stepped out of Marsh Hall's Tudor gloom, Letty saw that it was a fine bright day that would be truly warm only when the sun was at its height. As they waited for Victor to bring the car around, Astrid tapped her foot, looking for him, and Letty saw what Cordelia had been saying last night just before they went to bed—he was good for her, however abrupt their love might seem. Letty and Billie stood quietly nearby, trying not to feel funny about Cordelia's absence. The sadness and confusion over what had happened with Charlie must have been too big for her to sit still with, Letty supposed. Cordelia always had been restless when something was on her mind. And of course she'd want to make sure that she was at the finish line well ahead of Max. Except no one could figure out how she would have gotten all the way out there on her own.

"Don't you look like a spring flower!" Astrid told Letty, although they were dressed almost the same, in loose-fitting white shifts belted somewhat below the waist and pastel cardigans. Her tone flagged a little when she went on: "Feels strange, doesn't it? After what happened last night. But a girl has to keep moving, you know, and it's always better to be dressed for the occasion."

"Thank you."

A radio was on, somewhere close to a nearby open window, and news of the race drifted out to them.

"Mr. Darby wouldn't speak to reporters this morning," a man's voice was saying. His tone implied that he thought this made Max seem high and mighty. "But Mr. Laramie was happy to. He joked with the boys from the sports desk and let them climb inside his plane, which he said was the perfect bird for the job. He questioned Mr. Darby's choice of *air-o-plane*, however, saying it was much too big for this kind of race and that this was a sign that his rival, being a Negro, was too simple-minded and lazy to be a top-notch aviator . . ."

"Thank goodness!" Astrid exclaimed when Victor pulled the blue sedan up in front of the house, the rumbling of its motor drowning out the man's voice. "I've had enough of that nonsense."

Soon they saw Billie had been right about the traffic. They moved slowly behind a train of cars on a twisting, two-lane road, nobody saying very much and Billie occasionally exhaling cigarette smoke out the open back window.

"Who are all these people?" Astrid demanded.

"The Laramie–Darby race is all anybody's talked about for days," Billie replied. "Nobody wants to wait to know who the winner is. Lot of money down on this race, and a lot of fellows have talked big in the speaks and will be angry if it doesn't go their way."

"I hope I know who you're rooting for," Astrid said to Victor. "Cordelia's awfully fond of Max."

"Laramie's a loudmouth." It was the first thing Victor had said all day, but he said it earnestly, meeting Letty's eyes in the backseat. "I like Miss Grey's boy."

When they reached the Montauk airfield, they saw a huge crowd had gathered on the patchy grass, blinking in the sunlight and waving American flags and eating popcorn out of red-and-white striped boxes. The reporters were there too, in their brimmed hats and rolled shirtsleeves. As they stepped out of the car, Letty realized the airfield was close enough to the ocean that salt air was carried on the breeze. Billie strode forward, with Victor just behind, and Astrid took up Letty's arm so that they could trail at a more ladylike pace.

"Do you see Cord?" Letty asked.

"No. Surely she's figured the perfect place to watch from, don't you think? If we find that, I bet we find her."

There was the shifting of feet, the vague bark of a radio-man reporting enthusiastically, the sound of popcorn popping in the machine in the cart. And then as they arrived at the edges of the crowd, a noise went up. The crowd had looked like a big mass before, but now it revealed itself to have two distinct halves. One side had erupted in jeering and clapping, while the other gasped and booed. Discussion rippled between clusters of men, and children jumped up and down in excitement.

Letty cast her eyes up at the dome of the sky. Even out on the farm, she had never seen it look so vast as now—the color was that hopeful, thin blue of midmorning, uninterrupted by even a single cloud.

"What do you suppose it is?" Billie called. She had turned around and was walking backward now. The commotion had only increased in volume, but when the other girls shrugged, she began to search for another source of information. "Isn't that Peachy? Someone go over and talk to her. That fellow she's with looks in the know."

"That's Agent Dobbin," Victor blurted.

"Ooooo! Who's he?" Astrid squealed, as she let go of Letty and tucked herself against Victor's chest.

"He's one of the senior agents on the Grey case," Victor replied, incredulously. The two men made awkward hand gestures in each other's direction. Peachy was still wearing the dress from the night before—a plum-colored chiffon number that rippled around her calves—although she had since accessorized it with a man's jacket and fedora. Agent Dobbin had an arm fixed around her waist, while she practically hung from his neck.

"Well, isn't that spicy!" Astrid wheeled around to face Letty. "Come on, Larkspur, let's go see what they have to say for themselves."

The blues of Letty's eyes made a zigzag path before they met Astrid's. "I don't know . . . Peachy never liked me very much."

"Of course she does! What's that old adage? Competing for another girl's beau is the sincerest form of flattery? Come on, let's go get some dirt." Before Letty could protest that she didn't know if she really felt up to talking with Grady's fiancée, no matter who she happened to be with now, Astrid had her by the elbow and was dragging her across the grass. "Hey there, Peachy!" she was calling out. "Aren't you full of life this morning?"

Letty tried to smile as carefree as a summer day and wave, just the way Astrid had, rather loose and free, but so that the observer would get a good view of her long, slim arm.

"Hello, girls!" Peachy replied. To Letty's surprise, she seemed happy to see them and didn't try to hide the fact that she was in the company of a gentleman who was not her fiancé. In fact, she hugged Agent Dobbin rather more closely as the two girls approached.

"What are you doing here?" Letty was smiling with all her strength.

"Well, I'm here to see the race, of course!" Peachy replied, putting her left hand on the man's chest proprietarily. When Letty saw that the engagement ring was gone, she couldn't help the way her smile spread, natural and happy. "This is Clifford; isn't he a catch?"

"Indeed!" Astrid made a little curtsy. "Awfully nice to meet you, Cliff."

Agent Dobbin nodded his hello. "Sorry about your house, ma'am."

"Oh, that's all right." Astrid waved her hand as though it were all really nothing, before forging ahead. "*Well*, we were wondering if you knew what was happening. What's this noise?"

"Seems Laramie was up to some dirty tricks, ma'am. Darby was in the lead since they took off, and then Laramie tried to knock him out of the sky . . ." He broke off when another cheer went up, but now it was the other side of the crowd who were whooping happily. Letty glanced around at the crowd that cheered for Max—how happy they seemed. It was a mix of black and white faces, people who had idolized his flying prowess for a long time already, and perhaps some new admirers as well. Many of them were clearly from the city, and Letty marveled at this, that they had traveled to a remote end of the island to see the conclusion of the race.

"That must be good news!" Astrid exclaimed.

"If you like Darby," Peachy said indifferently.

"Don't you?" Letty asked.

Peachy turned away from the question, but Agent Dobbin met it earnestly. "I don't like how Laramie talks," he began in a rush, as though justifying his point of view. "I don't like what happened with those Laurel people. I don't like the idea that anybody would stop looking up to Darby because he isn't white. He wins this race, he proves them all wrong." Peachy slapped at his chest, and he shook his head. "I'm sorry, I've been going on. But don't you think so?"

Letty nodded. How brave it was of Max to ignore all the hateful things that were said about him, to move beyond the betrayal of the people who had been his benefactors, and to do exactly what he felt he was born to do. How like Cordelia to somehow involve herself in the most dramatic and consequential story of the moment. "Yes, I just don't think I would have known to put it quite so elegantly."

"Well, thank you Cliff," Astrid said. "We'll just be going back to our own federal agent now."

"Bye-bye!" Peachy singsonged as Agent Dobbin averted his gaze.

"How odd," Letty murmured, as she and Astrid moved away arm in arm.

"What is?"

"Last night she was wearing Grady Lodge's ring! He proposed, that's what he told me, and she accepted . . ."

Astrid made a clucking noise. "Can't say I'm surprised, really."

"How do you mean?"

"Well, the last time they fell apart it was because she had some fellow in France, and trust me, darling, it takes one to know one, a flirt doesn't change her ways on a dime . . ."

By then they were back with Billie and Victor, so Letty never got the chance to ask Astrid what she meant or to say what was on her mind, which was that Peachy really must be crazy if she'd had the chance to marry Grady and let it go. They had heard reports from others in the crowd, filtered down from the nearest radio—Laramie had lost control when he tried to knock Max out of the sky, and though he had managed to right himself before crashing, he was now far behind.

He never came close to the lead again.

They stood together in a tight cluster and listened to the crowd around them grow boisterous when it was reported that Max was approaching the airfield. Billie leaned in and whispered to Letty: "I think he's doing this for all of us."

In another minute they heard the roar of the airplane. Its silver fuselage glinted in the sun as it approached, and everyone around them began to cheer. If there were boos from the fans of Eddie Laramie, they were silenced by the loud shouting of Max's name. The whole crowd turned with the plane as it dipped down, and Letty's breath was stolen by the *whoosh* of the big silver craft swinging low. For a moment, she caught a glimpse of the cockpit: Max's serious face and next to him, wearing a wide, red smile, the girl she'd taken the overnight train with from Ohio. Letty raised her hand in welcome, but in the next moment, she realized the plane wasn't going to land.

A collective gasp rose up along with dozens of escaped balloons. Silence followed, even from the Laramie partisans, as the crowd turned again to watch the plane sail over the Grand Marina Lodge and in the direction of the sea. Letty followed its path for a few steps, feeling every emotion she'd ever known all at once, as her best friend flew into the unknown.

"He's going to do it," Billie was saying. "He's going to go all the way to Europe. I heard some crank saying it on the radio this morning, and everyone laughed at him, but I think he was right. That's why he needed that big plane. My God."

By the time Eddie Laramie's small red plane came down over the finish line, there were few left to see him. The grass was littered with empty popcorn containers and pamphlets and small flags on sticks. Those who had cheered for Darby were pleased that their man had crossed the finish line first, but without a hero in their midst to celebrate, they were confused and began to disperse. Like most of the people who had come to see the Laramie–Darby race, Letty and Billie and Astrid and Victor had returned to their car to get a jump on the traffic already snaking back to the city.

As they drove, Letty gazed out the window and knew what had happened. Cordelia had been her friend so long, and they had shared so many things. There had been times when they were almost like one person, when an insult to one girl was an insult to both. And with a flash she saw what Cordelia had done that morning, almost as though it were her own memory. How Cordelia had been unable to sleep, and with what joyful conviction she had hitched a ride to the airfield at dawn. What she had told Max, which was that the only place for her to be was with him, and the only thing for her to do was what he was doing. Her old best dream had been taken from her, and she had stepped into the next one without a backward glance.

The occupants of the car were silent as they left the East End, and so Letty was close with her thoughts, although she wasn't sure if the great, weighty thing she was feeling was a sadness at missing her friend or an elation that a part of her was with Cordelia as she soared into the bright, brave future . . .

Although the days following the strange conclusion of the Darby–Laramie race (the names had been inverted now) were lonely ones for Letty, she was somewhat heartened by the fact that she spent them in a place that was familiar to her, and that the name being shouted by the news barkers at Pennsylvania Station had been known to her for a long time already. By then everyone agreed that Cordelia had been with Max when he didn't bother to land at Montauk, beginning his daring flight over the Atlantic. Superstitiously, Letty chose the same small, round, marble-topped table where, some months ago, she'd sat deliriously sipping cold tea and wondering whether or not her father would let her live in his house, now that she was a runaway.

She didn't feel like a runaway anymore. Astrid and Billie had assured her she could stay at Marsh Hall as long she wanted, but they were all somewhat nervous together, with Cordelia gone and her fate unclear, and she'd explained there was important business she had to see to in town. The last time she'd sat in that spot, contemplating her future, the click of every pair of shoes that passed her had seemed superior, effortless, as though those fashionably dressed folks possessed some key to life that she could only dream of. They did not seem that way anymore, but she watched them anyway, more carefully, her eyes shiny with the hope that she'd catch one particular face among the stream of travelers flowing underneath the soaring iron and glass ceiling. She might have gone and stayed with Paulette or one of the other Vault girls, but it seemed like good luck to her, to be back in the place where she and Cordelia had first seen the city together. Anyway, she was afraid that if she didn't keep her vigil in Penn Station, she might miss him.

She knew that where she was going she'd need to watch every nickel, so she didn't buy a newspaper, but she didn't have to. The barker was shouting the latest headlines, and all the tables nearby were talking about it. There had been several first-person accounts from passengers aboard the *Aurora*, a luxury liner en route from Le Havre, France, to New York Harbor, of an airplane that looked very much like Max's passing overhead. Cheers went up when that one came across the airwaves, and for a moment the busy traffic in the grand lobby slowed. Max Darby was a hero again, immaculate in his bravery, and those who had let his race prejudice them against him kept quiet. He was as American as the rest, perhaps more so, and he had set off into uncharted territory to prove his countrymen's vigor and might. That was the moral of the story being told on the radio, anyway, and it had an aura of romance, now that it was suspected that his girl had been on board, too.

Letty felt buoyant with the news and smiled at everyone who passed.

But by afternoon she was hungry again, and though she continued to smile occasionally at strangers, she knew that it was a false expression and didn't really contain any joy. The sense of conviction she'd begun the day with slowly leaked from her limbs, and the light started to fade from the sky and the shadows that the iron struts made drifted across the marble floor. They'd started to make announcements for the 6:10 to the West Coast, and Letty saw, for perhaps the thousandth time, that she was a silly girl, raised on pictures to believe a

whole lot of nonsense. Her tea was gone, and what did she have
to show for it but a growling in her stomach?

"All aboard for Chicago, Denver, Oakland, Los
Angeles . . . ," the loudspeaker was saying.

"Would you like another tea, miss?" The boy was sweeping by her table again, and when she glanced up at him, she saw
that he didn't really mean it. He'd already asked her two times,
so she shook her head faintly and stood up to go, heaving her
duffel over her shoulder.

That was when she saw Grady, hustling through the
lobby.

She felt like her heart was a bell that had just been rung.

He was moving so quickly, and she stood there, still, the
reverberations of that first glimpse of him echoing through her
body. His straw boater was angled down over his fair face, his
seersucker jacket thrown over one arm and his suitcase swinging from the other. He was alone, and she felt so relieved by
this that for a moment she didn't know if she would ever be
able to move again, and she feared that he would pass her, and
board the train, and be gone before she managed to regain her
composure. But it didn't matter, because right then he turned
and looked at her.

The corners of his mouth trembled for a few seconds,
and afterward they were both smiling at each other across
Pennsylvania Station, just standing like that, too happy to

move. They might never have moved again, if a voice hadn't come crackling over the loudspeaker.

"Last call for California, last call for California. All passengers for Chicago, Denver, Oakland, Los Angeles, please board at track seven. Track seven for West Coast, last call, last call . . ."

"Come on!" Grady yelled, motioning for her.

They both started running, reaching each other halfway to track 7 and not stopping as they descended the steps to the waiting train.

"Can she buy a ticket on board?" he called to the first conductor they saw, but he barely glanced at them, only waved his hand and told them to hurry up.

They did as they were told, and boarded. The car was full of families and ladies in flower-bedecked hats and businessmen who had already unfolded their newspapers and settled in. They did not at first see any empty seats, and anyway they were both so breathless that neither of them managed words until the train had lumbered into motion.

"I hope you aren't—"

"Peachy, she—"

"I—"

"Oh—"

"You see—"

"Never mind." Grady beamed. "It doesn't matter. All that matters is that you're—"

"All passengers, please be seated!" barked a conductor, down at the end of the car.

But they didn't go searching for seats, not right away. Above their heads the sidewalks and skyscrapers, the delis and speakeasies and nightclubs of New York were squatting on the asphalt, stubborn and stationary, refusing to give up their places. Letty and Grady were flushed to be together, at the beginning of a long journey. They gazed at each other, trembling with their good fortune, afraid that if they blinked, their happy ending might fade too soon to black.

"Take your seats—," the conductor began again. But he didn't finish. They wouldn't have been able to hear him, anyway. The whole car had erupted in applause at the way the fellow in the straw boater put his arms around the petite girl with the sleek bob, bending her backward into a kiss that went on and on as the train rolled west.

EPILOGUE

FOR GIRLS OF MY GENERATION, THE MERE MENTION OF those days can cause gooseflesh. The memory of how we sat around the radio, listening for the latest details. Of course there weren't many details, and so a great deal had to be made up, and our best storytellers were inspired to spin epic yarns. The newspapers were full of all manner of speculation, and you could not go into an ice cream parlor or a shoeshine place without getting into a conversation about Max Darby and what he had been thinking when he flew off over the ocean and left Eddie Laramie in his dust, so to speak. Or how Cordelia Grey had come to be in the plane with him.

    I listened from the roof of my family's house. The air

was clearer up there, almost cool, and I could see a long way. The grand houses positioned on their knolls, the farms in the lowlands, the sailboats on the water. Somewhere out there is a crumbling pier on a marshy strip of coast—though I don't know precisely which one—where Cordelia once met Thom Hale at dusk wearing a red dress. I missed her more than I could have imagined, and I grew waspish with what they said about her on the radio, so I tried to remember stories she'd told me, when she still had that look of wonder in her eyes. That dress must have seemed like a dream to her by then. The breeze on the roof wasn't strong; it nudged the flossy clouds but couldn't really move them. In the days that followed the race, the weather was so lovely it ached, and I turned brown up there on the tar roof, even with the protection of my parasol.

Letty had left for Los Angeles—she and Grady called me, breathless, from Chicago in the middle of the night to tell me of their plans. The police didn't have enough to hold Charlie, and it began to look like they were going to have to let him out of jail. Victor told Astrid it would be wise for them to leave the country. Virginia thought this was a splendid idea—she said it would be best for Astrid's reputation to spend the fall and winter in Paris, and she gave them a little money, since Victor had lost his job with the Bureau. Once everyone was looking the other way, she said, a hasty divorce could be arranged; they sailed for Europe that afternoon. So I was by myself when the tenor of the radio announcers changed—after a few days passed with no sign of Max's plane—and when reports of strange metal hunks washing up on the shore of Ireland came across the wires.

There was no one to talk it over with, and I am not in any case given to displays of emotion, so I took one of Father's sports cars and drove as fast as I could through the lanes and back ways of White Cove.

That was how I found him.

I was passing Dogwood, without any intention of stopping, just to catch a glimpse of what she saw in the place. He was standing there, across from the gates, wearing worn pants and a black jacket that was too big for him, but that I suppose might have seemed fancy somewhere.

"You aren't from around here, are you?" I called out to him over the rumbling of the motor.

He kept on gazing up at the house. His hair was overgrown, but not long enough to cover his ears, and he was so unusually tall that I felt an uncharacteristic desire to protect him. Standing attentively at his side was Good Egg, Letty's greyhound. His face would be handsome, I thought, once he grew into it. "No," he said, after a while.

"Would you like to talk?" I asked.

"No," he repeated, although after another pause, he climbed into the passenger seat, slapping the side of his leg so that Good Egg would follow. "Can you give me a ride? No one but you has passed for a long while."

"Sure," I said, putting the car in gear. "Where are you going?"

"I don't care."

I laughed faintly. "My name is Billie Marsh, by the way."

"John Field."

"Were you at the party? The night they . . ."

He shook his head. "I was looking for Cordelia Grey. But I guess I was a day too late."

"Oh." I glanced at him and saw how he slumped when he said her name. "Do you know her?"

He had to put his fist over his mouth to say the next bit, which was how I noticed the ring on his left hand. "She's my wife."

"Oh!" I exclaimed, rather heartlessly.

"I haven't seen her since the beginning of summer. Then a week ago, I saw her name in an article about Max Darby . . ." When I saw how he covered up his whole face with those big hands, I felt even worse for sounding surprised.

"You're from Ohio, aren't you?" I went on, trying for gentle.

He nodded, and though I couldn't be sure, I think he wept a little after that.

"Listen, she was a friend of mine, too. In fact, she left a suitcase with some things, at my house. I haven't had the heart to go through it yet, but now that you're here . . . Perhaps there's something in it for you to keep."

He couldn't quite bring himself to answer, but neither did he ask to be taken anywhere else, so I steered the car back to Marsh Hall and told the butler to get us tea. To my great relief, he gave no more signs of tears, and stared rather unabashedly at everything in the house, which I suppose was somewhat grander than the houses where he came from.

"Well," I said, once it was painfully obvious we weren't going to gain in conversational fluidity. "Shall we go through Cordelia's effects?"

He nodded.

The suitcase was old leather, and he seemed to recognize it when I brought it out. "Her mother's," he said softly, letting his fingers linger against the brass handle.

"She never knew her?" I asked.

"No."

I undid the clasps and opened the suitcase. The collection of totems within was not what I had anticipated; they seemed so girlish, almost naïve, all there together. The hand-sewn white cotton dress, which John lifted and put to his face. The newspaper clippings, which so poignantly mapped the years that she'd followed her father's doings from afar. The worn notebook, which contained mostly outdated tourist information on New York City, as well as a few choice quotes that she diligently attributed to the radio character Cara Gatling. A love letter signed *DG*, matchbooks from nightclubs that were popular that summer, a humble gold wedding band.

Of course there was the revolver. After John put aside the dress, he picked that up, turning it over in his hand with a fearful, impressed quality in his features. Perhaps it was because none of these items quite fit with the Cordelia I knew that my attention settled on the folded piece of paper with the telephone number *HUnter-4201* scrawled on the back. Unfolding that piece of paper, I felt a wave of relief that John hadn't seen it first, because I think it might have ruined him, and also because what I found there explained for me why Cordelia did what she did. I stepped away, toward the window, and read what Max must have written to Cordelia on the night before his race:

Cordelia, he began in his grade-school penmanship, *I have never written a letter like this before and I don't guess I'll do it very well. You were always pretty good at knowing what I meant to say, so hopefully you will now. The main thing is I want to tell you how lucky I am I finally got to know what it is to love a girl. I never cared much about girls, and you took me by surprise, and that about tripled what I know of this world. You're pretty much the brightest thing I've ever seen and the only girl I can imagine ever wanting. But I've come to know you, too, and seen a few things about how you do things. For me it's always going to be about risking everything to break away and sail above it all. That's what I want from life. But you—you've lost too many people already and I wouldn't want to think you'd gone hard inside, on my account or for anybody else. You had better forget about me and learn to love somebody with their feet on the ground. Till then think of me up in the air, where you know my thoughts will be of you. Love, Max*

There were a few tearstains on the page, and I imagined how she must have felt when she read it. That is, I think her emotion must have been similar to mine, knowing I wouldn't see her again: cut open. But in the resulting chasm I saw for the first time the contents of my own heart. It was vaster than I could possibly have imagined. As I stood at the window—hiding that letter away so that John Field wouldn't ever have to know of it—I saw her everywhere, in the unfurling white streaks and in the ripening blue that surrounded them.

We spent a long time silently turning over her possessions. Dusk settled in as we did, making the edges of things murky. I asked John to stay for dinner, and he accepted, and after we ate I had the butler drive him and Good Egg to the train station. Though we pretended that we would write to each other in the coming months, we never did. I told him he should take her suitcase and its contents with him, and I suppose he brought them all the way back to Ohio, and perhaps even gave her a burial of sorts.

By the time the weather changed, the legend of Max

Darby and Cordelia Grey had taken hold. Of course no one really knew what befell them, if they weren't living on some island somewhere, or in Paris, or if they simply chose never to come back down to Earth. Schoolchildren across the country talked about his feat of bravery, and her act of love, and generally agreed that his brief encounter with the bootlegger's daughter had inspired him to break rules and reach ever higher into the clouds.

In the fall, *The Good Lieutenant* had its premiere, and I don't suppose you need to be told what a sensation Letty was after that. If the stories are to be believed, she was never paid for her work in Mr. Branch's film, but after its release she had her pick of studios, and of course everyone knows how when the era of talkies really took off, she and her husband made picture after picture together, he as writer and eventually director, and she as star. The partnership of Larkspur and Lodge is one of the most celebrated in Hollywood, even now. Out there in the land of year-round sunshine they were protected from many of the hard things that befell those of us who remained back East.

For months I got letters from Astrid, postmarked in Paris, saying that as soon as the Marietta Phonograph Company's stock tripled in value she would come back and set up house. The Feds did find Charlie's stores eventually, and he and Jones both got sent up to Sing Sing, so it would have been safe for them to come back. But then the crash came, in late October, and she didn't write for a long time. When she did, she never mentioned the Marietta Phonograph Company again. Father might have helped them, but he lost everything, too, and Virginia left him for a racehorse jockey, and I had to work my way through my last year of college but was very grateful afterward for my degree.

Some years later, a painter friend of mine said that he saw Astrid and Victor in a Paris market, holding hands and buying groceries for dinner, and that they were married and very much in love. When I asked how they got by, my friend only shrugged and mumbled something about Victor pickpocketing tourists and Astrid taking in laundry, adding that he had never seen two people so happy. The bit about the laundry is difficult for me to picture, but it would be a curious detail to make up, and so I am inclined to believe it.

At some point I did try HUnter-4201, and a pleasant man named Ogilvy explained that he had indeed been associated with Max Darby, very briefly, as the executor of the Max Darby Aviation Fund. At first he insisted he couldn't disclose who was behind the fund, but when I told him about the letter, he sighed, said it couldn't possibly matter anymore, and told me about Thom Hale's investment. It wasn't until after Prohibition was struck down that I saw Thom again—he had spent those last few years on his boat, bringing liquor down from Nova Scotia. After repeal, he lived in his father's house and didn't see many people, although I ran into him one day by chance on a street corner in the city. Manhattan was a different place by then—instead of nightclubs, people lined up for soup kitchens, and the girls couldn't afford panty hose anymore and had to draw the seams up the backs of their legs with kohl.

When I mentioned Cordelia's name, his face fell about a hundred stories, and I knew that he still loved her.

"Please don't ever say that name to me again," he said, before wishing me well and going on his way. Even then, in the depths of the Great Depression, he was wearing a fine, new suit—he went legitimate with his liquor-importing business and made the Hales far wealthier than they were even at the height of Prohibition.

Anyway, I don't say her name, or any of their names, very often. Only when the world seems a little too spare and impoverished, and then I will replay in my mind the finery we wore that summer, for no reason in particular, and the things that we dreamed of before the fall. You see? I told you how it would be. Those bright-eyed girls, flitting to the city like moths, how quickly they became embroiled in its madcap nights. Each of them escaped New York, in her own way—one of them is famous, one of them is married, and one of them is dead.

Although I don't like to think of it that way. When I remember Cordelia, I close my eyes and I am with her, out there beyond the land and nothing but the big, blue ocean ahead of her. What a riot of excitement she must have felt! To be so high up, free from all constraints, flying into the future beside a man as determined as herself. In my mind's eye she is still wearing that white silk evening dress, and thus she shall remain. Forever aloft.

ACKNOWLEDGMENTS

I am very grateful to have such wonderful friends and editors in Sara Shandler and Farrin Jacobs, who helped build this series into what it has become. Many thank-yous also to Emilia Rhodes, Joelle Hobeika, Josh Bank, Les Morgenstein, Catherine Wallace, Kristin Marang, Sasha Illingworth, Beth Clark, Sarah Landis, Christina Colangelo, Lauren Flower, Liz Dresner, Aiah Wieder, Melinda Weigel, and Laura Lutz. And thank you to all the bright young readers who shared with me these stories, characters, and great adventures.

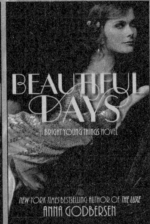
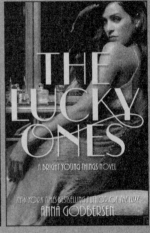